Ryan touched the wires together

The jolt of electricity made him gasp, and he was thrown backward with a blinding flash of light. The door squealed as the twisted metal tried to move in the straight grooves of the frame.

"Fireblast! I didn't expect it to hurt like that," Ryan groaned as he scrambled to his feet. Then he followed Jak's gaze.

A thin trickle of water was visible, running faster and then furiously down the crack between the two doors.

Without warning, a high-pressure stream of water shot through the gap and caught Ryan in the ribs. The force threw him against the wall of the corridor, and for a moment light exploded around his head.

Then it went black.

Other titles in the
Deathlands saga:

Eclipse at Noon
Stoneface
Bitter Fruit
Skydark
Demons of Eden
The Mars Arena
Watersleep
Nightmare Passage
Freedom Lost
Way of the Wolf
Dark Emblem
Crucible of Time
Starfall
Encounter:
 Collector's Edition
Gemini Rising
Gaia's Demise
Dark Reckoning
Shadow World
Pandora's Redoubt
Rat King
Zero City
Savage Armada
Judas Strike
Shadow Fortress
Sunchild
Breakthrough
Salvation Road
Amazon Gate
Destiny's Truth
Skydark Spawn
Damnation Road Show
Devil Riders
Bloodfire
Hellbenders
Separation
Death Hunt
Shaking Earth
Black Harvest
Vengeance Trail
Ritual Chill
Atlantis Reprise
Labyrinth
Strontium Swamp
Shatter Zone
Perdition Valley
Cannibal Moon
Sky Raider
Remember Tomorrow
Sunspot
Desert Kings
Apocalypse Unborn
Thunder Road
Plague Lords
 (Empire of Xibalba Book I)
Dark Resurrection
 (Empire of Xibalba Book II)
Eden's Twilight
Desolation Crossing
Alpha Wave
Time Castaways
Prophecy
Blood Harvest
Arcadian's Asylum
Baptism of Rage
Doom Helix
Moonfeast
Downrigger Drift
Playfair's Axiom
Tainted Cascade
Perception Fault
Prodigal's Return

JAMES AXLER

Lost Gates

A GOLD EAGLE BOOK FROM
WORLDWIDE®

TORONTO • NEW YORK • LONDON
AMSTERDAM • PARIS • SYDNEY • HAMBURG
STOCKHOLM • ATHENS • TOKYO • MILAN
MADRID • WARSAW • BUDAPEST • AUCKLAND

Recycling programs for this product may not exist in your area.

First edition November 2011

ISBN-13: 978-0-373-62611-3

LOST GATES

Printed in U.S.A.

Fear is a habit; so is self-pity, defeat, anxiety, despair, hopelessness and resignation. You can eliminate all of these negative habits with two simple resolves: I can! and I will!

—Author Unknown

THE DEATHLANDS SAGA

This world is their legacy, a world born in the violent nuclear spasm of 2001 that was the bitter outcome of a struggle for global dominance.

There is no real escape from this shockscape where life always hangs in the balance, vulnerable to newly demonic nature, barbarism, lawlessness.

But they are the warrior survivalists, and they endure—in the way of the lion, the hawk and the tiger, true to nature's heart despite its ruination.

Ryan Cawdor: The privileged son of an East Coast baron. Acquainted with betrayal from a tender age, he is a master of the hard realities.

Krysty Wroth: Harmony ville's own Titian-haired beauty, a woman with the strength of tempered steel. Her premonitions and Gaia powers have been fostered by her Mother Sonja.

J. B. Dix, the Armorer: Weapons master and Ryan's close ally, he, too, honed his skills traversing the Deathlands with the legendary Trader.

Doctor Theophilus Tanner: Torn from his family and a gentler life in 1896, Doc has been thrown into a future he couldn't have imagined.

Dr. Mildred Wyeth: Her father was killed by the Ku Klux Klan, but her fate is not much lighter. Restored from predark cryogenic suspension, she brings twentieth-century healing skills to a nightmare.

Jak Lauren: A true child of the wastelands, reared on adversity, loss and danger, the albino teenager is a fierce fighter and loyal friend.

Dean Cawdor: Ryan's young son by Sharona accepts the only world he knows, and yet he is the seedling bearing the promise of tomorrow.

In a world where all was lost, they are humanity's last hope....

Chapter One

Ryan Cawdor groaned as he opened his eye. It was gummed, heavy and felt as though a branding iron was being thrust repeatedly into it. Other than that, he was glad to be alive. As always, if he felt this bad, chances were that his opponent had to have come off worse. If he could remember who his opponent was....

At least lacking one eye spared him the pain of double vision. It was a grimly humorous thought that would, under any other circumstances, have made him grin. Not now, though. That would have been a signal to any potential enemy that he had regained consciousness. Besides which, it would have hurt too much. His face felt as though it had been trampled on by a herd of mutie cattle. The type that had razor-sharp hooves.

As the focus of his eye gradually came into some semblance of clear vision, Ryan could see that he and his companions were in a darkened wag. The jolting of the chassis as it bumped over either a rough road surface or a cross-country route jarred his vision, making it hard to pick out detail in the gloom. It also made his body ache. Every muscle and tendon felt rubbery and sensitive to the slightest impact. It felt as though each muscle and tendon had been taken out, rubbed in grit and then carefully replaced. He would have winced, if it wouldn't have alerted his captors to his conscious state.

Trying to keep as stable as possible, to improve his vision and stop the aches that ran up and down his frame, Ryan cast his eye over the dimmed interior of the wag. It was a basic wag, which looked as if it had been stripped at some point. There were no seats other than the two occupied by the driver and shotgun guard. He could make out three men, all armed with what looked like remade Armalite longblasters, who were hunkered down, backs resting against the shell of the wag. Between them were his companions. Jak, an albino, stood out because of his long white hair. Likewise Doc, whose head was down, his long silver mane shaggy as it banged against the floor of the wag.

With their darker hair and clothing, Krysty, Mildred and J.B. were harder to pick out.

The wag was a closed-in, metallic-bodied vehicle. It had no windows other than the windshield and the two on each door. There had to be rear doors, but these were solid. The pool of light from the front of the wag ended long before it reached the guards and the unconscious cargo in the rear. They were either not supposed to know where they were being taken—assuming the journey was long enough for all of them to regain consciousness—or no one was supposed to see in. Or maybe both. It kind of didn't matter right now.

But how did they get here? And why?

Ryan was mentally in a fog, and it was hard to remember anything from before the black curtain had fallen. Had there been a fight? Were they ambushed? Or was it…

Fireblast! It returned to him in pieces, and he wondered how they had been slipped the jolt derivative that had got them into this state.

And just what was Baron Valiant getting out of the deal?

SEVEN DAYS. Not a long time in the great scheme of things, but an eternity when you were stuck in a pesthole ville in the middle of nowhere. Hopping from convoy to convoy, running sec, the companions had made some distance from the last slice of trouble on the way overland to the next redoubt.

Hawknose was a strange ville, with an odd name and a baron, Valiant, with an odd name. The ville was no bigger than a few dozen huts and shacks, with a few buildings that were older scattered around. Mildred could see that it had once been a truck stop on a long-since-disappeared freeway. There was a diner, some old storage buildings that had been converted, and a gas station with the pumps still intact. The reservoirs underneath the pumps were still sealed, as they would find out. This was how Valiant kept his ville above the starvation line. It was a way station for passing convoys and travelers who knew the region. He could supply them with enough gas to get them from here to wherever. In return, traders would supply him at a discount.

It was just as well. The ville had nothing else going for it. The surrounding land was overworked and barren. When the rains came, they soaked in and stayed. Even when the surface was dry and cracked, just beneath was sodden. They would never get thirsty, but they couldn't grow any crops that wouldn't rot before they reached maturity. So any jack Valiant made on the gas was eaten up by the need to buy food. Usually from the very same traders.

But the baron was ambitious. And a baron with ambition but no jack and no manpower was a very dangerous thing.

RYAN WAS SLOWLY starting to feel like himself. The aches were still there, but through sheer force of will he cast the pain to the back of his mind. He concentrated on flexing every muscle in his arms and legs. His feet and hands were numb from the ropes that had been tied when he was unconscious—he assumed that the same was true of the others—but there was enough give in the ropes for them to burn on wrists and ankles as he flexed. Moments later tingling ached and burned in his fingers and toes as circulation began to return feeling to those extremities.

Still, there was a void where memory should be. He was aware that they were being taken somewhere for a purpose, but that purpose still escaped him. It lurked on the fringes of his consciousness, but was tantalizingly out of reach.

It looked, in the saturnine light, as though he was the only one to be awake. Maybe not. If any of the others had awakened, then they would be doing their best to disguise it, as he was, until they had worked out the how and why of being here.

Hawknose. Stupe name, he thought. Why was it called that?

Then it began to return. Slowly.

'SEEMS A WEIRD name, don't it?" Travis chuckled, and it wheezed its way from laughter into a cough. He hawked up a mouthful of phlegm and spit it out the door. "Mebbe it is, unless you know why."

"And you're going to tell us?" Mildred asked in a wry tone. It had been obvious that the grizzled man had been lacking in company, and was glad of the chance to talk.

"Since you ask so nicely, I will, little lady." Travis's eyes twinkled. He would, in all likelihood, have chuckled again if it hadn't run him the risk of another coughing fit. "See, if we hadn't had to move back in the early days, it would have been obvious. Originally, in the days before skydark, we came from a little place that was under the shadow of a bluff that was shaped like a hawk's beak. Least, that's what they say. I wouldn't know. I might look old, but I ain't really all that. It's just this fancy living that's made me so soft." He chuckled again.

"Not much story," Jak commented. He was tired, and hadn't taken to the old man who was providing them with accommodation. The sooner he shut up and let them sleep, Jak thought, the better. It would be an early start. The albino youth didn't mind hard work, but when it was monotonous it was that much harder to take the shit that went with it.

Travis shook his head. His graying hair hung in matted dreads that brushed his shoulders, putting his lean jaw into shadow.

"If that was all there was to it, then I'd agree with you. But it ain't. See, we'd been there for hundreds of years, they say. Since the white folks first come to the old lands, there'd been a Hawknose. Almost as long as the Indians—and look what happened to them. We were survivors. And so it was with skydark. There were caves, they say, under the bluff that went right into the earth. Our people took all they could carry, and they stayed there until it was okay to come out. Some tried too early, just to see, and that was the end of them. But they did it for all of us, and we remember them for that.

"See, that's what we do here. We look out for each other. Hell, most of us are related. It was such a small place. We get people stop by, drop kids or father them, then...well, some stay and some fuck off. Don't make no matter to those of us who have blood going right back. But I guess it stops us being all born with four heads and no legs, or some such shit."

That made sense. Since they had arrived, Mildred had noticed that most of the people looked like they came from a small gene pool. The men and women looked alike, and there was little to tell between one person and the next. And yet they hadn't shown the signs of mutie inbreeding that she had seen elsewhere on their travels.

So yeah, that made sense, Mildred thought. Unlike his story. Where the hell was that going?

Travis had to have seen the look on her face.

"The name. Why'd we keep it? That must be what you're wondering. Well, it's like this. After they came out of the caves, they saw that the old ville had been flattened by the hawk's nose. The fucker had blown off some time during the years they were hiding, and it had wiped out the whole ville. Too much shit there to clear and build. "Sides which, it was a sign. Leastways, that's how they took it. Time to move on. So they hit the road—what was left of it—and ended up here. Good place to be."

"You tried to dig that land?" J.B. murmured, his muscles aching in memory of his day's work.

"Listen, son, you say that, but look at it this way—would you rather try and dig wet earth or live on rocks that can't grow shit at all? And ain't got no water?"

J.B. shrugged. He guessed the old guy had a point. "So why is this called after the old ville?" he asked, wanting to hurry Travis along for the same reasons as Jak.

The old man sniffed. "Should have thought you could see where I was going with that. We're a loyal people. We stick together. We look after each other. And we remember the sacrifices of those before us. This was called Hawknose for where we come from, and in memory of the others. And one day, that name will be pretty damn big. Valiant believes in that. We all do."

There was something about the way that he said it—an almost messianic zeal—that would brook no argument. Not even daring to exchange glances, the companions let the comment slide. But when the old man had finished wandering the rooms of the shack they now shared with him, and had left to go to the communal bar that lay in the old gas station, Krysty let out a long sigh.

"This is going to be a long wait until the next convoy rolls into the ville," she said softly.

"That, I fear, is possibly the sanest and truest thing that we have heard all evening, my dear," Doc muttered.

"It is one thing for the baron of a ville to be so deluded and yet so firm in a conviction. But for this to infect his whole people?" He shook his head sadly.

"They don't seem to be a threat," Ryan said. "Unless you mean to themselves," he added with a grin. "We're just going to have to tough it out, people."

They had been in the ville a short while. Long enough, however, to know that it was a typical struggling settlement, going nowhere and fighting, like everywhere else, for survival. There wasn't enough jack to go around, and the land they lived on made raising crops and livestock an uphill struggle. The only thing they had going for them was the gas station and the reservoir. It kept them in business. Traders put them on the route as it suited them to have a way station here, but there wasn't enough trade, gas or traffic to make it anything other than a case of the ville paying out with one hand for the jack they'd just taken in.

The grandiloquent Baron Valiant was onto a stone-cold losing proposition. But if he was anything like his people—or they like him, however it may be—then he was stubborn, proud, a believer in his heritage.

A fool.

Yet it suited Ryan and the companions to stop here. They had been riding sec on a convoy and it had taken this detour to refuel, a stopover that was short by any convoy standard, and that said a lot about the way the ville was viewed. Hawknose was the last place a person would want to get stranded. But the convoy was uneasy. There were tensions between the trader in charge and the quartermaster, who was bucking to oust his boss and take over. He had the backing of half the crew, and was looking for the right place to stage a mutiny. From the time they had hooked up with the convoy, it was obvious that this was why they had been hired. With no agenda, no knowledge of anyone else on the convoy, the companions would just follow orders and collect their pay.

Except that the convoy was headed across Colorado, bound for the remains of the eastern seaboard, territory that Ryan and his people knew only too well, and were in no hurry to encounter again. As the long miles passed, they realized that the reason the quartermaster was able to gain support for his schemes was down to the attitude of the trader. He was triple stupe, and Ryan had started to doubt if they would even get paid at journey's end. They were there not so much to provide sec as to protect the trader from his own crew.

So when they reached Hawknose, and became aware that it was the last stop before a long haul into the east, Ryan figured that it was time to call it a day. The others weren't disappointed at the time. They were sick of looking over their shoulders on what should have been an easy ride. If convoys were regular through here, then it wouldn't take long to pick up another paying ride.

It had been almost comical to hear the alternating curses and imprecations of the trader when Ryan told him they were leaving his employ. Almost as blackly funny as the look on the face of the quartermaster as the convoy set to head out of Hawknose. It didn't need to be said out loud that the chances of the convoy having a new trader by the time they hit the next ville were roughly the same as those of a stickie beating the crap out of a mutie bear in a shitstorm.

Yeah, it had seemed like the best option. But nobody was thinking that after a few days of the monotony and rigor of life in Hawknose. Even Ryan was hoping that the next convoy would roll in during the middle of the night.

The people of Hawknose looked the same, and they had attitudes to match. Sharp-faced and suspicious, they were dour and ground down by generations of just about keeping body and soul together. Sure, they had the conviction of their destiny, but it was nothing they took joy from. Rather, it was as though they felt they had to suffer this life to find that state. Both Doc and Mildred could identify this with the attitudes of religious communities in their day, and although the people of Hawknose believed in a redemption that came in this world, not the next, it was as though they believed it was always just out of reach.

It made them hard—hard in the manner of their lives, and hard in their attitudes to each other. And particularly in their attitude to outlanders. That much was obvious from the moment that the convoy pulled away without the companions. There was no welcome for the newcomers—not that they expected it—but neither was there hostility. Instead there was a kind of grudging and grim acceptance. They were there in Hawknose—fine. But now they had to work and fit in. Or leave. Convoy or no convoy to carry you out.

Baron Valiant was a hands-on baron. Unlike the rulers of larger villes who surrounded themselves with a sec force and whatever wealth they could secure, using the one to enable themselves to indulge the other, Valiant was one of his people in a very real sense. He worked and lived alongside them. They showed him deference, but that seemed to come from a genuine respect and belief in his birthright. The ville of Hawknose was inherited, and he was merely following the footsteps of his forefathers. They were believers in tradition. They believed in order. That was evident by the fact that in their short time thus far in the ville, Ryan and his companions had seen no need for sec except in the rare case of a person who couldn't hold his or her brew. The sec seemed to be there purely for when convoys or outlanders passed through.

Maybe the law-abiding nature of the ville dwellers was more due to exhaustion than to any innate desire to walk a straight line, for life in the ville was hard. It soon became apparent that convoys weren't as regular as Ryan would have hoped when he made the decision to pull out of sec duty. Supplies of food that were bought from any convoy were stored and carefully rationed. Water was plentiful, and as a result so was brew. Anything that could be made to ferment was stored and used. Any roots, rotting crop, or plantlife that could be harnessed in such a way was thrown into vats that bubbled as the alcohol was boiled and distilled from the resultant sludge. It seemed that most of the people in Hawknose spent their evenings in the bar, which was as much a communal meeting area as one to get drunk and carouse. Even in their pleasures they were a dour people.

Dour, but hardened to the potent brew that resulted from their thrifty approach. They were hard drinkers, and their ability to rise with the sun the following morning and work just as hard was something that

Ryan and the companions soon found they couldn't keep pace with.

The old service station and diner around which the ville was constructed lay in a valley, a bowl shaped by a landscape that had once been a series of gentle inclines but had been disturbed by seismic shifts as skydark hit. Pushed and pulled by nature, the land had risen to form a steeply sided bowl that required the convoys that passed through to have sharp brakes. The freeway that had once passed this way had long since been reduced to ribbons by the seismic shifts, and little evidence of it remained. Instead a carefully hewn and beaten track ran close to the site of the old road and was marked by the rubble that had been cleared in making the new path. It guided any traffic down the incline and through the ville before gently guiding it up the opposite slope and out.

That left the ville in a basin. Was it simply that the land surrounding had risen, or had the ville itself dropped? It was impossible to say, but whatever the truth, it had left the people of Hawknose with a problem that they hadn't foreseen when they had taken possession of the old station and buildings and started to build around them.

The problem was that the land around had a high water table, and no matter what time of year it was sodden once you dug down a few feet. Any crop would rot. The land never really dried out, as the high ground around mean that the ville was in constant shadow. It was always damp and cold, even when the sun beat down from a cloudless sky. There was never enough to keep both the people and the livestock fed. Little grew wild. Both livestock and man were reliant on food brought in by convoy. Despite this, the people broke their backs on the land.

Belief in destiny was a powerful driving force. The people of Hawknose felt that in their very bones. They were in this place for a reason, not just because it happened to be the first place that was habitable that their forefathers stumbled across. And until that reason revealed itself, they would stay here. They would make it work, even if it would break the back of each person in the process. The one thing it could never break was their spirit.

Which was all very well if you lived there, and your roots were there. But, Ryan reflected as he settled on the hard bedding that had been supplied for them by Travis, it was bastard hard to get used to if you didn't give a shit about the ville and were just waiting for the chance to move on.

People had to work for their living. You eat, you put something back. There was nothing wrong with that. Except that these people drove themselves so hard… Ryan thought it was little wonder that the ville folk drank themselves into oblivion every night. Even the children worked like pack animals. It was a fair bet that you didn't make old bones in this ville. Travis looked as ancient as Doc, Ryan mused, but he wouldn't have been surprised to have learned that he was younger than he was.

The one-eyed man's head grew heavy as weariness overtook him. He could feel his mind slipping into oblivion as the fatigue of the day overwhelmed him.

RYAN WAS JOLTED back to consciousness by the sudden lurch of the wag. His attempt to recall how they had reached this point had driven him into a lapse of consciousness. It was only the whiplash of his neck and the sharp, painful crack of his head against the wag's bulkhead that had brought him back.

Everything was rambling, unfocused. There was a reason why they were here, and he had to remember what it was before they reached their destination. It was important that he knew why.

Ryan flexed his neck muscles. Thoughts were starting get blurred once more. Through a hooded eyelid, he took another look around. He was becoming accustomed to the gloomy light in the interior of the wag. Now he could pick out his fellow travelers with a greater ease. Doc was still out cold. His physical state was always precarious, despite his inner strength. It was impossible to know how his heavily buffeted body would cope with anything thrown at it.

Jak was conscious and, like himself, was seeking to conceal it. Ryan, though, knew the albino youth too well. There was something about the set of his body. He was poised, keeping balance perfectly as the wag swayed and dipped over the rutted ground beneath. Jak was scoping out his opponents, and was perhaps even now thinking the same things that Ryan was thinking about him.

Mildred and Krysty were still out. Ryan was only too familiar with every aspect of the Titian-haired beauty's body language. Her head lolled too loosely on her shoulders, and her sentient hair was limp rather than full or curled tight. As for Mildred, her body was jerking in muscle spasms. Her feet kicked in tiny arcs, her shoulders jerking uncontrollably. She was fighting the effects of the drug, and it was reflected in her body language.

That left J.B. The Armorer had his fedora pulled down over his eyes, at an angle that made it hard to see much of his face. But from the set of his jaw—a small sign but a telling one in a man that Ryan and known most of his adult life—it was certain that J. B. Dix had lifted himself from the depths of unconsciousness and was now observing his surroundings. Even as Ryan watched, the man moved slightly—a twist of the hip, shifting his weight on the floor of the wag. Caught from the corner of a guard's eye, it would have seemed to have been nothing more than a result of his being jolted by the movement of the wag. But to a careful observer, which J.B. obviously hoped Ryan was, it could be seen that he moved contrary to the shift of the wag.

Ryan responded by signaling back. He lifted his right foot as far as it would go without dragging his left. Which, in truth, wasn't much given how tightly they were bound. He then let if fall so that the heel struck the floor of the wag. He did this in short succession, paused, then again. Unless they were listening carefully, it was doubtful that the guards would catch this. But any of his companions would understand.

It was a code they had worked out in the past: a *J* and a *B.*

Ryan watched carefully, and saw the Armorer's fedora dip in assent. Switching his attention, he saw that Jak also moved in acknowledgment.

That made three of them who were recovering. Not

that it did them much good right now. But at least when they reached their destination, they should be clear-headed enough....

Fireblast! If only they had been clearheaded enough when they were back in the ville. They should have seen it coming. There had been warning signs, after all.

"WORK IS ALL. Without it we are nothing. And it will be rewarded my friend. When the time comes..."

"Mebbe we don't want to hang around that long," J.B. murmured as he slammed the blade of the shovel deeper into the mud.

For a moment Hardy stared at him with incomprehension on his long, lean face. Then he began to laugh, a dry, crackly sound as though it were being forced out of his lungs through layers of rustling leaves. His jowls shook, and his eyes ran with tears. He put down his shovel and took out a length of rag from his pocket, using it to blow his nose with a mighty honk before wiping his eyes.

J.B., too, stopped digging. He wouldn't need much of an excuse, as they had been attacking the same patch for three backbreaking hours. At least, that was what his wrist chron told him, though it seemed much longer by the ache in his back.

"What's so bastard funny about that?" he asked, genuinely puzzled. If anything, he would have expected the tall, skinny ville dweller to be angered by his dismissive comment. It had slipped out before he'd had a chance to bite his tongue.

"It's just what any of us would expect from an outlander." Hardy wheezed when he could speak. "You people are all the same when you first arrive. You can't see the bigger horizon, just what's in front of your nose. Then you get it, and stay."

J.B. was still puzzled. He knew that any kind of humor or levity seemed in short supply in Hawknose, but this?

"What about those of us who do move on?" he countered.

Hardy shrugged. "Well, who cares what you think when you're gone?"

J.B. furrowed his brow. There was a kind of logic in there, he supposed.

Hardy took up his shovel once more and gestured for J.B. to do likewise. "Listen, son, it works like this. Big work gets big reward. We make this ville into something, and we get the riches that will bring with it. But on a smaller scale, it works like this. We put in a hard day here and we grow stuff in a land that don't want to grow. So we, the workers, get rewarded by the baron, who oversees our homes and feeding. You don't work—don't pull together for the common cause—and you get jackshit. That's how life should be. You put in and you get given in return."

J.B. looked around and was dubious about the truth in that. They were about a half mile outside the main part of the ville. All around, for a distance of about three miles, spread across the rubble-and-rock-strewed landscape were fenced-off areas that were used for farming. Herds of scraggy livestock grazed on the perfunctory meadow that had been created for their use. The paddocks were waterlogged for much of the time, and the creatures looked out with doe-eyed and weary stares, the smell of decay palpable from the diseases that were engendered by the damp conditions.

Between the livestock meadows, protected by wild dogs that were housed in kennels on each corner, secured by long, rusting chains, lay the crop fields. J.B. stood in one of them, casting a weathered eye on his surroundings. What should have been fields of green and gold waving in the chill breeze that swept along the sheltered valley became nothing but stumpy pastures of brown, battered and rotting stalks. The root crops were immured in mud, and the wheat and grasses that were supposed to climb high were stunted and decaying at their base.

This was what they worked so hard for? And hard work it most certainly was. He and Ryan had been working on the farming detail for only a few days, but already he felt as though he had been a fight with an opponent who wouldn't give up. His ribs and neck ached, while the muscles down his spine felt as though they had been unnaturally stretched. His arms felt as though they had been pummeled with the shovel that he wielded. Looking down at the clods of damp earth that were matted to the blade of his shovel, he tilted and watched as the mud slid off with a squelch, revealing the paltry growth of root crop that lay beneath the discolored greenery that topped it.

The soil was a sea of mud, barely able to sustain any growth without rotting it. The root crops and wheat were ill-nourished and dying before they were even harvested. J.B. wouldn't be at all surprised if it transpired that the majority of what they used for food came from traded supplies.

In which case, why the hell did they put them themselves through this? Was it really because they had an almost preternatural belief in the value of their work to gain their prize?

He looked at Hardy, who had returned to attacking the unyielding, sludgy earth that just sucked at the shovel blade. There was a determination in the man's face that was unnerving. Given the right circumstances, there was little doubt that the people of Hawknose could be dangerous. Was there anything they wouldn't do for the good of their ville?

Meantime, J.B. felt that he should get back to work. Hardy had said nothing, but his silent return to his task had spoken volumes. As long as J.B. and the rest of the companions were in the ville, they would have to abide by the code of the ville, or risk the consequences.

The next convoy couldn't come along quickly enough for the Armorer.

As he continued to toil, he noticed the regular sec patrols came nearer and nearer to the spot where he was digging. There had to be some kind of pattern to how they worked. For nothing more than to relieve the boredom that threatened to crush his spirit, he tried to work out this route based on what he had observed on the previous few days.

Something nagged at J.B. as he continued to dig. Thinking back, it seemed that the sec patrols were sent out to scare off any kind of wildlife that may stray too close during the hours of daylight, and to scout for any approaching wags or travelers on foot. To do this, they sped through the areas that were used for farming, and were several miles from the ville before beginning their proscribed circuit.

But this day was different. For a while it was hard for him to pin down exactly why this was bugging him. Then as he tugged at the handle of his shovel, trying to free it from sludge that was almost like quicksand, it came to him. The sound was different. Sure, he'd seen them occasionally, out of the corner of his eye, but mostly his head had been turned down, facing his task. And the noise he had heard had been distant, a buzzing in and out of focus, as the wags came and went on their circuit, farther out and then closer in.

But this day they were much closer, and the sound was louder. They were coming into the area where farming was carried out, and from the revs of the engines as they passed it was as if they were slowing at various points.

So why were they coming in so much? And why were they slowing at certain points?

A tingling of apprehension prickled at the Armorer's scalp. There was something that worried him about this, something he'd have to mention to Ryan and Jak, if only to see if they had noticed anything similar.

J.B. ANGLED HIS HEAD BACK so that he could see from beneath the brim of his fedora. The guards were still unaware that he was conscious. Having Ryan's signal, and seeing Jak's response, he knew that he wasn't the only one conscious. He hurt like hell, but that wouldn't matter when the adrenaline started to pump. He was angry at himself for not realizing what was happening earlier. He should have known. It was all there in the attitude of men like Hardy.

The people of Hawknose would stop at nothing to further the cause of their ville.

Nothing.

Chapter Two

"This sucks. The sooner we can get out of this place, the better," Mildred grumbled as she and Krysty added another sack of meal to the pile that was growing in the dark shed used as a warehouse. They were at the back, unloading a cart so heavily laden that it had taken the two of them a great deal of time to pull it over the rutted planks of the floor.

Concrete lay beneath the wooden base. They could see the gray through the slats of the floor, and in places the planks had broken to show patches of the hard surface beneath. They had managed to avoid the worst of them, but in so doing had always seemed to run into a groove formed by two worn pieces of wood, causing the trolley to buck and stick, wrenching their arms and backs as it did.

They had spent the past two days on this task, gradually moving the supplies traded from their convoy. It was dull, monotonous and backbreaking work. It was easy to see why they—the newly arrived outlanders—had been allocated this task.

Krysty straightened as the sack hit the others with a dull thud, raising a cloud of dust that caught in her throat. She was too exhausted to even sneeze or cough with any alacrity. Every spasm made her back twinge.

"These guys are tough, I'll give them that," she said

with a wince as the spasms passed, and she stretched to allow her aching muscles to uncramp. "I have no idea what they'd be like as fighters, but if they were well organized, they'd be tough to take down."

"They're not that type, though," Mildred reflected, leaning against the bar by which they alternately dragged or pulled the cart. "They believe in hard work, living simply and keeping to themselves. Lord knows that's a rare enough commodity in this pesthole land."

"Yeah, but what if someone comes looking for them?" Krysty countered. "There's a whole lot of people here who don't...ahh—" she winced as she stretched to one side "—who don't believe in live and let live. What would they do then, and where would their work ethic be then?"

Mildred pondered that between feeling the disks in her spine contract as the muscles tightened. "You know, there were people like that back before I got frozen. Religious sects. They were pretty much left alone. The only difference between these guys and the ones from predark is that the old ones believed in God rather than a sense of destiny."

She stopped speaking as she noticed movement in the shadows. Krysty caught the change in her companion's demeanor and immediately snapped out of her relaxed state. She turned so that she was facing the same way as her companion.

A woman came out of the shadows. Sharp-faced, tall and angular, she looked like so many other people in the ville. Her lean, long face was lined, although she probably was younger than either Mildred or Krysty.

Her clothes hung off her, not because she was thin but rather because they were recycled castoffs.

There was something about the way she moved that made Krysty's nerves tingle. It seemed as though she had emerged from the shadows, where she had been still, observing.

But why?

"Going well with that load," the woman noted, her voice flat and neutral. "Soon be done. You'll be glad of that." It was a statement rather than a question.

"Damn right," Mildred murmured. "Anything you wanted?" Like Krysty, she, too, was suspicious of the woman, although equally she would have been hard-pushed to say why. Instinct.

"Just came to tell you that the next shift won't be yours. Baron wants to see you all later. That's a real privilege. Means you get some time out."

"Like a reward?" Mildred asked with heavy irony.

"Yeah. Anyone with a private audience with Valiant has time out before they go. Need to be sharp, not tired or hung over. So you have time to rest."

Krysty suppressed a smile at the way in which the irony had flown over the woman's head. Still, if it meant she could have a bath and soak her back....

"Why does the baron want to see us?" she asked.

The reaction wasn't quite what she had expected. The woman shrugged in an exaggerated manner. "I don't know. Stuff like that is private. Between him and the people he sees. Anyhow, you just finish up here and get along. I can find a replacement." Abruptly, she turned and walked away into the shadows.

Mildred waited until she had seen the woman's silhouette disappear through the double doors.

"That was weird. I don't like the sound of an audience with the baron."

"No," Krysty said slowly. "And I'll tell you something else. I'd swear she was there watching us before she came out. Why?"

Mildred smiled grimly. "We won't have to wait long to find out, sweetie...."

AS THOUGH WADING through a sea of mud, Mildred grimly fought her way to the surface. She had been kicking and screaming for some time, the images of memory running through her head.

She wanted to groan as she regained consciousness and the pain washed over her like the final spray of water on emerging. But she bit her tongue, a reflex action triggered by the knowledge that she was tied up. Before she could even form the thought, her instinct told her to keep silent.

She kept her head down, opening one eye and knowing, by the way they brushed across her face, that her beaded plaits would shield her. At first, she could see next to nothing. It was incredibly dark in the wag. She knew it was a wag because of the noise and movement. Then the vague shapes took substance, and she could see the others: Doc's head banging rhythmically on the floor of the wag beside her; Krysty still unconscious.

She knew J.B. so well that she knew he was awake and feigning unconsciousness. Jak and Ryan she wasn't so sure of, but it was a fair bet that they had also come around. All of them had to have received approximately the same dose of whatever sedative that coldheart Valiant had administered. It had to have been in the food, as he had drank from the same brew as they had. Hell, she was angry with herself for being suckered so easily with that. A child should have seen it coming.

There was no time for recriminations now. She had to think about what was going to happen, not what was already past. She tested the rope on her wrists and ankles. Tight, but maybe not tight enough. Her joints were supple enough to perhaps allow for some manipulation. It was just a matter of being able to balance the maneuver with the necessity for stealth.

While she worked at it, to distract herself from the burning of the nylon rope on her skin she tried to recall exactly how they had come to be in this situation.

After all, for all its strange ways, Hawknose had hardly seemed the type of ville where this behavior was the norm. Events were still swimming in confusion, and if she could somehow decipher them, then it would allow her to be ready for whatever lay ahead, at the end of the journey.

TRAVIS WAS STILL at his work when Krysty and Mildred arrived at the shack. They were alone, and both bathed in silence, letting the hot water soothe their aching limbs. It was only after they had dressed that Doc and Jak arrived from their own labors. As they entered, they were bickering.

"I am sure that you cannot be right, dear boy. Why would they wish to keep us under surveillance when we are right in their midst? Surely if they had some suspicions about our intent, then they would not allow us to move so freely among them? If that were—"

"Doc, shut up." Jak sighed. "Not care why, just saying."

Both Krysty and Mildred's interest was piqued by this exchange, as it mirrored their own feelings.

"You think you were being watched?" Krysty asked, following them into the room where Travis kept his primitive bathtub. A hand pump welded to a pipe that ran through the walls to a central tank behind the gas station supplied the hot water for the ville. As Jak began to pump vigorously at the handle, he turned to Krysty.

"Sure of it. Same two men pass by every five, ten minutes."

Doc paused in stripping off his dusty clothing. "Come now, that's an absurd leap of assumption, lad. They may simply have been going about their business."

Jak paused. "They carry anything?"

Doc thought about this, poised on one leg. "No," he said slowly as he finished discarding his clothes, with the exception of his drawers. "No, I don't recall. And if you all don't mind…" The others turned their backs, giving Doc a moment to shuck his underwear, enabling him to preserve his modesty.

"No one walk empty hand to and from anywhere," Jak said with emphasis. "So why them?"

"But why do it?" Doc countered, climbing into the bath.

Jak shrugged as he discarded his own clothes, turned and joined Doc. "Dunno. Don't matter. Just know it's happening. And not good."

"Jak's got a point," Mildred interjected, joining Krysty in the doorway.

"Madam, a little privacy," Doc murmured.

"Too late for that, you old buzzard." She grinned. "More to the point, something happened to us today..."

She went on to describe what had transpired, with Krysty adding detail while Jak and Doc cleaned up. Their own tasks, in the maintenance of the gas pumps and tanks, left them dusty from the earth, and smelling of gas. The primitive cleaners used by the people of the ville were hardly strong enough. You could always tell those who worked on gas detail by their distinctive odor. Fortunately they still had in their own supplies, some soap and shampoo taken from a redoubt some time before.

By the time Jak and Doc had cleaned and dried themselves, Mildred and Krysty had finished their own tale.

"I take back my own doubts," Doc mused as he dressed. "I fear I did you a disservice, young Jak. For reasons that are best known to themselves, they have started to watch us.

"Tell me," he directed to Krysty and Mildred, "did you notice this before today?"

"No," Krysty said firmly. "You?"

Jak shook his head. "Just today."

Doc frowned. "It is as though they were suddenly directed to keep an eye on us—perhaps so that we would not stray? Might there be a convoy due in, and that is the cause?" When the question brought forth no response, he added, "I will be most interested to hear what Ryan and John Barrymore have to say about this, and whether or not they have encountered a similar phenomenon."

Doc didn't have long to wait. To save gas—so important for trade—the workers in the fields walked to and from their tasks. Only the sec patrols got to use wags and bikes with any regularity. To trudge back after a hard day's work was hard enough, but to be sent home early with an instruction to see the baron was ominous.

BOTH J.B. AND RYAN had been told to quit their tasks at about the same time that the others had also been dismissed. However, the greater distance told on them. They met about halfway back to the ville, the paths through the fields crossing so that their routes coincided. For some time they walked in silence, both too exhausted by their morning's labors to spare the breath. It was only as they neared town that J.B. spoke.

"Think the others were called back to the ville?"

"Yeah," Ryan replied shortly. "And I don't like it."

"Because we're being watched?" J.B. asked.

Ryan looked at him. He'd thought he was being overcautious in noting the sudden frequency and change of the sec patrols.

THEY BRIEFLY exchanged details of what they had observed. It gave them much to ponder by the time they arrived at Travis's shack. As they stripped and bathed, Ryan and J.B. listened to what their companions had to say before adding their own experiences.

"Whatever's going on, it's something that's only just happened," Ryan mused as he dressed. "We're agreed that it's only been today, right?" There was general assent, and he continued. "So Valiant has decided to take a closer interest in us. Why? Has anything happened?"

"As far as I am aware," Doc said, "there have been no arrivals or departures since the convoy left without us. Jak and myself have been central, so would have seen any arrivals or heard commotion."

"And I'm sure we could have seen anything coming from a long way off out in the fields," J.B. added. "No, it's got to be something from the inside."

"Well, we haven't had time to do anything except work like dogs then sleep," Krysty said. "Nothing to draw any attention to ourselves."

"Then I'd say we be on the ball and alert with Valiant, and don't give anything away." Millie sighed. "It isn't much, but it's all we got for now."

RYAN WATCHED carefully. His muscles cramped and he wanted to grimace, to grunt through the pain. But he couldn't give any sign of being conscious. He was pretty sure now that Doc—whose head was still banging rhythmically on the floor of the wag with every lurch and bump—was the only one of them who was still suffering the effects of the drug.

Krysty had regained consciousness. She hadn't moved, but her hair betrayed her. While her head still lolled, her hair falling over her face to disguise any movement of the eyes, he could see that her prehensile hair was no longer hanging limply. Now it had become suffused with a life of its own. It moved subtly, waving in tendrils that seemed to curl around her neck and then reach out, as though seeking something. The movement seemed to be in sync with the rhythm of the vehicle, so that it would be unseen to the guards that sat, bored and unmoving, between them. Only someone who knew Krysty would appreciate what it meant.

So, only Doc was still out.

At least the majority of them would be ready for what lay ahead.

"COME, SIT WITH ME and eat, drink. We must talk, but only after you have sated yourselves. The day's work is hard, and you aren't yet used to our ways."

Valiant gestured them to be seated. He lived in what had once been the diner near the old freeway. The tables still remained, as did the bar and grill. In one corner, where there had once been space for jukeboxes and slot machines, a drape-hidden area now housed his sleeping quarters. Some of the nearby tables used for business were covered with papers and boxes of goods and jack. Only two sec men were in the diner with them.

The other tables were bare. The booths along the windows facing the gas station had their padded seats covered with all manner of colored drapes and throws. This area was undoubtedly where the baron would relax. But even then, it was austere by the standards of most barons, even if luxuriant by the harsh standard of the ville as a whole.

The table he directed them to was in the center of the diner. The fluorescent lighting running overhead had long since ceased to work, and illumination was provided by tallow candles in beaten metal holders. The light from these formed a shallow pool that threw the rest of the diner into darkness as the evening began to close in. In the distance, they could hear the people congregate at the old gas station, a distant buzz of background noise.

Food was prepared for them at the grill behind the old counter. Some sort of brew was placed in front of them in jugs. After tasting their food and brew, Doc in particular had formed the theory that the food was nothing more than nutrition to the ville people, their taste buds having been scoured since birth by the harsh alcohol on which they were raised.

The food that was carried out from behind the counter and placed in front of them by two women and the man who prepared it did little to dispel that theory. But the companions ate, washing it down with the raw spirit, each waiting for the baron to reveal his purpose.

Two courses had been served from a communal pot, the indeterminate meal served onto their plates with ladles. The first course had contained some kind of pickled meat in a sauce that looked a little like the mud from which they dug the vegetables. It tasted a little like that would probably taste. Doc steeled himself, having no expectations. Jak could eat anything, and so passed no comment. But for the others, it was an effort to force down the food, which Valiant seemed to enjoy so much.

As, indeed, he relished the second course. Rice, which tasted as though it was seasoned by the gasoline that was their staple, was heaped on their plates. There it was joined by overcooked vegetables in a sauce that once more seemed to be made of mud, and some stringy lumps of fiber and gristle that may have been meat. Again, only the nullifying fire of the raw spirit could erase the cloying taste from their mouths.

While they ate, Valiant spoke to them of the ville,

his plans for it and how he hoped to fulfill the dreams and hopes of his ancestors. The only thing that could hurry the process beyond hard work, he had decided, was to bring more jack into the ville. Jack meant power in the world outside their valley. It may not reflect on their own codes of behavior, but if they were to use the world around them to further the aims of their forefathers, then they had to adapt in some ways.

By this time, despite the best efforts of each of them, the brew they had ingested to ease the passage of the food was beginning to take effect. The light from the candles seemed to grow haloes of luminescence that spread out in ripples. The distant sounds of the gas station bar became distorted and echoed. And the long, rambling plans of Valiant seemed to grow more and more incomprehensible.

The third and final course was laid in front of them. Sweet meats in individual dishes that had been sugared by the raw cane that grew limp and rotting in the mud, colored by who knew what kinds of dyes into lurid colors that were still matt and dull, like all else in the ville.

They were doughy, stodgy and indigestible. But, unwilling to offend the baron before they had some idea of exactly why he had asked them to this meal, they forced them down.

Licking his fingers, Valiant sat back with the hint of a smile playing around his lean, hatchet features. It looked uncharacteristic, and set alarm bells ringing at the back of Ryan's brain, fogged as it was by the potent brew.

"Your plans have something to do with why you pulled us out of work and got us here," Ryan said. He spoke slowly and carefully, aware of the way in which the brew had crept up and fogged his brain. His voice sounded distant and echoed to him. "Why you were having us watched."

"You noticed that, then?" Valiant questioned. "I was hoping my people were a bit more subtle that that. Guess I shouldn't be surprised. We don't really do that sort of thing."

"Then why start now?" Ryan countered. "And why not when we first got here?"

Valiant took a hefty drink of the brew in his cup. "It didn't occur to me for a day or two. I don't know why. But then it just sprang into my head. I guess it had been there since I first saw you all, but it had to come to the surface. See, there's a baron less than a hundred miles from here who has this mission in life. I guess we all have them. Mine's about fulfilling the destiny that our forefathers foretold for us. His… Well, it doesn't really make that much sense to me, but it has to do with this trader who knows something about secret places that are left from before skydark. Now, he's long gone, but he had this right-hand man. Well, two of them. One was a big guy with one eye. The other was smaller. Hat, glasses, liked blasters. Now you tell me, who does that sound like to you?"

Alarm bells and sirens went off in the one-eyed man's head. Ryan and J.B. were pretty unmistakable. But who was this Baron? He tried to move but found that his limbs were sluggish. It was as if he was trying to make himself move from a very long way off. The commands from his brain, as urgent as they were, seemed to be taking aeons to filter through to his arms and legs. Even then it was as though the message was diluted so that the desire to spring up came out as a feeble twitch.

He tried to look around at the others. Even moving his head required an effort that it took supreme will to summon. From the corner of his eye he could see them—they all looked to be in a similar state to himself.

Valiant picked up one of the sweetmeats. "The only part of the meal that was served separately. Yours had an extra, added ingredient. I had to leave it till now so that you could get enough brew in you not to notice." He sighed. "You know, I really do hate doing this. It goes against all the ways we usually do things here. But Crabbe will pay me big jack for you. I had to keep an eye on you all day, make sure I knew where you were. I can't mess this up. Pity, though..."

Ryan wanted to call him a coldheart bastard, wanted to rise from his seat and plunge the panga into his heart. But he couldn't move. As everything faded to black, he could see Valiant beckon his sec men.

DOC WOKE with a jolt as the wag pulled to a halt. The cessation of blows to his head jolted him back to awareness.

His head was spinning, the pain enervating as he lifted it up and looked around him at the interior of the wag.

"Are we there yet?"

Chapter Three

Brilliant white light poured into the interior of the wag as the double doors at the rear were flung wide. The sec men inside raised arms to protect their eyes, rifles held at an angle. All of the companions squinted, torn between protecting their vision from being seared and maintaining the ruse of being unconscious. One thing was certain—any chance of taking the guards by stealth had now been eliminated.

"Illuminated," Doc whispered, the sole exception to the rule, his eyes wide and pupils reduced to pinpricks as he was temporarily blinded. "And the light pours out of me..."

"Yeah, they got to be the right ones—that sure as hell sounds like the crazy fucker," a voice boomed from beyond the wall of light. It was followed by the sounds of laughter. Three, maybe four, male voices.

"Shit, you got to do that?" one of the sec men whined, his eyes still protected by a ragged sleeve.

"Just want to make sure you got the cargo, and it's the right one," the first man said patiently, as though speaking to a child.

"The people of Hawknose don't double-deal. It isn't our way," said another of the sec men in the wag's interior, his tone as pompous as his words.

"Yeah, sure you don't," the man replied, barely able

to keep the humor from his voice. "Thing is, it ain't me you got to convince. Crabbe don't trust no one. Not even your precious Valiant. Seems a straight enough guy to me—you all do," he added placatingly. "But it ain't down to me. I'm just doing my job, just like you."

The sec man who had complained sniffed hard. It would seem that his pride had been appeased. "That's okay, then. Chill that engine, no sense in wasting gas," he added over his shoulder to the wag driver, who complied. "Right, now let's get these fuckers out of here and get the transaction over and done with."

The sec men rose stiffly to their feet, no longer shielding eyes that had grown accustomed to the light. They hustled their captives to their feet, none of the companions making the pretence of unconsciousness. Now that their eyes, too, were becoming accustomed to the light, they could see that the sec men who had brought them were also augmented by five men, clustered within the arc of lights that cast such an illumination into the interior of the wag. The lights illuminated a semicircle of dirt that was about five yards in circumference. Beyond that, and the bank of lights, it was hard to see anything. They could be in a ville, or they could be in the middle of nowhere at a randomly chosen rendezvous. Until any of them had any idea of their location, it was best just to play along, a decision that none of them needed to consult to make.

None except Doc. The old man was last to his feet, staring around him in awe and wonder, as though seeing the world for the first time. Which, perhaps, in some ways he was. Mildred, casting him a glance as she was hustled by, wouldn't have been surprised if he had a slight concussion from the constant banging of his head. Certainly, his dazed expression did nothing to dispel that notion.

The old man was the last to be hustled out of the wag and onto the hard ground. The others had stood idly as the sec men struggled with him—his balance seemed genuinely impaired and he had trouble keeping his feet—trying to scout their position without being obtrusive.

As they became used to the arc lights, the darkness beyond began to slowly coalesce into a series of shapes and shadows. They weren't in the middle of nowhere—this was a ville. It was quiet, and now that the noise of the wag engine had ceased, they could hear in the background the familiar noises of people going about their business. It was late evening, almost dark. An overcast sky let little light from the moon seep through. Chem clouds hid a near full moon, and only the very occasional shaft of moonlight pierced the oppressive darkness.

The companions were, at a guess, on the edge of the ville. The sounds drifted only from two directions, the others yielding nothing but silence. Was this a compound of some kind where they were to be kept prisoner?

They would find out soon enough. For now, at least Doc's bewilderment had given them the time to take some kind of stock.

"Line them up and step back, lads. We want to see what we've got here."

Now they could see the man behind the voice. It was surprising. He had the voice of a big man: barrel-chested and tall. Yet the man who addressed the Hawknose sec force in such booming tones was actually a short, squat man with a mop of curly gray hair and a straggling beard, almost dwarfed by the battered Kalashnikov he cradled in his arms. Yet despite his lack of physical stature, he had a presence that told he was in charge of the sec men who flanked him, each man standing taller and broader. They looked like a handpicked team designed to deter any arguments. As they stood, in a parallel arc to the lights that were at their rear, it certainly seemed as though they were having the desired effect on the Hawknose team, who stood back toward their wag a little defensively.

The small, squat sec man stepped forward, squinting at the six bound people now arrayed in front of him as though examining them closely.

"Yeah, they look like it to me." He stepped back and said over his shoulder, "You reckon as much, boys?"

There was a general muttering of agreement.

Mildred, looking at them, wondered if this was because they really were in agreement, or as part of some process to soften up the men clustered by the wag. To make them more amenable to whatever may come next.

Meanwhile, the squat sec man snapped his fingers, and two of the men bent down, reaching behind them. They each withdrew three sacks, which they tossed into the center of the dirt patch, so that they landed at the feet of the companions with a clinking that betrayed the contents.

Solid jack.

"Yep," he continued without missing a beat, "I reckon these are the dudes that Crabbe has been looking for. Stupe, really, all those missions he sent us out on, and the bastards roll up down the way apiece without us even having to do anything. Valiant did good, and so did you."

"Then why have you only thrown in six sacks?" asked the pompous Hawknose sec man. Even if he wasn't the senior, he had taken it upon himself to be spokesman. Like the others, he was lean of face and grim of demeanor. His face gave nothing away, like his compatriots, though none of the six betrayed by them would have betted that the others weren't secretly relieved that they weren't the ones on the firing line should his opposite number not like his tone.

The squat sec man sniffed heavily, growled in the throat, then spit out a phlegm ball that landed with a dull splat by one of the sacks.

"It's like this. They look right. That's good. We got—" and he pointed to each in turn as he reeled them off "—Brian Mordor, the one-eyed leader. Jock and Snowy, the old guy and the albino. One's crazy as a mutie coot. The other's a shit-hot hunter and real dangerous. Had my way, I'd shackle the little bastard at all times. Can't trust them… Krysty, the mutie with the weird strength. Gonna have to watch her, boys. Millicent, the one who's a healer. Don't let that fool you, boys. Heard she can fight like a man. Kinda looks like one, to my eyes. Krysty looks more my type, though I hear she's Brian's woman. And then we got J. T. Edson, the blaster man. They say there ain't shit he don't know about weapons. Useful guy."

"You know a lot about us," Ryan said slowly. "We don't know shit about you. Want to tell us?" He kept the irony out of his voice. The man seemed to know something about them, but with a strange twist. Like that old game Chinese Whispers that Krysty had told him about, where information was passed on from person to person, half heard. He wondered what else they would know, but yet not know.

The squat sec man sniffed and spit again.

That's one hell of a sinus infection the guy's got, Mildred thought, but held her peace.

"Listen, Brian, I ain't got nothing against you personally, see, but unless you shut up I'm gonna have to bust you in the jaw. My baron wants you, and he's got you. But that don't mean that a little accident don't happen between here and him getting to see you, especially if you can't keep your yap shut. You don't talk unless you're asked something, you see?"

Ryan bristled at being spoken to in such a fashion. He could see the smug looks on the faces of the surrounding sec men, and he was seized by a desire to wipe it from their faces. But his hands and feet were still bound, and he had no weapons. He gritted his teeth so hard that his jaw cramped as he fought down his temper. Although he knew he shouldn't rise to the bait, there was something about the squat man that irritated him—an assumption of superiority based on nothing more than the fact that he held a blaster.

And something about the way that sec man looked at him. As though he was sizing him up.

Just what did Baron Crabbe want from them? Want enough to have been searching for them, and to have collated information that seemed to be almost but not quite right? That was a cause for concern. Did he want something that they would be unable to give because they had never had it? Any further rumination, taking his mind off his anger as it did, was interrupted by the further supercilious tones of the sec man who had escorted them this far.

"Are you going to argue with Ryan—" he pronounced the name with emphasis "—or are you going to tell me why you're not paying up in full?"

"I was in the middle of telling you when one-eye here interrupted me," the sec man snarled, raising his blaster and checking it pointedly. Behind him, the other guards moved menacingly. "Thing is, Brian and his boys—and girls, if you'll excuse me," he directed at Krysty, "have got a little task that Crabbe wants them to undertake for him. Now, much as he appreciates the fact that Valiant sniffed them out, and that you've brought them here, he feels that it would be a little remiss of him to pay in full before they've undertaken that task. After all, they look right, but if they ain't, then that's a lot of jack to throw away. Y'see?"

"But we've brought them here in good faith—" the sec man began.

"Ain't saying nothing against you or Valiant," the squat man interrupted. "How many times? Shit, get the point. You keep the half no matter what. Turns out that we all made a mistake, then that's it. If these're the right guys, then you get the second half of the payment. Look at it my way—you already called out Brian as Ryan. That don't inspire me, you know what I'm saying?"

The pompous sec man's voice held a quiver of fear as he spoke once more. "Valiant will not like us returning empty-handed."

The squat man coughed a laugh that was filled with scorn. “You ain’t returning empty-handed. You got half the jack. You get the other half if the task is completed. Shit, way I see it ol’ Crabbe is being pretty good to you. He’s taking you on trust ’cause he knows you fuckers wouldn’t lie if your lives depended on it. Don’t think you know how,” he added reflectively. “So if it turns out that ol’ Brian here is really Ryan, like you say, and he ain’t the man Crabbe is after, you don’t deserve the full jack. But you didn’t try to deceive him, so you get to keep that half. I’ll say it again, stupe boy—if I had my way, and these ain’t the right people, I’d be after your asses with all blasters blazing. So why don’t you be a good little man and fuck right off before I really lose it.”

There was something about the way that his tone changed over the last couple of sentences that signaled a barely concealed anger. Not one of the companions had to exchange glances with another to know that the pompous Hawknose sec man had overstepped. Without turning, they could hear the shufflings that indicated at least some of their former guards were preparing for retreat.

“Before you go, ain’t there something you forgot?” the squat man asked with a hint of mockery in his voice. From their rear, the companions could hear two of the men move forward. They appeared in front of the group, gathering the sacks of jack before hastily moving back to their wag. They didn’t look at the people they had betrayed, but Ryan could see enough to notice that both guards were sweating with fear.

The squat man watched them, the ghost of a smile

playing around his lips. He put the blaster over his shoulder, as though to indicate his lack of fear and knowledge of his superior status. "Something else you forgot?" he added, waiting until the Hawknose men were almost ready to leave. There was a pause, and then one of the long-faced men stepped past the companions, carrying a clutch of weaponry. As soon as they had been rendered unconscious, Ryan and his people had been stripped of their blasters and blades. Even Ryan's weighted scarf had been taken, and used to bind the weapons together.

They were dropped in an unceremonious heap at the feet of the squat sec boss. He nodded—a barely noticeable approval, whether at delivery or horde was impossible to tell—before speaking again.

"Yeah, that's it. You can go now. You'll be hearing from Crabbe if things go well. Don't come asking."

The sec man who had dropped the load looked up briefly as he passed Ryan. The one-eyed man caught him in a stare for the briefest of seconds, and was astonished to see the naked fear in the Hawknose man's face. Whatever Crabbe wanted from them, he would obviously stop at nothing. His ruthless reputation was foretold in that one glance.

While the group stood, still bound hand and foot, facing the semicircle of sec men who covered them, they could hear the wag in which they had been transported start up and leave. Even the pitch of the engine seemed to have a whining note to it, as though it couldn't get away quick enough. As it faded into the distance, they were left staring at the men who were now their captors.

"You don't say much, Brian," the squat man said. He looked quizzically at the one-eyed man, as though trying to peer into his very soul. "Hope for your sake that you say more when Crabbe questions you."

"You told me to shut up when I spoke before," Ryan said calmly. "You're the man with the blaster. What do you expect?"

The squat man sniffed. "Don't know. More fight, mebbe. But mebbe you're just biding your time," he added with a knowing look.

"Mebbe..." Ryan answered slowly. "Meantime, shouldn't we know what this is all about?"

The sec man laughed. "I'm going to watch you very carefully, Brian...Ryan...whatever the fuck your name is."

He gestured, and half of the lights went out. It took a moment for the companions to adjust to the sudden change, facing as they did the full glare of the arcs. In that time, the sec men fanned out so that they covered the group from all sides. As their eyes adjusted to the darker night, they could see that they were on the edge of the ville. Behind the lights lay the spread of buildings that housed the ville folk. Looking around for the first time, they could see that to the rear—where the wag from Hawknose was now nothing more than a memory—there was nothing but wasteland.

There were more men than they had originally thought. Behind the arc lights had been an additional six, who had been operating the arcs and standing in reserve. Now, with the lighting reduced to a level where they could see clearly beyond and around, it was plain to tell that these men were deployed to surround them.

They might be unarmed and bound, but their reputation had obviously preceded them.

"Okay, chill the rest of the lights, and keep them covered," the squat sec man ordered, almost casually deploying his blaster so that it now covered Ryan. The meaning of this gesture was clear to the one-eyed man—the squat sec man considered Ryan his own personal charge.

Three of the six lights operated at half beam. These were pulled down slowly until they were extinguished, allowing the sec force to keep full observation on their charges.

"Okay," the squat man barked when the lights had faded. "Louie, retrieve the arcs come morning. Pickup accomplished. Keep the bastards covered, and let's move on out. Aw shit, better free them up a bit," he added, looking at their hobbled ankles.

One of the sec men moved forward silently, observed by the others who kept their blasters carefully trained on the companions. Quickly and with deft fingers he loosened the knots around their ankles, one by one. Feeling that had been restricted to pins, needles and a dull throb now flooded back into their extremities, making it easier to move and yet at the same time more painful.

The squat sec leader waited until the task had been completed and his man had fallen back into his place in the circle. With a grunt of approval, he gestured that they move.

If being drugged and spirited away to a strange ville while bound and stripped of their weapons could be called a surprise—and Ryan would be more inclined to term it stupe bastard carelessness—then this was the second one to assail them in the space of a few hours. For they didn't move toward the lights, shapes and sounds of the ville, which was what they had expected.

It was difficult for the companions to move at the pace that the sec men tried to set. Their bonds made it difficult to move with more than the smallest of steps, despite their being loosened. Blood flow to previously numb feet made them tender and treacherous. J.B. stumbled into Krysty, who found it hard to keep her own balance. Doc fell over many times, face-first into the dust before levering himself up by his elbows. Mildred went to help him up the first time, but the barrel of a Kalashnikov jabbed in her ribs dissuaded her. Only Ryan and Jak kept to their feet with any sign of ease. That was deceptive in the one-eyed man's case. It took all of his concentration to maintain the appearance of ease. Despite the pain and the effort, he didn't want the sec leader to see that he was struggling. When the time came, he wanted the man to have seen no chinks in his armor. But for Jak, there was no such effort required. The innate skills that made the albino the hunter he was were more than enough for him to compensate for a minor—and temporary—disability.

The guards around them tried to force the pace, but it was of little use. The shackles of returning circulation and the bonds that were still in place made it impossible. Finally the sec leader had to compromise. With a curse and a sigh he stopped the party, directing that the ropes around their ankles be severed. He even allowed them a few moments to massage circulation back into aching ankles.

Krysty's glance flashed across the circle, catching Ryan's eye. He knew what she was asking, and shrugged. He had no idea why they were being led away from the ville when the baron had paid for them to be delivered to him. Was this some kind of plot by the sec boss? Or was there something else that they couldn't as yet know?

Ryan thought that both he and Krysty had been discreet. Obviously not as much as he had thought, for as they shuffled and stumbled to their feet once more, the sec boss spoke.

"Yeah, weird that Crabbe wants to see you so bad, yet you ain't getting to see the baron's palace. Am I right?" He paused, then laughed harshly. "Yeah, sure I am. But you'll see soon enough. And if you're who he hopes you are, then you'll understand."

With a gesture to his men, he ushered the party onward. There was no chance for the companions to communicate in any way, even though that was what they most urgently needed. Thoughts were whirling inside their heads. They were being marched across terrain that was rough and uneven, uncertain under their feet. Their weapons were achingly just beyond their reach, carried by one of the sec men ahead of them in the guard circle. It would be so easy to just make the effort—to stumble the short distance and make a grab—and yet if they did, any one of them, they would all be cut down before anxious fingertips could touch gunmetal.

The sky overhead was dark and unforgiving. Chem

clouds scudded across the void, whipped along by winds that were at high altitude, in contrast to the stillness through which they trudged. The near-full moon was only briefly and fleetingly revealed, its wan shafts of light revealing nothing that seemed to matter. The ville lay far behind them now, and ahead there was only wild and desolate wasteland.

Still, it seemed that the sec boss knew where they were going. Whatever his aim, at least it was possible to see that he had one. And, by the pace that he was setting, the goal was still some distance away.

They continued on through the night, their energy sapped by the after-effects of the drug and the cramping, crippling effects of the subsequent confinement and constriction. As the chem clouds became suffused with the light of early dawn, turning from gray and black to a gray that was tinted orange and red as the sun attempted to signal a new day, it seemed that they had walked at least as far as they had been driven. It was almost impossible to determine direction without the map of stars denied by the cloud cover, and so it was ludicrously possible that they may be walking all the way back to Hawknose.

That idea vanished when the sec boss turned to them and, with a sly grin, said, "Well, what do ya know, kids. Looks like we're here."

For some time they had been ascending a shallow incline. Now they had reached the summit and could see that it fell away sharply beneath them. At the bottom of the drop was the remains of an old road, a single-lane blacktop that led through the rusted tangle of a chain-link fence until it came up against what had once been a disguised doorway. Concrete, receding into the earth, and roughly seven yards in diameter, it was now as plain as the dawning day—the entrance to a redoubt.

"Thought that might make you jump," the squat man observed as he closely watched the companions' reactions. Despite themselves, all except Jak had registered some sense of surprise. The albino teen had remained impassive, as ever, despite his inner feelings echoing those of his friends.

Ryan's jaw set hard. He should have expected this. There had been hints in what Valiant had said before they had been drugged. Crabbe had pieced together a kind of history. He knew some facts, had made leaps of imagination between others, but had the basic ideas. There had to be a reason why the story grabbed him. Why not because he had found his own, personal redoubt?

So where was this going to lead them?

The squat sec boss's face broke into a grin. "Yeah, the looks on your faces, I'd say that names and shit aside, Crabbe knew what he was looking for. And that cob-up-his-ass jerk-off Valiant is a lot smarter than I'd give him credit for. Looks like his people are halfway to the rest of that jack."

With a gesture, he bade them to start down the slope. It was dry and dusty, the loose earth rising in clouds around them and making it hard to keep a foothold. Small rocks and stones turned at their ankles and slipped away from under their feet. Each of them was concentrating too closely on keeping their own footing to notice that the sec force surrounding them had spread out a little to allow them more room.

With good reason—the squat man knew what would happen, and wanted to keep his own people out of the way of the impact. Choked and blinded by the dust that rose around them, ropes pulling at ankles forced apart by slipping feet, balance proved to be an impossibility. Doc was, inevitably, the first to go. His feet shot out from under him and he fell heavily, rolling on his hip and pivoting sideways.

Despite catching him from the corner of her eye, and trying her best to avoid being taken down by his falling frame, Mildred couldn't move her own feet quickly enough. A combination of uncertain terrain and limbs dulled by constriction made her clumsy where usually she would be sure.

The pair began to tumble down the incline, gathering momentum and dislodging earth and stone as they fell. It made the ground around them begin to move. For J.B., Ryan and Krysty—all of them, like Doc and Mildred, disabled to a degree by the binding and constriction of their limbs—it made things that much harder. The already unsteady ground beneath their feet was now treacherous, and the way in which Doc and Mildred had fallen made it that much more apparent that it would be all too easy for each to follow.

All of the sec men had fallen back so that they were at the rear of the group. They were surer on their feet, partly because they were unshackled, and also because they were able to pick their way around unsettled terrain with greater ease. They took the pace more slowly—no need to hurry when your captives were in no condition to make a break.

The only exception to any of this was Jak. The albino

youth was always fleet and sure of foot. Even with the remnants of the drug in his system, and his ankles still partially numb from their binding, he was able to pick up speed, nimbly jumping the larger rocks that sought to disturb his balance. He rode the scree of stone and earth that began to move like a river beneath him, using the currents within it and adapting his own rhythms to run with it. When he reached the bottom of the sharp drop, bringing himself to a halt before he hit the remains of the black ribbon, he turned and looked back up the incline.

The sec force were three-quarters of the way down, picking its way carefully over the wake of the companions' descent. The sun had now risen enough to light their way with ease. They were strung out in a line, with the squat, bearded sec chief in the center.

He stopped short when he saw that Jak was glaring at him. Their eyes met, and in the early light of morning the albino's red eyes glowed with a passion that he usually kept masked. A shiver ran down the squat man's spine. The albino teen had said nothing, and his face remained fixed. But those eyes said it all—if ever he had the chance, he would take vengeance for this humiliation on himself and his friends.

By the time the sec force had reached the bottom, Jak had long since turned away. He helped Ryan to his feet, and then between them they assisted the others to right themselves. Limbs ached and were bruised, there were a few contusions, but there was no major damage. Mildred murmured that she would tend to the wounds when her hands were freed. Ryan wondered why the sec men had been content to watch them fall.

When he looked toward the exposed concrete of the redoubt tunnel, there was an answer. There was a wag to one side that hadn't been there before. As the area around was flat and open, and they had seen nothing approaching for several miles from their initial vantage point at the top of the incline, it could only have come from inside the redoubt. That impression was reinforced by the way in which the men standing on either side of the wag were dressed. There were three of them, two on the left, one on the right. Two cradled Kalashnikovs, while the third was carrying an SMG of some sort. At this distance, even J.B. couldn't tell the model. But it was a blaster, nonetheless. As was the canon mounted on the back of the wag. No one was manning it at present, but it looked capable of serious damage over serious distance.

No wonder the sec force following them was in no great hurry.

The sec men from the incline reached the bottom and fanned out to cover them once more. The three men by the wag, two with rifles, began to move forward to reach their compatriots. The man with the SMG slung it and climbed up onto the back of the wag, covering them.

"You're taking no chances," Ryan observed wryly as the sec boss approached.

The squat man shrugged. "You should be proud, Brian or Ryan. Shows we take you seriously."

"I'll remember that next time I see a shitload of blasters ready to take me out when I'm unarmed. Makes me feel real proud."

The squat man grinned. "I could grow to like you, Brian…if I could be bothered. Now get moving."

He gestured to them to move. Slowly, the captive group moved toward the entrance to the redoubt. Seeing that their guards were in control, the two sec men from the wag returned to it, one of them getting behind the wheel and firing up the engine. He maneuvered the vehicle so that it faced the redoubt entrance, the SMG on its back swiveling with the movement so that it always kept the captives covered.

The companions walked slowly up to the redoubt doors, which stayed resolutely shut.

"So what now?" the one-eyed man asked, turning to the sec boss.

"Little test for you," he called. "See if you're who we think."

"I thought you knew that," Ryan countered.

The sec boss laughed, a short, barking cough. "Reckon I do. But mebbe Crabbe would like more proof. He suggested this, and who am I to go against my baron? Now stop fucking about and open the doors. If you are who we think, then you'll know how to do it."

"And if we're not?"

"You'd be triple stupe to try and bluff it out, if that's what you're thinking. We'll just chill you now, and not waste any more time."

Ryan surveyed the sec force facing them. All were armed. And then there was the SMG.

They'd do it, all right. He was certain of that.

"J.B.," Ryan muttered.

The Armorer stepped forward, raising both bound

hands so that he could remove his glasses and wipe the dust and dirt from them before placing them back on the bridge of his nose.

The keypad, discreetly hidden, was directly in front of him. He punched in the three-digit entry code that was common to all redoubts.

The doors groaned into action, opening to reveal a tunnel that sloped gently down to a dogleg corner. The brightly lit interior was clean and empty. It looked like any other redoubt they had seen.

Except it was far from empty farther down.

Baron Crabbe was waiting for them.

"Move on in. Slowly," the sec boss ordered. "Wait," he added as the companions began to enter. "Four in front. We don't want them to be pulling down any of those other doors and leaving us on one side, them on the other, do we," he added.

"Smart. Wouldn't get us anywhere when you've got people in there already," Ryan said, as four of the black-clad sec men moved in front of them, reversing so they could move backward, keeping the companions covered all the while.

"Mebbe. Wouldn't want to look stupe in front of the baron, though," the sec chief replied. "Now you can go."

They moved down the tunnel and into the interior of the redoubt.

Chapter Four

The wag followed them as far as the first dogleg, where it turned off to go into the vehicle maintenance bay. J.B. followed it, noting that there was only one other wag in the bay. If that was any indication, there were few sec men at the redoubt other than those they already knew about. That information could be useful.

Moving down the corridors from level to level, they began to move deeper into the bowels of the earth. All the sec doors within the redoubt had been propped open, and apart from a few areas of darkness in the distance, where lighting had failed, it seemed that the redoubt had been in good condition when discovered and hadn't been ransacked. As they descended past the level where the armory was housed, J.B. once again cast a look toward the closed rooms that he knew would house the redoubt's weapons. Had this Baron Crabbe stripped it, he wondered, or were there rich pickings that would serve them well? Always assuming, of course, that they could escape their captors long enough to reach the armory. Looking at the limping, dirty and exhausted group around him, it was an option that seemed a thousand miles from possible.

While J.B. was thinking of the armory, Mildred was wondering about the medical facilities. Meds and dressings would make it a lot easier for them to handle the pain and the minor injuries they had sustained. And handle it was exactly what they would need to do if they were to leap on any avenue of escape that might present itself. Krysty and Doc, meanwhile, thought of the dorms and showers they had passed. A hot shower would soothe many of their aches, and clear their heads. And they'd need clear heads if they were to make a break.

Ryan was thinking of all that, while at the same time trying to observe his companions and assess the level of punishment they could risk. There was no doubt that the night had taken a toll on them. Whatever Crabbe wanted, the longer it took him to explain, then the better it might be. At least time would give them the opportunity to snatch some recuperation.

Jak wasn't bothered by the dirt, the pain or the need to rest. He just watched everything carefully, noting the areas where the sec men were weak or sloppy, noting where the lighting had dimmed, providing places to hide and strike. As soon as the chance came, he would be ready.

With all these thoughts preoccupying them, the companions were silent as they were led farther into the military installation.

Finally they reached their destination—the control room of the mat-trans unit.

The sec man in front of them pulled back, revealing an open door. There were noises from within: low, whispery voices and the shuffling of movement. At a gesture from the squat sec man, the companions moved into the room.

Two men stood by one of the comps. One was tall

and thin, slightly stooped and balding, with long strands of hair falling around his shoulders in contrast to a pate that shone under the lights. He had a list in his hand, and Ryan recognized the type of paper. They had seen these before: single sheets, laminated to protect against constant use.

Did the sheet tell the two men something about the mat-trans? Had these men worked out how the mechanism worked? Ryan knew from experience that the companions weren't the only ones who used the mat-trans system.

As the group entered the control room and shuffled to a halt, the two men turned. Ryan had assumed that the tall man was Baron Crabbe, but as the second one turned to face them, there was something about his expression that said otherwise. He was shorter, and stout, yet there was a hardness about his frame, and the squaring of his shoulders, that suggested the fat had formed a layer over solid muscle. He was clean-shaved, with hair cropped close to his bullet skull. Scars showed through, as did some on his face under the stubble. As he saw them, his face broke into a satisfied grin, his mouth raising only on one side, the other paralyzed by the scar that ran from the corner and down his chin.

But it was his eyes—they bored into the group, examining them minutely and flickering from one to the other. At each, he paused before nodding shortly. His eyes blazed brightly with excitement.

"At last," he said finally. "All this time, and then you go and land virtually at my bastard feet. It seemed too good to be true."

"They passed the code test, Baron," the squat sec

man reported. His deference was in complete contrast to the way he had spoken to his captives, and Ryan found it both amusing and instructive. Another clue on how to handle the man when the moment came.

"I knew they would, Nelson," Crabbe snapped with a tone that veered between irritation and anger. "Stand back, let them settle. Please, be seated," he added with a more unctuous tone, although only indicating the floor.

"It would help if we weren't tethered like a bunch of pack animals," Mildred said as they started to lower themselves.

"Of course, of course," Crabbe said, although in a tone that suggested it wouldn't otherwise have occurred to him. He gestured to his sec chief. "Nelson, cut them loose."

The squat man moved carefully in front of the group. He had holstered his blaster and held J.B.'s knife in his hand—a deliberate move, no doubt—and used it to cut free their wrists and ankles. He brandished the knife close to Ryan's artery as he sliced at his wrist, a grin flashing across his face as he caught Ryan's eye. A provocation, and then he was gone again, vanished to their rear.

Crabbe, satisfied that they were now comfortable enough to listen, began while they each massaged life and full feeling back into their hands and feet.

"This must be a familiar room to you all. At least, if you're who I think you are. You have knowledge I need. Mebbe I have knowledge that will help you make sense of what you know. It's like that," he added, appearing to go off at a tangent, "what's left of the predark world. Bits and pieces, some of which make sense, and some of which makes none at all. And then you get some small glimmering that suddenly makes the previously insane seem somehow sane. Things that make no fucking sense at all suddenly seem to be transformed into things that are just so blindingly obvious that you think you must have been a stupe not to see it before.

"Like the stories of this guy, Trader," he continued, emphasizing the name and watching them carefully. After Valiant's explanation, they were expecting this, and so Crabbe didn't get the reaction he wanted. His words were met with a blandness that did nothing to inform him, and little more than irritate him.

"Have it that way, then," he said softly. "See, the thing I could never understand about the legendary Trader was his seemingly limitless supply of stuff. A hidden predark stockpile my ass. He had an underground base. I just know it My men found this one when we had a quake. The shit covering it dropped off like so much crap. Took us a long time to figure out a way in. Now that I know how it works, it's a marvel to me that we did it all. Punching those fucking keys in any order… Now that I know how these doors work, I take it as a sign that we got in here. It's meant."

"What is meant?" Doc asked.

"Why, my using my knowledge and the knowledge that I get from you to run the whole of this pesthole and make it great again. I know, from what I've seen in here, that this land used to be the one that everyone else looked up to. Now there must be a whole chunk of world out there that's still got people, even if it's like us. We should be great in their eyes."

"Ah, glory…" Doc said absently.

From the slightly glazed expression, which puzzled Crabbe, Mildred could tell that the old man was still slightly concussed.

"But not gold?" Doc added.

Crabbe's brow furrowed. "Gold? Well, yeah, of course I mean that, too. Hell, I'd be stupe if I didn't. Ain't that what everyone wants? Ain't that the same thing as glory? Glory gets you respect, and so does jack, gold. Goes hand in hand, I'd say."

"If it's the way to glory and jack, then why didn't Trader take that? Why haven't we? Suppose we are the people you say. Ask yourself why we were doing shitty jobs in Hawknose waiting for the next convoy out," Ryan said.

Crabbe eyed him shrewdly. "Fair point, Brian. But this is the only place like this around these parts. I know that 'cause I read that there map." He indicated the area behind them. On the wall over a row of comps lining one side of the room was a clear glass screen, outlined with a map of the predark United States. On it were marked the locations of redoubts across the continent. "The way I see it is this—somehow you wandered away from one of these places. I bet you've been to lots of them. Mebbe that's what you do. Go to one of these, see what you can pick up, then move to the next. Mebbe you got a stockpile in one of them, mebbe you're looking for the next big stockpile. Whatever, I reckon you left one of them, got into a fight and ended up stranded in the middle of nowhere. Fact is, you ending up at Hawknose may have been no accident, now that I think about it. Mebbe the reason you landed there is because you were headed for the nearest one you knew…here."

He finished with a triumphant flourish. In the silence that followed, Ryan was unsure as to whether the baron expected them to cave in and admit that he was right. The demonstration of reasoning that had got Crabbe to this point was disturbing. What other assumptions had he made about Trader? About them? And what, as a result, would he expect from them?

Ryan decided that the only way to find out would be to play him at his own game.

"Okay, so you got us. And you're right. Question is, where does that get you?"

Crabbe looked at Ryan closely, studying him as though to somehow discern whether he was being deceived. Ryan held the baron's gaze, steady, impassive.

The baron's weathered features creased. "Knew it. I fucking knew it. Didn't I tell you, Sal?" he asked, turning to the tall, thin man.

Sal simply nodded, his face unreadable.

"So where does that leave us then, Baron? All cards on the table."

"Huh?" The baron looked confused for a moment. "Ah, you mean everything out in the open, right? 'Cards on the table'—what kind of a stupe expression is that? Something you've picked up from the old ways in your travels?"

"Yeah, must be," Ryan answered blandly. In truth, he'd heard it all over Deathlands, and had no idea where he'd first started using it. But if that was what Crabbe wanted to believe, then that was just fine.

Crabbe shook his head, laughing. "There is just so

much that I need to find out, but first, we need to get down to basics. Am I right? There's a whole network of these underground bases, like on that map. Was that Trader's secret?"

"Not exactly," Ryan began carefully. "There are a number of these places, like you've worked out. Getting from one to the other is difficult, and some of them have been looted or are damaged in some way."

"What ways?" Crabbe snapped, as though suspicious of anything that may deviate from his own ideas.

Ryan knew that was worth bearing in mind. "Well," he said, "you saw how this place was exposed. Sometimes quakes bear down deep, cause cracks in the tunnels. Some places just collapse in on themselves."

Crabbe nodded slowly. "Right…and looted, you say. So there are places where others have got into these bases." He looked at Ryan, who merely nodded. "Then if that's right, how come there ain't people appearing from everywhere?"

"I told you. Getting from one to another is difficult."

"But you do it," Crabbe said quickly. "So you must have the secret."

"What secret?" Ryan asked slowly.

Crabbe smiled slyly. "One of the legends of Trader. There was a disk that was part of the old tech. It showed where the big stockpile was. Where all the jack and weapons predark were hidden when they knew the nukecaust was going off. It showed where it was, and how to get there. How to get there, Brian. Which means the secret of moving between the bases. And that's got everything to do with this."

Crabbe turned and strode the few paces to the mat-trans unit.

The baron once again getting his name wrong was another reminder that the man's half-assed assumptions spelled trouble. He had worked out that the mat-trans was a means of transportation, but not how it worked. That, presumably, was part of the information that he wanted to extract from the group.

More worrying was his assumption that so much knowledge was contained on one old comp disk. Again, it was rooted in a piece of truth. There once was a disk, but it had contained nothing more than a few codes for redoubts. It had been damaged, and was, in all likelihood, nothing more than a piece of tech that housed some mundane and routine information. The disk was long gone, lost during one of their mad scrambles for survival.

How could they explain that to a man who had already decided to believe what he wanted? He was certain that Trader had had a disk, but he was dead wrong.

Crabbe was on a roll, and so Ryan remained silent. The baron turned back to them, snatching at the sheet in Sal's hand. The tall, balding man let it go quickly, so as not to anger his baron. Crabbe brandished it at them.

"You know the secret of moving, but you don't have the disk. Think about it. If you use your knowledge to help me find the disk, how far could they take us?"

Ryan was bemused and relieved, but managed to keep this from his voice as he said, "We? An alliance?"

Crabbe grimaced. "Not exactly. A deal, sure. I like to deal. Who doesn't? But not really what you'd call an alliance. See, I didn't get to be baron by cutting people in on the deal. You know how it works, right? You did learn from the great Trader, after all. And I'm betting he wasn't the kind of guy to make an alliance where he could make a bargain. You know what I'm saying?"

Ryan stole a look at his companions. Doc still looked dazed, but the others had their attention on the baron. And there was no doubt that they, like Ryan, were totally clear on what Crabbe's meaning might be.

"Okay," Ryan said slowly, "let's just say that we do know how to get from one base to another. Are you saying that the disk you're looking for—the one that contains all the information you want on how to find the kind of stash you're looking for, and how to go from base to base easily—is in one of the places on that list?"

Crabbe smiled slyly. "I think you know it is, Brian. But if you want to play it that way, then fine. I believe the marks on this paper show the bases where the disk might be. And they also have something that shows you how to work the thing—" he gestured at the mat-trans unit "—but I don't understand the way that they used to write stuff down predark. There ain't no one in the ville who does. That kind of stuff has never been any use to us before."

"Couldn't you just ask someone else to read it for you?" Mildred asked, breaking her silence. She could barely keep the sardonic edge from her voice. "Seems a whole lot of bother just to look for us to read a list for you."

Crabbe stared at her. He seemed to be torn between towering rage and astonishment. The latter won out.

"For fuck's sake, how do people as stupe as you get to be the keepers of the secrets? Fuck's sake, Brian, haven't you ever thought that it might be an idea to keep Millicent from opening her stupe mouth?" Before Ryan had a chance to answer, Crabbe sighed then continued. "Of course they know how to do it in places around here, but you think I'm going to let any of them in on the secret? I'd be forever looking over my bastard shoulder. Sure, I could say little about it, but there would always be questions. I don't want to be distracted by those fucking insects while I'm about my work."

"So you want us to read that list for you, then go to all of these places and try to find the disk you want," Mildred stated, bristling at the way in which Crabbe had spoken of—rather than to—her. The fact that he kept getting their names wrong was also irritating her out of all proportion. "So what, Mr. Smart-ass, is to stop us finding your disk and then not coming back?"

Crabbe stared at her as though he couldn't believe she could speak to him in this manner. "Brian," he said softly, "you should really keep a better hold on your people."

Ryan, on the other hand, was content to let Mildred lead, to see where it took them. "She has a very good question," he said. "I would have asked it myself. So would any of us."

Crabbe snorted, shook his head and turned away. It took him some time to compose himself. When he had, he turned back to them, shaking his head again.

"Shit, just how stupe do you think I am? Look around you. I got men with blasters aimed at you, could take you out anytime, and yet you still talk to me like I was shit. You've either got balls the size of a fucking boulder, or you're triple stupe. And that I don't believe. Is this your way of pushing me, see how far I'll go?"

Okay, Ryan figured, maybe he wasn't quite the stupe he had him figured for. But still, how was he going to work this out? And why the nuking hell did Crabbe assume the nonexistent disk was in one of those six redoubts out of the dozens in the Deathlands? It just didn't make sense.

Crabbe stood over them. He gestured to the rear of the room. "You've seen the sec. McCready doesn't like you, I can see that from his face. Nelson's a mean bastard. That's why I put him in charge. He'd gladly blow you all away now. He's sick of chasing you and getting nowhere, so he might be relieved that you're here now, but he still fucking hates your guts for all the trouble you've caused him. All I've got to do is say. But if I do, just 'cause you're all a pain in the ass, I have a problem."

"What we know," J.B. stated. "You want it. And not just that."

"No," Crabbe said softly. "Not just that. What then, J.T.?"

"You want us to go on the hunt because you don't want to leave here. You want to stay at the center of things."

"Smart man. I don't know what lies at the end of each journey. Might be nothing, might be someone like me. I'd rather you faced that. You're used to it. And you'll come back. I can make sure of that."

Again, the sly smile crossed his face.

"See, you don't think I'd go to all the trouble that I have and then just let you go off as you are, do you? Do

I really look like that kind of a fuckwit? No, I have a real simple plan. I might not be able to read, but I can count. Six lines on this sheet," he said, holding it up in front of them once more, "and six of you. So I pair you up, and while one of you goes and searches, then the other four are my prisoners here. If you don't come back, then say hello to the farm."

"What's to stop any of us taking our chances?" Ryan questioned.

Crabbe laughed. "From what I hear, with you people it's all for one and one for all. That's your strength. Thing is, it's also your weakness."

Chapter Five

Crabbe was, as he was so fond of telling everyone, a fair man. Certainly, he had continued to say that to Ryan and his companions many times, until they had reached the point where it was like the drip of water torture, the syllables like spikes to the brain. It was an interesting definition of fair under which he worked. In essence, although he would give them no real choice over the undertaking of the mission—do it or buy the farm—he wouldn't expect them to embark without some kind of rest or recuperation. Because he was fair. Not because it had been his sec men who had dragged them across wasteland while bound hand and foot.

So, it was fairness that came at a price, and with a large amount of provision. But tiredness and the erosion of spirit that came with aching weariness could do a lot to alter perspectives. What would have seemed very little, if not an insult under any other circumstances, was now welcomed.

Crabbe decreed that it wouldn't be fair to his new "partners" in the business of finding the disk if he didn't allow them to rest and prepare for the task ahead. It occurred to all of them that this may have had something to do with the fact that a rested and prepared team was more likely to succeed. But to say as much would have been pointless at best, and provocative at worst. Leave it until the time was right to strike.

After all, Crabbe did have a point. None of them was in a fit state to take on anyone. Sore, aching limbs were matched by a fuzziness of the mind, an after-effect of the drug that had enabled Valiant to sell them like so much feed.

So it was with an overwhelming sense of relief, rather than anything else, that they allowed themselves to be led to the redoubt's dorms. McCready escorted them himself. He was hostile and suspicious, and so would trust none of his men not to screw up. After Crabbe dismissed them, McCready and three of his men accompanied the companions to the level on which the dorms were housed. Before they left the baron and Sal to pore over the sheet that held, allegedly, the answers sought by Crabbe, Mildred stopped to ask if she could visit the medical facilities. When Crabbe, suspicion showing in his tone, asked her why, she indicated Doc.

"If you know anything about us, then you know that he's a little crazy at the best of times. I think he took a hell of a blow on the head, and the last thing you want—shit, that we want—is him going a little more crazy on our ass."

Crabbe had looked at the still dazed Doc, who grinned blankly when he saw the baron focus on him, and had decided that she was right. So two sec men accompanied Mildred while she went to the medical facility. To her surprise, it hadn't been looted.

"So you boys don't believe in the power of medicine?" she asked idly while she rifled the room for supplies.

The sec men didn't answer. Undeterred, she continued, even though she figured that she may as well be talking to herself.

"I'm really surprised. This stuff is at a premium out there. Good jack for some of it, and a hell of a lot of use for it among your people. I would have thought that Crabbe would want to use it, rather than let it go to waste."

"Can't do that when this place is still under wraps," one of the sec men mumbled.

"Shut the fuck up," his partner snapped.

"Don't matter if she knows," the first man replied in peevish tones. "Ain't like she's gonna get the chance to mouth off about it, right? They ain't going nowhere near the ville."

"Shithead, don't say no more," the second sec man said in an exasperated voice. The first man took the point and clammed up. But the exchange had told Mildred something—Crabbe was keeping the existence of the redoubt secret from the majority of his own people. He had some obviously high hopes for what he would find, and how it would increase his power. So much so that he felt the need to keep it a close secret. So much that hardly anyone knew that they were here. So much so, perhaps, that hardly anyone knew that the baron himself was here.

It was this knowledge that she carried back, along with the medicines, to the dorms. Once there, she set about treating Doc, biding her time before sharing her thoughts with the others. As she tended to the bump on the old man's head, which had now swollen and reddened showing the extent of the bruising from the repeated blows on the floor of the wag, she kept an eye on the two sec men. They watched her closely, as if expecting her to practice some deception.

"I'm only tending to his head, boys. Nothing to see here," she said with a heavy irony. "Why don't you just leave us to get some rest? Your boss has pulled the rest of you out of here, and there's no way we can escape, right?"

The sec men exchanged looks. The woman had an undeniable point. McCready had stationed men outside the dorm, and there was only the one entrance and exit. They looked uncomfortably at each other and then withdrew.

Mildred sighed with relief. Sure, there was no way out. But who knew what the companions would discuss if left alone? Good at following orders, but not too bright could be said of both the sec men and their leader, she guessed.

Having tended to Doc, Mildred was glad to strip off and get in the shower, feeling the needle-sharp points of hot water beat at her skin, massaging away the tiredness and tension. Her wrists and ankles smarted as the water hit them, but soon the water became soothing. She could feel the waves of torpor roll over her, and she wanted nothing more than to sleep. But as important as rest might be, she couldn't allow herself to succumb until she had discussed what had happened in the medical facilities.

Doc followed her into the showers, his head now clearing. He was, to be sure, a trifle uncertain of what had happened to him over the previous twelve hours, knowing only for sure that his head hurt like hell. But while Mildred had been showering, Krysty had filled him in. Doc firmly believed that he had been concussed. He knew what his crazy moments were like, albeit fewer of late, and they didn't fit with what he had experienced or felt. There were parts of the past twelve hours that were clear, and others that were hazy, as though he had been struggling to move and breathe through cotton wool. He could only hope that he would be of more use in the hours to come.

The time it took him to shower allowed Mildred to gather her thoughts and listen to the others. Left alone, they had reached a consensus that now was not the time to act, but that it would be necessary to keep triple red for the slightest opportunity. None was under the illusion that Crabbe wished to use their knowledge—as he saw it—and then keep them around. He currently had the whip hand. It was up to them to see that it changed.

When Doc emerged, Mildred told them about what had happened in the medical room. It was a small enough thing in itself, but the import of it wasn't lost on the rest of the group.

"If, perchance, we can engineer an opening in which we can reverse the positions between ourselves and the baron and his men, then an escape from here would be relatively simple. After all, who is there to follow us should we disable the forces he has down here?" Doc grinned. "And then perhaps we should pay that conniving knave Valiant a brief visit, to pay him the remainder of his blood jack in kind."

"Easy, Doc," J.B. said. "One thing at a time. Besides, if Crabbe disappears, who are his people going to blame?"

"Agreed," Ryan added. "We look out for ourselves first and settle scores second. A long way settled."

Doc pondered that. "A fair point, uh, Brian. But a man can dream. Besides which, I think I would prefer to be Brian, rather than Jock. Or even Snowy," he added with a grin directed at Jak.

"Thing is, we should forget this for now, if we can," Mildred said. "Keep alert for the slightest break when we're out there, sure. But right now, rest is what we need. We're not going to be any good to each other unless we get some of that right now."

They retired to the beds, having dimmed the light to an acceptable level. Jak and Doc slept alone, while Krysty and Ryan, and Mildred and J.B., took the opportunity to share, and silently move closer to each other. Words weren't necessary, and although each of them was far too weary to consider a more intimate embrace, it was nonetheless sweet for each to feel the other close.

Sleep came swiftly to the companions, but not so swiftly that something of importance occurred to Ryan, and would have kept him awake if not for the pull of inertia from his lead-heavy limbs.

Crabbe believed that they knew the secret of using the mat-trans to journey from place to place. In this, as in all things, he was only partly correct. They knew that to close the door would trigger a jump. But to where? The comps that controlled the mat-trans were subject to codes that were long-since lost. Destinations were decided by figures that were long forgotten.

In this instance, apparently, moving to a destination

would be determined by the figures on the paper that Crabbe held so dear. That was simple enough. Trouble was, each destination code would be known only to the person, inputting the data, not those making the jump. It was always forward, never back. Without the code, the only way you could return was if you hit the Last Destination button inside the mat-trans.

And the last destination was only stored in memory for half an hour before the automatic default settings were restored. After that, you were at the mercy of wherever the mat-trans comp decided to send you.

That meant one thing. Whatever situation you were pitched into at the destination for each of Crabbe's codes, you had just thirty minutes to recce and deal with it. If you did this, you could come back.

But if it took longer, then you were lost.

"GET YOUR ASSES out of bed now," McCready roared as he turned the lights up full. "Baron Crabbe wants you."

"Asshole," Ryan muttered under his breath, disentangling himself from Krysty's embrace and rolling out of bed. "So he's ready to begin, is he?" he asked in a louder voice.

McCready grinned, a mirthless death's head. "What do you think, bright boy? One eye, and half a fucking brain, eh?"

Laughing to himself, McCready strode out of the room, leaving two sec men to stand in the doorway, blasters ready, while the companions dressed hurriedly.

"I wonder if we will be forced to go into battle with no weapons to light our path," Doc mused. "It is bad enough that we are already facing the unknown. To be at the mercy of it is untenable."

"I don't know what you mean, but I'm figuring he's going to have to give us our blasters if he wants us to fight for him," J.B. said quietly. "Otherwise we don't have the chances of a stickie in a shit swamp."

"That is rather what I said." Doc grinned. "Although your words are a little more colorful. The question is, how will he handle the distribution of weapons? To just give them back would be—"

"Nice, but real stupe," Krysty interjected. "My jack's on him just handing back to those he's sending on a jump."

"Makes sense to me," Ryan agreed, "in which case we should watch how they do it. Any chinks…"

"Are to be mercilessly exploited," Mildred finished. "Now I guess we should get going. Huey and Duey over there look like spare parts, and they'll get pissed about that soon enough."

"One more thing," Ryan added, remembering the thought that had kept him awake for part of the previous night. "Don't forget that wherever you land, you only have half an hour before the mat-trans won't send you back."

"Better check those chrons," J.B. stated.

They had been talking in low tones, with the sec men just far enough away to be out of earshot. But now they finished preparing themselves, taking a few seconds to check that their individual chrons were still in working order, then moving to the doorway, the sec men parting to allow them through and keep them covered. As they reached the corridor, Doc laughed quietly to himself.

"What?" Jak asked with a puzzled glance.

"Huey and Duey… Very good." The old man chuckled, shaking his head.

Jak just looked at him blankly.

They walked in silence to the mat-trans unit, the two sec men falling in at their rear, the remaining men lining the route at junction points.

"Don't know where they think we'd go," J.B. said.

"They know that we're more familiar with these places than they are," Mildred whispered. "Fact is, they think we know all there is to know about them. They're terrified—or Crabbe is—that we'd be able to hide, or mount an attack."

"Nice, Millie," the Armorer replied. "That's worth bearing in mind."

McCready was waiting for them at the entrance to the control room. He said nothing as they passed him, but the malevolence coming from the man was almost palpable.

Inside, Crabbe and Sal were waiting for them, looking as though they had hardly moved since the day before. The baron beckoned them.

"Let's not waste time. You know the offer. You get me what I want, you live. You don't, you buy the farm. So what do you say?"

Ryan looked over his shoulder. Apart from the sec chief at the door, they were alone with the baron and his companion.

"What's to stop me from grabbing you by the neck and just stepping into the mat-trans unit right now?"

Crabbe grinned. "You really think I'd be that stupe? What do you think Sal is doing here?"

Mildred eyed the stooping, balding man who had so far remained silent. "You know, I've been wondering that myself," she said gently.

"See, Brian, you should pay more attention to Millicent. Not what I was saying yesterday, I'll grant you. But then she was just mouthing off. There's a lot of intelligence there, and you should just get her to focus it."

"How about you focus on answering the question," Mildred said flatly.

Crabbe grinned, a full, shit-eating grin the like of which Mildred hadn't seen since the days before the nukecaust. It was the grin of a man who held all the winning cards, and was enjoying the feeling.

"See, Sal here don't know much about reading and writing. So I ain't got him here for that. But I ain't never seen anyone with such a gift for engines, wags and tech. I got a shitload of old vids that I can watch because of Sal's gift. He can take any heap of junk and fix it. Anything that's already working, he can figure out how it does it. I really like those vids, by the way—" he leered in Krysty's direction "—'cause they got a lot of girls who look just like you. And they do anything, sweets."

"Are you telling us that he—" Mildred indicated the balding man "—has worked out how the mat-trans unit works?" She could barely keep the incredulity from her voice.

Sal coughed and looked bashful. Despite the incongruity of the situation, he was obviously not used to being praised by his baron. His voice, when he did speak, was somehow higher and more fluting than seemed right for his lugubrious appearance.

"I wouldn't go as far as to say that," he said modestly. "The principles on which the actual process works seem to be more than purely mechanical, and so are outside the realm of my particular skills. Science has gone back to the Dark Ages, and we have a lot of catching up to do. Despite that, I have to say that I've found that much of the base operates on mechanical principles that aren't so far removed from those anyone would encounter on the outside. A little more complex and developed, perhaps, but despite that not really hard to assimilate. So it has to be said that it didn't take me long, if I may be boastful, to work it out."

Crabbe shook his head. "Sal watches too many of those other vids, the ones where guys with spectacles like yours—" he indicated J.B. "—talk shit about the world before skydark. Too many words. To make it simple, Sal can turn the power on and off, stop the fucker from working."

"Okay," Ryan admitted, "you hold all the weapons, and they're all cocked and loaded. So what's your plan?"

Crabbe smiled and nodded. "Glad you see it that way, Brian. We'll do it like this. You people sit yourselves down over there, backs to the wall." He indicated the far wall of the room, farthest from the mat-trans, and waited while they moved over and seated themselves.

Once they were in position, he beckoned McCready to enter. The sec chief turned to his rear and beckoned his men from the corridor. Two of them entered the control room with their blasters raised, while another two carried between them a tarp that bore all the weapons that had been taken from the companions in Hawknose.

They carried it between two desks and dumped it on the floor, stepping back as they raised their own blasters to cover the seated group.

"Now, we've got you, and we've got your weapons. Like I said to you last night, the way I'm gonna handle this is simple. Two of you will go off to one of the locations on the list while the others stay here, to make sure they return. The two going will be handed their weapons by a sec man. The rest of you will be covered by two more of my men. You so much as even look at any of us wrong, and their trigger fingers are gonna itch. Then when you get back, you hand over your blasters to my boys straight away. You might take some of us out if you get the urge, but be sure that the remainder of you will get shot to shit if that happens. Am I clear?"

Ryan looked at his companions. To an outsider, their expressions would have been unreadable. To Ryan, it was clear—they would play along for the sake of keeping themselves alive until such time as any one or two of them could find a way out for the group.

"You're clear," he said blandly to Crabbe.

"Good." The baron nodded. "Now, like I said, I'm gonna send you out in pairs. Seems to me that it'd be a good idea to match Snowy with you, Brian, as I hear he don't say much and might be the simple one."

Ryan tried to suppress his amusement, both at how wrong the baron was and also at the anger he knew would be seething behind Jak's calm visage.

"And I also figure that Millicent should go with Jock. I know he's a crazie, for sure, and she's the one who knows how to control him. I also figure that he ain't so great at the moment, so mebbe he needs her to help him out."

Mildred figured that the baron wasn't far off his assessment, no matter what Doc may think of it. His concussion from the night before hadn't done anything to change the baron's preconceived notion, and although babysitting the old buzzard wasn't on her favorite list of things to do, she still felt that his head injury could make him the most vulnerable. As such, she was kind of relieved that she could keep an eye on him. But seeing the look of thunder on Doc's face, she knew his thinking had stopped at the phrase "he's a crazie, for sure." The rest was lost to him.

"Which just leaves Kirsty and J.T. to pair up. The strongest pairing, by all accounts. The blaster expert and the mutie. Hellfire, I'm surprised they need the rest of you. So that's how we do it. And you go first…."

He indicated Mildred and Doc, both of whom looked surprised, particularly given the terms with which he had addressed Doc.

"Yeah, thought that would surprise you," he said. "My way of thinking is this—get the crazie into action first, see how the bastard holds up. 'Cause you got two bases each if you're gonna clear my list, so best to see if some of you are gonna have to double or triple up."

"My dear sir," Doc intoned, mustering as much restraint and dignity as he could manage, particularly as all he really wanted to do right then was to rip off the baron's head. "You need have no fear of my failing. Not for you, for I do not give a fig about your worthless and putrid opinions, but for my friends. For I have never let them down, and nor do I intend to start now."

"Good, good." Crabbe smiled. "I don't give a shit why you do it, Jock, just as long as you do. Now you and Millicent point out which of that little stash is yours," he continued, indicating the inventory on the tarp, "and then get yourselves over to the thing there." He waved at the mat-trans unit. "And one of you can go and punch in the code that powers it…just one of you, and you'll be covered."

Krysty stood and moved to the comp, nervously scanning the keys and displays. She breathed an inner sigh of relief when she realized that it was the same as any she had seen. There were a few minor variations, as there always were, but the basics were those that she understood. As she stood there, Doc and Mildred stood slowly, always mindful of the blasters that were trained on them. Both hesitated.

"Move to the blasters slowly, then point yours out to my men," Crabbe said in a low, clear voice. His demeanor had changed. Now that it had come to the business end of things, there was an iciness about him that defined why he had become a baron. While he observed, and his men covered them, Doc pointed out the LeMat and his lion's-head swordstick. They were handed to him carefully, along with spare ordnance that was taken from J.B.'s capacious munitions bag. It amused Doc that they had defined his cane as being more than it seemed. The point wasn't lost on Mildred as she indicated her Czech ZKR, and was handed it along with extra ammo.

"Now step over to the glass room," Crabbe murmured. "Weird kind of glass, Brian. Mebbe you can tell me more about it."

"Mebbe I can. Later, though, when this is done," Ryan answered carefully.

Crabbe's eyes shifted to him. "Sure...when this is done," he replied in an ambivalent tone.

Then, switching his attention to his mechanic, he said firmly, "Power it up, Sal."

The stooped, balding engineer nodded and strode rapidly to the far side of the control room. Only now, by following his passage, could Krysty see that the mechanic had put a circuit break into the power lines. It looked crude and primitive, but she marveled at the skill he had shown. It seemed that Crabbe was right about him.

Sal threw the switch and the previously dark and silent equipment hummed and pulsed into life. The monitors flickered, and Krysty could see information scrolling on the screens.

"Well?" Krysty said. "Where are the coordinates you want them sent to?"

Crabbe grinned and handed her the list. "We just gonna work from top to bottom, Kirsty. You send them to the first one."

She nodded, scanning the paper. It was a list of six redoubts with their locations across the old United States, and the mat-trans codes that would enable her to send her friends to each one. Keying in the codes would be simple. There were no commands for return, as she had feared. It would be up to each of them to make sure they could hit the Last Destination button in time.

There was one other thing. It made her want to laugh, although it was too bitter even for that. She knew, as they all did, that the disk sought by Crabbe wasn't in any of these locations. The whole operation—their capture, confinement, and the charade of the mat-trans jumps—was ironic beyond words.

There was more than a series of locations and codes on the list. Crabbe couldn't read them, but Krysty could. And it made her want to weep.

The list was a routine maintenance roster. The six locations were all within one old state. They held nothing of importance, but were maintenance and storage redoubts to service the central location. The redoubt in which they were now confined was less, even, than this. Its purpose was nothing more than to house a staff that would routinely jump to these redoubts and perform the most basic of maintenance and mopping up.

The whole of Crabbe's fantasy was reality in reverse. All they would be performing in this pantomime was a simple janitorial rota from a time before the nukes came down.

She wished that there was some way that she could communicate this to Mildred and Doc. But as they sheathed their weapons and stood on the threshold of the mat-trans unit, there was nothing she could do or say. Her eyes locked with Mildred's. The physician gave the briefest of nods: time to do it.

As Krysty watched—as they all watched—Mildred opened the armaglass door and stepped inside, followed by Doc. They stood on the threshold, looking out, as Krysty fed the coordinates into the console. She looked up and nodded.

With a sharp intake of breath, Mildred pulled the unit door until it clicked shut.

Chapter Six

"This, then, is the moment of truth," Doc said softly as the they heard the locking system slide home.

Mildred nodded. "Better get ourselves ready."

Neither of them relished the jump, and knew only too well the rigors it would place on their bodies. As the air crackled around them, the sharpness of ozone filling their nostrils, they picked places to sit on the chamber floor. The disks that were inlaid into the floor of the chamber began to glow. Wispy columns of white mist, so frail and slight as to be almost invisible, seemed to grow from nowhere. The mist started to appear more solid as the moments passed and the air around them became charged. To just breathe seemed like a static shock to the lungs. Nausea rose in their chests, choking like bile. And then the blackness overwhelmed them.

So THAT'S WHAT it looks like when that thing works," Crabbe breathed in tones of awe as the room glowed momentarily, the light shining through the armaglass walls in an incandescent flash that had an afterglow on the retina.

"I must work out how that works," Sal said softly. From the look on his lugubrious features, now suddenly alive, it was plain that the marvel of the machine had infused him, rather than the avarice of the baron.

Even McCready was stunned to silence by what had occurred. He looked down at the companions as they sat along the wall. Ryan could see that the sec man was viewing them in a different light.

"What does that feel like?" he asked quietly.

Ryan grinned slowly. "Like nothing on earth," he replied. "Like every last little piece of you is being ripped to shreds, flung across the world and then glued back together again by a stickie with the shakes."

"Sounds like crap," McCready breathed.

"It is," Ryan said simply. "But how else are you going to get around?"

MILDRED WOKE with a start. Her head jolted forward, although her brain felt like it was still in the same spot. She felt her stomach heave, and she turned her head just in time to puke on the floor rather than over herself.

Unsteady, she pulled herself to her feet. The unit spun around her. She tried to shake her head to clear it, but it was too disorienting. She stopped, fearful of losing her balance. Reaching out to place a hand on the armaglass wall, she winced as her palm came into contact with the surface. It was almost pulsing with heat.

A low moan to one side distracted her. She turned to find Doc stretched out on his side, his hair splayed around his head, his limbs at angles that looked almost unnatural.

"Doc," she croaked, her voice nothing more than a dried-up husk of its normal self.

The old man raised his head, supporting himself on his forearms before trying to sit up. His eyes were a little cloudy, but there was some light breaking through. He flashed her a crooked grin.

"I confess, I had forgotten quite how...shitty, I think is the best epithet...these jumps could be. I tried to stand a little too soon. Could you, if at all possible...?" he added, almost embarrassed.

Mildred slowly moved toward him, and gingerly assisted Doc into a kneeling position. Already, she was beginning to feel better as the worst excesses of the jump process began to recede.

Doc gave a short, barking cough of a laugh. "Some force to be reckoned with, eh, my dear Dr. Wyeth? Once is bad enough, but to make the return in just half an hour?" He shook his head. "The stresses must be—"

"Something we don't need to think about, Doc," she cut in. "We need to recce this place and see if we can get something together so that we can better that bastard Crabbe."

Doc nodded, breathing heavily and deeply as he got to his feet. "I shall be fine in a few moments. The sooner we get out there, the better. Who knows what we'll find."

"Exactly. That's why we need to be sharp," Mildred said softly, drawing her ZKR and checking it. "Can't do the usual routine when there's only two of us. Have to wing it."

"I shall follow your lead, dear lady," Doc agreed as he examined the LeMat.

Mildred moved to the door of the mat-trans unit. "Cover me, Doc. I'll hail you when it's all clear."

She didn't bother to look back, knowing that Doc would assume the position without comment. The trust between the companions was strong, bonded in the blood of themselves and others.

She hauled the door open as the automatic lock cleared. Using the portal as a shield, she scoped the interior of the antechamber and as much as she could of the control room beyond.

It was empty. And quiet. It had the air of a place that had been empty and undisturbed since before the nukecaust. There was a stillness about the atmosphere that bespoke of a long emptiness. They had spent too long being pitched into redoubts for Mildred not to recognize it. But there was more than that. The air itself had a staleness that could only come from being too long recycled without any other elements. If the redoubt had been breached, then there would be some fresher air coming into the atmosphere. But this had a flatness, almost producing a dull metallic taste at the back of the throat and nose.

Still, she would take this cautiously. Moving swiftly and keeping low, Mildred moved out from behind the cover of the door, seeking the cover of the banks of comps that lined the room. Her blaster was in her raised hand, her finger lightly resting on the trigger.

The only sound in the room was her own breathing, which was loud and almost overwhelming in her own ears—partly, she was sure, because she was still not operating at one hundred percent. But mostly because the redoubt was empty.

Checking the rest of the control room was easy. It was a small room, in what was probably a small redoubt. She had seen one like this before, a long while back. The purpose of such small redoubts was lost to her. It didn't matter much, except that in this case it decreased the chances of either of them finding much that they could use against Crabbe.

"Doc, it's clear," she called. Then added, as the old man emerged from the mat-trans unit, "It doesn't look like this place has been visited since before skydark."

Doc sniffed the air experimentally, then looked around. "Unusual layout, too. Our captor would be very disappointed."

"Yeah, and we might be, too. Unless we find it was some kind of ordnance storehouse, that is."

Doc smiled slowly. "Now I do not think we're likely to get that lucky, do you?"

She shrugged. "Probably not, but we can hope, right? Let's get this done. Best stay alert, just in case we're wrong."

"That goes without saying," Doc assented.

Mildred keyed in the code that would open the door onto the corridor, keeping herself behind the frame as she surveyed the empty and desolate expanse of concrete beyond the chamber. Even by the austere standards of most old military bases, this was stark. The floor and ceiling were of rough concrete, and the lighting overhead was on red emergency, waiting for a repair that never came. It was as empty and chilled as the control room.

"Some systems failed, then," Mildred commented as they began to move toward the next level.

"Could be why the air is stale," Doc mused. "Perhaps it is as well we do not have that long to tarry."

Almost certain now that the redoubt was empty, they moved at a greater speed. There were three levels to this redoubt. A small dorm and washroom on the next level up revealed that only four people could be stationed here, and from the lack of anything personal it was almost certain that it had been empty when the nukes fell. On the same level were the medical facilities and the armory. Where the dorm had been open, the doors to these rooms remained stubbornly locked, even after entering the codes scratched on the lock keypads.

"Dammit, why aren't they responding?" Mildred asked, frustrated.

"It could be that the light is not the only circuit to fail with age," Doc mused. "It could be that a fail-safe has been triggered."

"Just our luck," Mildred said, punching the keypad to vent her anger.

"Let us try the next level to see what we can find," Doc said hurriedly, consulting his wrist chron. "There is not much time."

Still taking precautions, even though now sure that they were alone, they moved to the top level. They found the purpose of the redoubt. It housed large fuel reservoirs within a bay area designed for military wags—instruction plates and haz chem warnings on the walls confirmed this—and a small control room in which the cameras on the interior and exterior were monitored. They could see this through a bay window of reinforced Plexiglas, tinted against the lighting that should have suffused the bay—except that now the bay was a dull red, and the interior of the sec room, much like the mat-trans control room, was still lit by a fully working circuit. Within the room lay the panels that controlled the entire redoubt. To gain access to these would have unlocked the armory and med room. Mildred had no doubt about that. She knew that to fire on it would be futile. The glass was bulletproof, without doubt. And there was nothing in the refueling bay to use against it. From the pristine look of the tanks, she doubted that the fully equipped redoubt had even seen use before the nukecaust. Certainly, the floor was unmarked by any vehicles that may have used it at some point in the past.

"Dammit," she yelled, hammering the butt of the ZKR against the Plexiglas window. "So close…"

"But forever out of our reach," Doc counseled, "and particularly during the time we have left." He indicated his wrist chron. The thirty minutes grace they had was fast slipping away.

Mildred grimaced. "You're right. We'd better be getting back."

They moved toward the back of the refueling bay and the exit to the lower levels. Suddenly she stopped.

"What is it?" Doc asked.

She looked puzzled. "Can you hear that?" she asked. And then, when he failed to answer, but merely appeared quizzical, "That buzzing. It's like insects." She set her head to one side, banging her ear with the heel of her hand. "Like they're inside, but…"

She looked up, the words falling silent on her lips. She couldn't believe what she was seeing. A mosquito swirled in the air, almost dancing, then buzzed around her head, so close that she could feel the air disturbance. As she watched, it flew toward the exit, turned once more and was joined by another. A slow trickle of them emerged from the red darkness, growing to a stream that began to swell in volume, both physically and aurally.

"Doc, where the hell did they come from?" she whispered.

But Doc only looked bemused.

The swarm was large and menacing now, moving with a perfect symmetry that allowed them to circle in flight with a race that was awesome to watch. Or at least, it would have been if not for the fact that their perfect circle was designed purely to bring their flight in line with an attack on Mildred.

She made to turn and run, figuring that if she could angle that run, she stood a chance of reaching the level exit before the swarm, and maybe shutting them off.

Doc…

She glanced over her shoulder as she ran. Doc was standing there, watching her, seemingly oblivious of the swarm as it passed him.

"Run!" she yelled, breath catching in her throat. The metallic tang to the air made it hard to breathe.

Doc tilted his head. Why, he wondered, was Mildred headed off at such speed? She was acting like a spooked horse, running blind with panic. And yet he couldn't see anything that could account for that.

The bay was empty and silent.

Mildred reached the level exit and turned. In the red light it seemed as though the mosquitoes hung motionless for a moment, then dissolved into thin air. She panted heavily, gulping down air. The tang rasped at the back of her mouth, and made her sinuses feel as though they were being sandblasted.

"Doc, what..." she breathed.

The old man strode toward her, a look of concern discernible on his face when he came within the red illumination.

"I do not know, my dear Mildred. But I do know that I did not see whatever it was that you saw. That being the case, I suggest we make speed before such a thing happens again."

Mildred shook her head as though to clear it, although the vision and the sound were now gone. "Yeah, I guess you're right, Doc. What the hell happened there?"

Doc sniffed the air speculatively. "I am not sure, but I suspect that the quality of the air may have something to do with it. Have you noticed a change?"

Mildred gave him a wry grin. "You're asking me that after what just happened?"

"A fair point," Doc conceded as he hustled her into the corridor leading to the next level down. It struck him, as they moved, that it had been an incredibly stupid question for him to ask. So ridiculous, in fact, that it was laughable. He chuckled. The sound was low and mellifluous, rumbling deep in his chest and stomach, a ripple that ran through his whole body, making it hard for him to move. The band of muscle across his abdomen seemed to go into spasm, bending him over with the sudden pain. And yet, despite the agony, he felt compelled to laugh.

It came out of him now in gouts, overriding anything else he might feel. Even rational thought was hard, overwhelmed by the need to laugh and the pain it was causing him. He couldn't breathe, his ribs constricted by the spasm in his gut.

Mildred stopped and looked back. Doc was convulsed in fits of laughter. Literally—he looked like a man in the throes of a fit. As she watched, he doubled over and fell to the floor, twitching, laughing all the while, despite the pain that he had to be in as he spasmed. She hurried toward him, her mind racing. First the mosquitoes, now the uncontrollable laughter. What could be causing it? They knew that the redoubt was empty, so there was no human hand that could be behind the strange effects.

She realized what was happening. The air has tasted different to her shortly before she had seen the first mosquito. Doc had remarked on a similar sensation shortly before he had started to laugh.

They both knew that the air was stale and recycled. It hadn't been breathed by humans for over a century. And the redoubt had been evacuated before skydark, as there was no sign of habitation. What if there had been a reason for that? Suppose that the redoubt had been more than just a refueling depot? Suppose it was home to chemical weapons? Nerve agents of some kind? Suppose there had been a leak of these agents, and they had infected the redoubt. Perhaps an evacuation had been ordered until the problem had been resolved.

But what if skydark had put an end to any such action? The nerve agents would be in the atmosphere of the redoubt, being recycled and cleaned again and again by the filters in the air purification system. All chemical weapons had some kind of shelf life after which their effects diminished. That, with the constant recycling, could account for why it hadn't hit them straight away. And for why the effects were so low-level.

There was no time to try to explain her theory to Doc. No point, either. It was only supposition, and if she knew anything about the old buzzard he would try to argue the point with her, even though there was no time for the niceties of debate. She just had to make sure that he got up, got moving, and then stayed moving.

"Doc… C'mon…" she gasped as she tried to help him to his feet. But he was frozen, almost in rictus. His muscles had gone into such tight spasm that it almost seemed he was made of iron.

"I…I can't… Good grief, it's not…even funny…" he managed to gasp as he tried to move his rigid limbs and assist her in helping him to his feet. He got as far as his knees before another spasm in the gut doubled him over so that his head smacked on the concrete floor.

"Doc, time's moving," Mildred yelled. "Now move, you old bastard, or else you'll buy the farm for both of us."

"Leave me," he yelled in a voice strangled by his own laughter. "Go now."

"The hell I will," she snapped. "You don't get left behind. None of us do. Ever."

"I cannot move." Doc forced the words out between pained laughter. He looked at her, and his eyes were clearer—even in the red emergency light—than she had ever seen them.

"Shit, no," she breathed. "Not on my watch."

Doc was looking up, still on his knees, but with his torso straightened. In truth, his spine was almost bent at a backward angle by the muscle spasm. It flashed into Mildred's head, and she acted before she even had time to consider whether it might work. No time to wonder, just act. With a vicious upward jab she leaned down and punched Doc in the pit of his stomach, driving the air up and out of him. In any other circumstance, the expression that crossed his face would have been comical.

Not now. The wide-eyed and puckered-mouth surprise as the air was expelled from his body was exactly what Mildred had hoped to see. As the last of the air left him, the shock of sudden oxygen deprivation made him collapse. His body went limp and he slumped to the floor.

Limp. That was the key word. The spasm-induced rigidity had gone.

Struggling to raise himself as quickly as possible, despite the agony he felt, Doc reached for Mildred's proffered hand.

"Thank you, Dr. Wyeth. Quick thinking. I may be a little slow because of it, but at least I am moving."

Mildred took his arm and began to pull him in her wake as she half walked, half ran along the corridor. She looked at her wristwatch as they moved down another level. Only one more. Less than ten minutes remained until the last destination default kicked in.

They should do it. The place was empty.

That was when the floor began to shake and break up beneath their feet.

"What the—" she yelled in surprise, the rest of the question cut off as she was thrown off her feet, dragging Doc with her.

With a wordless scream, she found herself thrown into a fissure opened up in the ground by the tremors in the earth.

"HOW DO YOU THINK they're doing?" Crabbe asked Sal.

Ryan suppressed a grin. He could see from the look on the mechanic's face that it was the last question he wanted to answer. If he said good, and they either didn't come back or came back empty-handed, then he would be facing the wrath of Crabbe. Equally, if he answered in the negative, it could do little except bring on more opprobrium.

"Hell, we'll find out soon enough," Crabbe murmured to himself, answering his own question. The relief on Sal's face was almost laughable.

But still, it was a question that Ryan had asked himself. He was sure that each of the other three companions in the room was thinking the same. The Armorer would be worried about Mildred in the same way Ryan knew he would worry about Krysty when it was her turn. He knew that he shouldn't value one of his team above the others. His head said that; his heart said otherwise.

From Krysty's hair, he could tell that she was concerned. It lay flat on her scalp, the filaments slowly coiling and uncoiling around her neck, like the tails of agitated wild cats.

What were Mildred and Doc facing? he wondered. Had they jumped straight into disaster, or into a chilling? It was something they faced every time they jumped. But usually they were together. Now, being forced to sit and wait, the full import of what they faced was hitting him.

And he didn't like it.

He looked at his wrist chron, moving slowly so that it wouldn't draw attention.

Just over five minutes remained until they would know for sure whether Mildred and Doc had made it.

AS THE FISSURE widened and she fell into it, dragging Doc behind her, all she was aware of were the jagged edges of rock as they plucked at her clothes—and the heat, growing by the second, as though they were plunging into the heart of a volcano. The molten heart waiting to swallow them up.

A quake that had hit just when it would be least welcomed. That was some kind of coincidence.

Too much of one.

Mildred's mind raced. They—she was certain that Doc was falling behind and above her—had fallen into the fissure as the floor crumbled, and had passed walls of rock that towered above them. But how could that be?

For surely, if they had fallen through the concrete floor of the redoubt as it opened up, the first thing they would have passed would have been the floor and walls of the lowest level.

But she hadn't seen that. What had passed in front of her eyes was little more than rock. Unadulterated, and bereft of anything that resembled concrete, or empty space.

The damn gas. The traces of the nerve agent that remained in the recycled air had got to her mind once again. There had been no quake, and they weren't plunging into the bowels of the earth. The trouble was, although her mind knew this, everything else told her that it was happening. She could feel the jagged rock edges plucking at her clothing, could feel the air whistling past her face, pushing at her skin. It was so real.

Drive the air out of her body, so that the trace effects would rapidly be expunged. That was the only way. It had worked when she had run and become breathless. It had worked for Doc when she had punched him in the gut. But how could she do it when she felt like she was in freefall, and her limbs wouldn't respond to any instruction she tried to give them?

She had to scream, loud and long, and not drag in any breath. Get it all out.

So she screamed. And kept on screaming.

Doc stood over her, barely able to keep himself upright as the effects of the laughter and of her assault made it hard for him to breathe and move. One moment he had been trailing behind Mildred as she pulled him, the next he had shot over her prostrate body as she fell. Now she was flat to the floor, screaming loudly and incoherently while he tried to yell at her, the words and volume lost in his own strained thorax.

Time was of the essence. She had told him that, and as he looked at his own chron, he could see that she was correct. If he was right, they had only a little over five minutes. They were one level up, but he couldn't move quickly. Mildred wasn't moving at all, by the look of her, and if he couldn't get her to stand, then all was lost.

He was about to stand back and take a wild swing at her ribs with his foot, unsure as to whether it was worth breaking a rib to deprive her of breath in the same way as she had punched him—and whether she would see it later as some kind of revenge—when she suddenly stopped screaming. Doc tottered uneasily as he stayed his foot.

"My dear Mildred, are you with us again?"

Mildred raised her head. The floor and walls around her were solid enough.

"Shit, that was so real."

"I shall not ask," Doc said quickly, partly because of shortness of breath and partly because he didn't wish to waste time. "Come."

Mildred gratefully took his proffered hand. Although he was weak, and in truth did little to assist her to her feet, the fact of his being there helped her find that strength within herself.

"The sooner we get out of here the better," she whispered through heavy, deep breathing as she sought to gain the strength to move. It was, as she was aware, a double-edged sword. She needed the oxygen to move, and yet at the same time the very air she craved ran the risk of driving her imagination into overdrive.

Stumbling over their own feet, the desire for speed outstripping the strength in limbs that were now leaden and lungs that were running on empty, they half ran toward the lowest level. Twice, Doc stumbled and fell, scrabbling to his feet as Mildred turned back to help him. Once she toppled over, her momentum outstripping the alien feet attached to numb legs.

It was only when the entrance to the mat-trans unit was in sight that they both realized that the heavy breathing necessitated by their flight was allowing too much of the trace agent to enter their nervous systems and brains.

"Lori?" Doc breathed out slowly, stumbling to a lesser pace despite himself. The blonde was standing in the doorway. The notion was ridiculous, as she had long since bought the farm. Yet she seemed so real. His companion and solace in this world, snatched from him as he had been snatched from the bosom of his own family.

"Dad?" Mildred also slowed. In the doorway, she could see her father, the Baptist preacher who had taught her of the hell on earth that she now lived.

"Come with me. Don't go back. What is there to go back to?"

The words were the same, even if delivered in different voices. For a moment both Doc and Mildred halted. Perhaps those were wise words. What was there in this land for either of them? Displaced and not belonging…

They looked at each other.

"Who can you see?" Doc asked.

"My father," Mildred answered. "I heard him, too."

"Strange how it plays on our deepest fears. True as they may be, we cannot give in now."

Mildred laughed without humor. She grabbed Doc's sleeve and pulled. The two of them broke through the doorway, each feeling the phantom of their own deepest doubt plucking at them as they passed.

Ignoring the imprecations from behind them, they plunged forward and into the chamber. Mildred pulled the door closed, the lock clicking, shutting out the voices that still called from beyond. She pushed the LD button, then sat on the floor beside Doc.

As the mist began to gather, and the air crackled, Doc checked his chron.

"Thirty seconds on a one-way ride..." He laughed, in relief rather than amusement, holding up the chron for her to see.

As blackness closed in, all she could hope was that it was thirty seconds on the right side of thirty minutes.

Chapter Seven

Time. There was never enough time. Ryan bit down hard on his lip as he eyed the second hand of his wrist chron. Only a few seconds and it would be past the half hour mark. Whatever had happened to Doc and Mildred at the redoubt they had been sent to, it would be unimportant unless they managed to hit the last destination time limit.

The air became taut and tense around them. Within the sealed chamber, lights began to glow, luminescent as the wisps of mist that began to form and spread into a cloud. The light increased suddenly and without warning, going from pearlescent glow to blinding flare almost before he had time to avert his eye. He heard J.B. mutter something that may have been a prayer, or may just have been a sigh of relief.

"They're back!" Crabbe exclaimed in a statement of the obvious that Ryan found all the more irritating because of what was running through his mind. They may be back, but in what kind of condition?

Leaving Sal behind the comp desk close to Krysty, Crabbe rushed toward the mat-trans unit and tugged at the door. He swore heavily when it failed to yield to him. Krysty's eyes flickered to Ryan, J.B. and Jak. She knew what they were thinking.

"Dammit, why the fuck don't they come out?"

Crabbe yelled at Ryan as he tugged once more at the door.

McCready leaned over and prodded Ryan with the end of his Kalashnikov. “You people better not be screwing with Crabbe,” he whispered. “Fuck with him, and he’ll let me handle you just how I want.” He smirked, indicating Krysty as if to make his intentions quite clear.

Ryan’s voice was low, growling with barely contained anger. “Keep your mind on the job, boy. Just one slip…”

McCready was about to answer when the yell from his baron cut him off.

“It’s opening!’

The door to the mat-trans unit slowly swung open, and Mildred staggered out. Her eyes were glazed, and she stumbled twice before collapsing into a heap.

“Shit!” Crabbe stepped back, as though scared of contamination—of what was a mystery. Nonetheless, his fear was palpable.

Krysty rushed forward. J.B. tried to struggle to his feet but was beaten down by the barrel of a blaster, swung by a sec man. Jak’s hands snaked up and grabbed the blaster, twisting it so that it was jerked from the hands of the sec man. The Kalashnikov spiraled in the air, whistling past J.B.’s head as the Armorer was caught between half standing and falling back down, reeling from the blow. Ryan reached across him, and suddenly it became apparent to McCready what was happening. He raised his own blaster, but was too slow. Before he had it level at Ryan’s chest, he was staring down the barrel of the blaster taken from his own man.

"Something to say?" Ryan growled.

Crabbe looked wildly around him. Things had happened suddenly and had taken him by surprise. But he wasn't a baron without reason. Thinking on his feet was something that kept him from buying the farm.

"Brian, think before you do it. Unless you want Kirsty and Millicent to get blown away. I don't think J.T.'ll like that too much, either," he added.

"Jak?" Ryan asked, unwilling to unlock his gaze from McCready's.

"Got handblaster. Smith & Wesson. On Krysty and Mildred. Both prone. Take 'em before you turn," the albino youth said calmly.

Ryan's mouth quirked. "Guess you got the whip again, Crabbe. Get your boy here to back off, and he can have his toys back. But let Krysty see to Mildred. A mat-trans jump isn't much fun."

"Okay. You take it easy, Nelson. Shouldn't have been such a damn fool in the first place," Crabbe said easily. He held up the barrel of the blaster, so that it pointed at the ceiling. "Tell him, Snowy."

"Not on now. Good as word," Jak affirmed.

"Okay." Ryan lowered the barrel of the Kalashnikov, turned it and held it out sideways to the sec man. He snatched it, almost dropped it, then made a point of leveling it squarely at Ryan. The one-eyed man took note. The man was easily rattled.

Krysty leaned over Mildred, ignoring what went on around her. The black woman's pulse was fluttering, and bile flecked the corners of her mouth from the rigors of the jump. Her eyes rolled in her head as she tried to open them. Her mouth moved, but no sound emerged at first, as if it was on a ten-second delay.

"Doc..."

It was then that Krysty realized Doc hadn't yet emerged from the mat-trans unit. She scrambled to her feet and ran inside, shrugging off Crabbe's hand as it reached for her.

"Hey—"

She ignored him and looked around. Was Doc actually here? With a mixture of relief and fear she saw what appeared to be a bundle of black rags in one corner. Doc was slumped and seated with his black frock coat pulled tight around him, his head low to the floor.

"Doc?" She approached him carefully, reaching out to touch him, not knowing if he was conscious, or even alive. When he suddenly raised his head and beamed munificently at her, she jumped back with a gasp.

"Fear not, my dear Krysty," he murmured in a small yet strong voice. "I am fine. It's the good doctor you should be worried about."

"That's kind of what she said about you," Krysty said, reaching out to assist him as he started to struggle to his feet. "But she's almost out cold, while you're—"

"Feeling like death. But then that's only to be expected. Pray assist me, I shall only be able to speak of this the once."

When she led him out of the mat-trans, his weight supported on her shoulder, she saw that Mildred was being attended to by J.B., while Ryan and Jak were being covered heavily by the sec men. The implication was clear. If she, or J.B., should try anything, it would be the big chill for Ryan and Jak.

Crabbe was standing back behind one of the comps, next to Sal. The mechanic looked nervous. Sweat lined his brow, and his anxiety was transferring itself to the baron, who twitched as he held his blaster at an angle.

"Well?" he snapped. "What the fuck went on? Have you got the disk?"

Doc laughed. It was a hollow sound from the center of his chest. "You really think it will be that easy?" he asked in a mocking tone. "You have no idea, but while the good doctor recovers herself, let me explain something to you."

Doc told the baron what had happened from the moment they had landed at the redoubt. He told him in detail not because he cared what the baron thought, or even that he deserved the whole story. He told him because he knew that his companions would be listening intently, and any information about redoubts would be invaluable—particularly if it revealed something that they hadn't encountered before.

By the time he had finished, Mildred had recovered enough to have gotten to her feet. Her breath still rasped, but at least she was now free of the hallucinations generated by the contaminated air.

"This is true?" Crabbe asked her.

"I haven't got anything to add," she rasped in agonizingly raw tones. "Except maybe this—if you think it's going to be easy to get what you want, then you're sorely mistaken."

Crabbe's face hardened. "It's there. It's in one of the places on that list. You better do the job properly if you want to get out of here alive. Now get your asses over there where we can cover you." With which he indicated the area where Ryan and Jak were seated. "As for you, Brian, you and Snowy are next in line. Anything you wanna say about that before you're sent off?"

There was plenty that either of them would have liked to say. But one look at the way in which they were covered, its futility was obvious. They exchanged the briefest of looks, of nods, and then made their way to the tarp housing their weapons. They waited patiently for the sec man to hand them their blasters and blades. Ryan sheathed the panga, while Jak secreted his leaf-bladed knives. They checked their handblasters, and Ryan chambered a round in the Steyr before shouldering the rifle.

"Count yourself lucky," Ryan murmured to McCready as the sec chief watched them. "Come the time..."

"I'll be waiting," McCready replied, sneering. "Have a good trip."

Ryan ignored him. He looked at Jak, who nodded, and they made their way to the mat-trans unit.

"We'll back. Disk or not." Jak spit on the floor, as if to express that which he couldn't speak.

"Do that and things'll be fine," Crabbe replied.

Krysty watched them enter. Jak went in first. Ryan didn't look back at her as he pulled the door shut behind him.

"TRIPLE FROSTY when we come out the other side," Ryan said to the albino youth.

"Yeah, long as unit still there," Jak replied with a grim smile.

Without another word the two companions hurried to settle themselves on the floor. The air was already charged, the mist rising from the disks. Having now seen a jump from the other side of the armaglass walls, Ryan was more amazed than ever by the swathes of mist that formed from the briefest of tendrils. The light didn't seem to him to be as bright as when he'd seen it from the exterior. Maybe that was the point at which their very being was ripped into its constituent atoms and flung across some kind of void, before being reconstituted.

The thought made him nauseous. He felt like he would puke. Or maybe that was just the feeling that came in that briefest of moments before the black of unconscious claimed him. That moment that came...

"LORD—THAT'S WHAT it looks like?" Mildred whispered, averting her eyes from the lightning flash, but not before it had seared itself on her retinas.

"You get used to it," J.B. said in a laconic tone. The briefest of smiles flickered at the corners of his mouth.

"Get you—blasé already," she said. Then, on seeing the puzzlement crossing his brow, she added, "Acting like you've seen it every day of your life."

"I hope I have more every days to come," he muttered by way of reply. "Wonder where they'll end up?"

"Whatever or wherever, I just hope that they exact due caution," Doc murmured.

Crabbe had been listening to them with interest. Standing beside him, Krysty could see that he was having trouble coming to terms with their attitude. He turned to her.

"What's with you people? You act like there's no danger at all. Now that I've seen that thing in action—" he pointed with disdain at the mat-trans unit "—I'd be damned if I'd trust myself to chance it."

"But you'd send your men through it?" Krysty asked him, ignoring his question and keeping an eye on McCready and his men as she did so.

Crabbe shrugged. "Sure. That's what they get their jack for. Don't mean I have to, though. That's what being the boss is all about, right?"

"If you say so," she said noncommittally. But she noted that the sec men looked at their chief questioningly. And that McCready himself looked uneasy at the prospect.

Another little chink. When the moment came, then these would all count against Crabbe.

RYAN'S EYE WAS STICKY, gummed together and difficult to open. It felt like some kind of stickie gloop, as though one of the muties had punched him in the eye and left something of itself behind. He felt the lashes pull against skin as he forced the eyelid open. The eye behind it felt little better. Perhaps he had been punched in the face? The mat-trans had somehow slugged him as it pulled him apart and glued him back together again. Maybe this was part of the glue?

Considering how dry and sore his eye felt, it was amazing that any kind of gloop had been produced at all. Come to that, the rest of his head felt like that, too.

He moved it slowly, flexing his neck and testing just how far he could push it before the pain kicked in.

Good. The more he did it, the more it began to clear. It was as though he needed the movement to kick-start his reconstituted body. Feeling stronger by the second, as a sense of being himself rather than someone stuck in an alien body began to return, Ryan hauled himself to his feet.

The armaglass was dark, the lights in the chamber beyond chilled. In the gloom, he could hear Jak retching. The albino teen always suffered from a jump in this way, and Ryan was sure that once he had thrown up he would feel better.

"Jak." His voice was a dry husk. He coughed phlegm and spoke again. "Jak, how are you?"

"Okay. No—feel like crap but okay soon," Jak replied. In the semidarkness, Ryan could see his companion's stringy white hair and the blazing red of his eyes as he shakily raised himself up. Ignoring his own condition, the albino youth continued. "Dark. Lights fail, or waiting for us?"

Ryan grinned. It was the grin of a predator. "Only one way to find out. You ready for this?"

Jak's teeth shone white and sharp. "Do it."

Ryan opened the door of the mat-trans. He stood to one side, using it for cover, and gestured for Jak to dart into the control room. Like Mildred and Doc, they were met with silence.

But there was something different about this redoubt. Jak sniffed the air experimentally.

"Empty, Ryan," he said, standing from a crouch. "Were people, but long since gone."

Ryan had stepped through the anteroom and into the control room. He held the SIG-Sauer ready, but he could feel the emptiness, too. He looked up at the ceiling. The lights were out because they had been smashed, not because of a power failure. As their eyes adjusted to the gloom, they could see that the lights on the comps around the room were still illuminated, flickering as the programmes ran their preprogrammed course. They may have still been working, but there were other signs of damage. The floor was littered with broken chairs, and the sides of the desks looked dented, as though they had been hit in incoherent frustration.

"Think it was the original inhabitants went a little crazy?" Ryan questioned.

Jak shook his head. "Smell too fresh. Not taken out yet by air con. Recent, but not much."

Ryan nodded. "Should be okay, but stay frosty."

The pair moved toward the exit. The door showed signs of taking a beating. Someone had been in one hell of a hurry to get out. Presumably they had. Otherwise, it would be a real pain if the mechanism was broken, and Ryan and Jak were stuck in the control room. The one-eyed man held his breath as he punched the standard numbers in to the keypad…then sighed with relief as the door slid open, showing no signs of damage.

The corridor was brilliantly lit. The floor was littered with detritus—paper, wood, metal, pieces of equipment that had been mangled and smashed, and the remains of what might have been food but could equally have been waste.

"What the fireblasted hell happened here?" Ryan murmured.

"Looting," Jak replied simply.

"Yeah, but who and why?" Ryan asked, puzzled. "Why make a mess like this and try to break up the mat-trans control room? They haven't smashed these lights like they did in there."

Jak looked at him. "Mebbe some got in unit."

Ryan considered that. He could remember the shock he had felt the first time he had used a mat-trans. And then how he had felt just a short time before when he had been on the outside of the unit as the jump process started. Jak could have a point. Say someone stumbled in and the door closed. The comp would automatically trigger the jump, and who knew where the poor bastard ended up? But those with him, on the outside trying desperately to free him… How would that feel?

"Yeah, that makes sense," he agreed. "It could be why they got the hell out instead of staying. Assuming they didn't stay, that is."

Jak shook his head. "No one here, Ryan. Chilled like grave."

"Yeah, reckon you're right. But a little caution never hurt anyone." The one-eyed man shrugged. "We'll keep our blasters on red."

Jak nodded. He had little doubt that the redoubt was empty, but was always mindful of the fact that caution had kept him alive this far.

They headed upward. This redoubt seemed to be smaller than many of the ones they had visited in the past. On the next level up they found dorms and washroom facilities for about fifty people. The dorms were empty. The bed frames remained, but the mattresses and linen had been taken away. Whatever wasn't looted had been ripped up and dumped in corners of the rooms, some of it smeared in excrement.

The washrooms were in a similar condition. The cleaning materials had been left, or randomly broken and scattered around, while the shower areas had been used as latrines. Disgusting as it was for them to see, Ryan and Jak checked the detritus left behind. By the hardened state of the feces that had been smeared or dumped randomly, it had to have been some time since the redoubt had been invaded.

"Scum," Jak murmured simply as he examined the mess.

"Agreed," Ryan stated. "Wonder how much other damage they did."

They left the dorm and shower areas. Next was the clothing stores. As they expected, these had been thoroughly looted. Those clothes that hadn't been looted had been left lying on the floor. They had been tried on and then randomly discarded, some spoiled and ripped. One pile of clothing was discolored by dark stains that looked like dried blood.

"Fucking animals," Ryan muttered. "It's like they couldn't even find what they wanted without trying to split each other's guts over it."

"Good. Less scum better," Jak stated, emphasizing his view by spitting on the mess.

Ryan sniffed. "Wonder how much else they've fucked up in this place. You reckon they'll have looted the armory?"

Jak snorted and shook his head.

"Yeah, me, too," Ryan replied. "Might as well check it out, anyway. Time check?"

Jak looked at his chron. "Eight minutes since arrived."

Ryan nodded. "Let's get this done."

They left the wreckage of that level behind them and pressed forward. The next level housed the kitchens, food stores and dining area. Any foodstuffs that hadn't been looted were spilled around the whole area. The level itself looked as though it had been coated in a layer of food, all now dried and caked on every surface.

"How the fuck did they manage to do that?" Ryan blurted, exasperated and bemused.

"Like that?" Jak asked with a wry smile. Ryan followed the line of the albino teen's hand. One area of the floor, in front of an open floor-to-ceiling storage cupboard, was littered with self-heats that had been opened. The correct way to open them was to use the tags to trigger the heating mechanism, but there had been no attempt to employ this on the packages that lay on the floor. Instead, it looked as though the looters had been frustrated in their attempts to open the packaging, and had opted to shoot the hell out of the self-heats with their blasters. The sudden release of the high-pressure system that heated the package and its contents had caused them to explode with a release of inner tension, propelling the foodstuffs across the kitchen and dining areas. There were also ragged holes of blasterfire in the plaster of the walls, as though the blasters had been fired randomly.

"Waste of good ammo," Jak commented pithily. "Good food, too," he added, looking around.

"Yeah," Ryan agreed. "How much other good stuff did these assholes waste?"

"Much as they could," Jak sniffed.

They left the kitchen and food stores behind, moving up another level. As they did, it became clear that there was less random mess and destruction the higher they got. It was as though the looters had frustrated themselves in the kitchens and taken out their rage on the levels below, culminating in whatever had happened in the mat-trans unit. For now, as they gained the working heart of the redoubt, there was little obvious damage. The floors were clean.

But the gaping maw of the armory and the medical facilities dashed any hopes they may have held. The looting had been thorough, no matter how stupe the looters.

As they approached, Ryan could see that the doors of both sections had been jammed open. Light from within flooded out into the corridor, which had been cast into shadow because random lights had been shot out. Another display of temperament or just a casual testing of the weaponry they had found within? It didn't really matter. The scattered shell casings, ammo magazines, and boxes in which they had been stored told their own story.

"We're not going to find jackshit here." Ryan sighed.

Jak shrugged. "Least no danger."

"Guess so," Ryan mused, "but we've got to try to find something that we can use against Crabbe. He's got all of us by the balls right now. Outnumbered back there, and undermanned out here."

Jak agreed. It was a problem. Distributing blasters

only to the pair embarking on a mission and keeping a strong sec presence made it almost impossible for any of the companions to cut all risk. Jak had considered the possibility of just coming out of the mat-trans blasting on their return, and using the element of surprise. But the way he had felt when the jump was completed reminded him of why it was a stupe idea. To make the return jump in under thirty minutes would probably leave him spilling his guts on the unit floor again and of no use to anyone.

By this time they were under the shadow of lights that had been blasted out. It put the medical facilities into stark relief, and as they stood outside and looked in they could only imagine the anger and frustration that Mildred would have felt, had she been with them.

It didn't look as though any of the medical supplies had actually been taken. It was doubtful whether the looters had any idea what most of them were for. Target practice, judging by the carnage they had wreaked in the medical room. Bottles, jars and vials were smashed, shards of plastic and glass littering the floor. The surface was sticky with the mingled meds that had run together and congealed over time. Pills were scattered around in a profusion of colored capsules that were part-melted, part-trampled into the floor. Bandages, lint and gauze were scattered and ripped. The equipment that had once been precision made, and used for healing wounded and sick bodies, was smashed beyond repair in an orgy of mindless destruction.

For Ryan and Jak, it was a waste that was more than just pitiful. There had been times when their lives had been saved by the materials they had found in places such as this. The desecration represented chances of their lives being lost.

"Figure point looking in armory?" Jak asked.

"No," Ryan said sadly, checking his wrist chron, "but we've got some time, so we might as well."

If anything, the armory presented an even more depressing sight. For a redoubt of around fifty people, it had been—at the time of skydark—well-equipped. The racks that had once held rifles and SMGs attested to this. They were, however, long since empty. The boxes that had once nestled in neat and serried rows, containing grens and explosives, were now either hollow and broken husks, or simply missing with only a blank space indicating that they had ever existed. Boxes of ammo were broken open and scattered across the interior of the armory, just as they were across the corridor outside.

"What kind of stupes were these?" Ryan said almost to himself as he stepped across the discarded ammo magazine and shells to pick up an H&K MP-5—the predark SMG of choice for the old military, it seemed to him—from where it had been discarded on the floor. The mechanism had been stamped and battered until it was dented and jammed. Or had the beating it had taken been part of some misguided attempt to unjam it? Come to that, he wondered how this polycarbon mechanism had been jammed in the first place. Uzis, like the one favored by J.B., could be bastards when on rapid-fire, but H&Ks were usually reliable. Just what had they done to make it jam in the first place?

"Some people just don't deserve good blasters," he said, again almost to himself.

Jak had been examining some handblasters and a few longblasters that had been discarded in a similar manner. He figured it was what you'd get when you had men deprived of ordnance who then had the chance to pick and choose from what had to have seemed like a treasure trove. Act like stupes, like animals. No, unfair on animals. He'd never known anything he hunted to be so wasteful. But he didn't bother voicing any of these thoughts. What was the point? Only one thing to do.

"Let's move," he said simply.

Ryan nodded, and they made their way out of the armory with no little regret for chances lost. Picking their way over the ammo, resisting the urge to scoop some up, they carried on until they reached the next level. Here, they found what had to be the redoubt's operations center. Sec monitors for the whole installation and the outside were housed in a darkened room. Most of them, inside and out, were dark.

"Guess they shot out all the cams," Ryan mused. "Just as well they left this level mostly alone..."

It was as if they had walked past these rooms, seen the banks of comps winking seemingly at random as the automated mechanisms of maintenance ticked patiently on until their masters returned, and passed swiftly on, fearful of that that they didn't understand.

In truth, Ryan and Jak didn't really understand the way in which most of this old tech worked. But they respected what it did, and how it kept the redoubt alive.

Ryan looked over the comps, trying to glean some clue as to what the redoubt had been used for. As always, lazy predark soldiers had marked up the comps and desks with shortcuts and reminders for passwords, key codes and the functions of different comp displays.

This redoubt had housed a local defense force, which was to enforce military law in the locality in the event of a national shutdown. What that meant he wasn't too sure, but the coming of skydark would certainly count as some kind of shutdown. He also figured that the term "defense force" was fluid—who or what were they actually defending, and from whom?

Maybe that was what had happened to them—they'd ridden out into the teeth of a firestorm, never to return. And what of those who had been left behind, if any? Perhaps they had just bought the farm with age, wandering belowground, unable to emerge in daylight. Maybe the long wait had driven them crazy, and they'd gone outside anyway, preferring to face the hostile elements rather than go slowly mad. Thinking about it, Ryan wasn't too sure which he would prefer.

"C'mon, Ryan, get moving. Time..."

Jak's words shook him from his reverie. Whatever had stopped the stupe looters from breaking up this section, he was glad. It meant that the redoubt could actually support them.

"See this," Ryan murmured, indicating a yellowing piece of paper taped to the surface of one desk. "It says that the level above this is a wag garage with armored wags. Mebbe some of them are still there. And mebbe the looters were too stupe—or couldn't be bothered—to get at their ordnance when they were here."

Jak's expression didn't change, but his voice was clear. "Long shot."

Ryan blew out his breath. "Yeah, mebbe. But if we

can just find something to use, then I'd feel a whole lot better." He checked his wrist chron. "Halfway mark. We've got time."

The albino youth nodded, and they headed up to the next level.

"Sec door's closed," Ryan murmured as they took a dogleg in the corridor. "You'd think the looters would have blasted it open."

"Wait," Jak said, turning and running swiftly back to the last junction, where there had been an elevator. Like Mildred and Doc, they had forgone the use of the redoubt elevators to keep themselves aware of all that could occur around them. Jak returned a few moments later.

"Elevator out," he said.

"Guess they could have shot them out like they shot out the sec cams," Ryan mused. "You want to check it out or go back?" he asked, indicating the sealed doors in front of them.

Jak breathed in heavily, and stood looking at the doors for what seemed to be an age. Ryan guessed that the albino teen was weighing any possible dangers that may lay behind the doors being closed and the elevator being out. To Ryan, it seemed unlikely that they would be at any risk. The stupes who had looted this redoubt had long since departed, and there was no sign of anyone having been left behind even then. Let alone there being anyone around who could give them trouble now.

"Place empty. Mebbe something useful next level. Just how long it takes to open door?"

Ryan checked his chron again, mindful of time.

"Thirteen minutes," he affirmed. "If we can't get this bastard open in three, we give up."

"Sounds good," Jak agreed.

They walked up to the door, and Ryan tried the code that had been etched on the keypad's plate.

No response.

They exchanged glances. Jak shrugged at Ryan's unspoken question. He took one of his leaf-bladed throwing knives from within his patched camou jacket and, using it as a screwdriver, deftly unscrewed the plate that was set into the concrete frame housing the sec door. Within moments, the workings of the control panel and keypad were exposed to view.

"Everything seems to be connected okay," Ryan mused, eyeing it carefully. "No reason I can see why the bastard isn't working. It must be some kind of mechanical jam in the door itself. Hang on. Let's see if I can override the emergency function."

It was something that he hadn't done in a long time, but hot-wiring was an old trick. It might just work. He could remember the sequence as clear as the first time he had seen someone do it. He took two wires and pulled them from their mounts, ignoring the sparks that hissed and fizzed at him.

"Ready for this?" he asked Jak, looking back. The albino teen had taken a couple of steps back, and at first Ryan thought it was because he wanted to be out of range of the possible charge when the wires touched. But he could see that Jak was studying the doors.

"Ryan, doors buckled at top. Jamming 'cause that. Wonder why?"

They'd soon find out, Ryan figured as he touched the wires together.

The shock of the wires coming together made him gasp, and he was thrown backward with blinding flash of light. The door squealed as the twisted metal tried to move in the straight grooves of the frame.

"Fireblast! I didn't expect it to hurt like that," Ryan groaned as he scrambled to his feet. Then, following Jak's gaze, he added, "What the—"

A thin trickle of water was visible, running faster and then furiously down the crack between the two sections of the sec door.

"Oh, fuck!" he yelled, trying to turn away. But it was too late.

A high-pressure stream of water, like a blunted spear, shot through the narrowest of gaps and caught him in the ribs as he turned. The force threw him against the wall of the corridor, and for a moment light exploded around his head once more.

Then it went black.

Chapter Eight

Jak took two steps back as he saw the water pressure build, then threw himself to one side a fraction of a second before the pressurized jet broke through and flattened Ryan. He hit the ground in a roll, and despite the impact knocking the air from him, he was dragging in breath before he had gotten back to his feet,

Spray soaked him and flew into his eyes, making it hard to see. But not so hard that he couldn't spot Ryan, prone and on one side where he had been flung back and hit against the angle of wall and floor. The one-eyed man was facedown, and water was starting to gather in rivulets on the floor. Not deep enough to drown a man, perhaps, but who knew what would happen if he inhaled while unconscious.

Jak made his way over to where Ryan lay.

"Ryan, c'mon," he yelled, turning the one-eyed man so that he was on his back and slapping him across the face. He barked the man's name a few more times, hitting him as he shouted. The water was less high pressure now, but that was far from good. It only meant that the weight of the water had pushed the doors farther apart. The water was flowing fast and free, starting now to run in wider and wider rivulets that grew to small streams, eddying and flowing around Jak as he knelt beside Ryan, rushing up and welling around the man's face and neck. His eye opened, sightless and unfocused for a moment. His mouth opened and closed with no sound. Then, with what seemed to be a supreme effort of will, he forced himself into some kind of awareness.

"What's—"

"Quick. Flooding," Jak snapped. It was stating the obvious, with water pouring over them, but he figured the sooner he shocked Ryan back to himself, the sooner they could get out of the redoubt.

"Fireblast and fuck!" Ryan jolted into full consciousness, and although his head ached and his neck muscles felt as though they'd been twisted backward, he scrambled to his feet, splashing violently in the water and slipping once or twice on the way up, despite Jak's assistance. When he was on his feet, he had to resist the urgent desire to vomit, his head spinning and his ears humming. He tried to shake his head clear, but that only succeeded in making things worse. He clung to Jak for support as the albino youth started to make tracks back toward the lower levels. They only had a short time in which to move. Not just because of the time limit that had already been imposed on them.

With a hum and a crack, the lights went out above and around them, plunging them into blackness for a moment before the emergency circuits cut in and red light flooded the corridor. The water around them, now swirling to their ankles, was as red as the blood that thundered through their veins as they ran full-tilt toward the next sec door.

How the hell had the levels above become flooded? Was it something that the looters had done, or was it some kind of natural freak that had happened after? It would at least explain why no one had come back to the redoubt to use it after the first looting.

The thoughts rushed through Ryan's confused and still aching head, but he tried to dismiss such speculation. It would serve no purpose, and at this stage would do little other than slow him and dull his reactions.

Jak cast a look over his shoulder as they skidded and splashed around the dogleg of the corridor. There was no way they could have stayed and tried to close the sec doors to stem the tide. The warp in the doors had turned into a full buckle. Above the sound of the water, and the sirens that had started to sound an alarm when the red lights had come on, he could hear the squeal of twisting and protesting metal as the weight of the water bent it out of shape and pushed it free of the grooves that had contained it for so long.

The sirens and the red light had been triggered when the circuits in that section of corridor had been shorted. Was it a fail-safe? Maybe it was possible that the upper levels could cut out without interference to lower levels. That had to have happened where the closed sec door had acted as a dam.

That also had to have been why the sec monitors for the upper levels were blank. The lower level monitors blanked by looters' blasterfire had only muddied the waters. At any other time, Jak would have considered that one of his rare jokes.

Except this race against the water was far from funny.

Behind them, they could hear the water start to rush faster and faster as the gap in the twisted sec doors began to grow larger. At any moment a wave would hit. They needed to get to the next interior sec door, and quickly. Not just to avoid the wave, but because the automatic emergency procedures would start to kick in.

The water was rushing around them now, reaching up to their calves. At least it wasn't flowing against the direction of their movement. It wasn't acting as a resistor. But it was making the floor beneath them treacherous, and it sucked at their boots. They found themselves slowing as they tried to stay on their feet. To fall in these conditions meant the risk of losing consciousness and thus losing all hope of making the mat-trans unit in time.

It was only when they turned the corner that they could see the lights beyond the next sec door were still as normal. The water was flowing fast ahead of them, making the floor slick.

And the sec door was beginning to close.

DOC SIGHED HEAVILY and looked up at the ceiling.

"Something bothering you, Jock?" Crabbe asked him.

"Beyond the inability of people to hail me with my given appellation, I think not," Doc mused. "Although the manner in which stories can become distorted by the telling and retelling so that they resemble nothing so much as myth is also somewhat of a concern."

"What the fuck did that crazy old coot say?" McCready asked, looking at his baron.

Crabbe shrugged. "Jock's like that. That's the way I hear it, anyways. Got no reason to think any different from the way he's been acting. How's the power doing, Sal?"

The mechanic had been running a routine check, just as he had while Doc and Mildred were away. He was a proud man, but his nervous demeanor betrayed a self-doubt concerning his abilities.

"It's fine," he stated. "Everything's holding. They'll have no trouble coming back."

Krysty wanted to laugh, but held her peace. It wasn't this end that they had to worry about. It was whatever they might have found at the other end of the jump. Doc and Mildred had only just gotten back, and they'd been lucky. Would any of the others find it as simple? She looked across at J.B., and his gaze met hers. There was an understanding there. They would be next, and there was a mutual—what? Fear? Trepidation? Yes, perhaps that was it—trepidation about what they might find. At least the others had already faced that.

She looked at Mildred and Doc. Both of them looked as though they had aged ten years and had gone weeks without rest. A one-way jump was draining enough. To jump back in half an hour was putting an immense strain on the body.

But it was to be worse than that. They would all have to make two trips. Four jumps. She looked at her wrist chron. Ryan and Jak had been gone just over twenty minutes, and it was just under an hour and a half since Mildred and Doc had been the first to jump.

She wondered if Mildred and Doc had been able to find anything to use against Crabbe and his men. How the hell could they communicate, with the baron and so many sec men in such close proximity? Would Ryan and Jak be able to find anything? Would she and J.B.?

Even if they did, even if they were able to somehow let one another know about any discovery, even if they had the chance to take the enemy by surprise… After so many mat-trans jumps in such a short time, would they be up to the fight?

She could only hope so. Looking at Mildred and Doc, she wondered how she and J.B. would feel.

"THIS ISN'T GOOD," Ryan gasped as he floundered in the water, struggling to keep his balance as he ran. The sec door in front of him was closing too quickly for them to reach at their current pace. And yet it was an agonizing irony—the way in which it was grinding shut was, perversely, almost too stately for the rising tide of water. They needed it to close fast and cut off the flow before it hit the circuit breaker and that level, too, was reduced to emergency power only. The water would run faster the more that poured in. If it outran them, outran the sec door mechanisms, and reduced all levels to emergency power, then they would be stuck. There would be no way to make the jump back, and nowhere to go to escape the rising waters.

A slow chill by drowning awaited them.

"Panga," Jak said at Ryan as they ran. He still had hold of the one-eyed man and was pulling him. Ryan was aware that he was slow, more in brain than body. It took a second for him to realize what Jak meant, and he should have thought of that himself.

No time for recriminations. He unsheathed the blade, flipped it and thrust the hilt into the albino teen's free hand. Acknowledging him with a nod, Jak dropped Ryan's arm and forged ahead. The water was shallow on the floor, but not so shallow that it didn't enable Jak to dive and skim across the surface like a pebble, his momentum and that of the water incrementally increasing his speed. He was able to reach the sec door when the opening was down to a few inches. With all the strength he could muster from such an oblique angle, Jak thrust the blade of the panga between the bottom of the door and the floor. There was barely enough room for the thickness of the blade, but he pushed with all his might. In dry conditions the metal would have sparked on the concrete. Not now. But it did have an effect—the door squealed as the obstruction worked against the movement of the mechanism. It didn't halt completely, but it did slow almost to a standstill.

Jak could feel the tension singing in the blade. It wouldn't hold for long, but perhaps just long enough.

He was still listening for the distant crash of the last set of sec doors finally giving way totally, and the wave of pent-up water to be unleashed.

Ryan pushed himself forward with all the strength that he could muster. The gap in the door was narrow, and even as he hit it he could feel it constrict his chest. The pain was immense, his ribs being slowly squeezed as he struggled to push his muscular frame through a gap that was far too small. He yelled in agony and frustration as he seemed to get stuck. One last, supreme effort of will, and…

Perhaps it was that, or perhaps it was nothing more than the expelling of air in rage and frustration that enabled the one-eyed man to constrict his chest cavity enough to forge through.

He fell onto the other side of the door, aching and sore and aware both of the fact that there was still another battle ahead and that there was a pool of water beneath him, running swiftly ahead.

Before he had a chance to gather his thoughts, Ryan could feel Jak tugging at him. The smaller frame of the albino youth had made it easier for him to squeeze through, even though he was second in line. He had also managed to pull the panga out from beneath the door, which now closed in stately motion, cutting off the water.

Ryan looked up. The lights were normal, not red. The circuits hadn't been shorted on this level. With a bit of luck they could make it back to the chamber without any further perils.

"C'mon," Jak urged, handing Ryan the panga as he pulled him to his feet. "Hurry."

Ryan clambered to his feet. "Wait," he wheezed, his breath coming slowly and painfully, "I can't—"

He was about to say that he couldn't hurry, and that there was little need. The words died in his throat as he heard a thunderclap and an ominous rumbling from above them.

"Door finally gone," Jak said simply. "Move."

The albino teen was already on the move, and Ryan stumbled after him, hearing the onrushing tide of water, finally let free, hurtling down the corridor toward them. The weight of it had to be immense. The sec door at their rear was shut, but how long would it be able to hold against the battering ram of water that was about to hit?

Every step for Ryan made his lungs burn. The impact of boot on concrete drove acid bile into his throat. He spit it out when it became too much, and tried to focus on moving. Jak was a few paces ahead of him, looking sporadically over his shoulder. The sound of the sirens in the distance was now lost to the rumbling of the water as it approached.

It hit the sec door with a crash like the explosion of a ton of plas ex in an empty tank. The sound was almost physical in the impact it had on them. Partly because of that, and partly from a reflex desire to seek cover, Ryan threw himself forward as the crash reverberated around the corridor. He expected to be consumed in a wall of water that would wipe life from his body.

Yet nothing followed the crash other than a jarring impact on his already bruised body as he hit the floor in a roll. There was no wall of water. No lights turning to red as the circuit was flooded, no alarms sounding off in his ears.

"Fireblast—it held!" he exclaimed.

"How long?" Jak answered, coming back to help Ryan to his feet. The albino teen had also dived when the sound had hit, but he was quicker to his feet. He suspected that the first jet of water may have broken a rib or torn muscle in the one-eyed man's chest. No way did Ryan normally move so slowly. And the crack on his head had also disoriented him. Ryan had never left any of his people, and Jak felt the same about his leader, even though his instinct screamed at him to run.

Ryan let Jak pull him up, and he shook his head violently, as though the action would clear it of the torpor that threatened to overtake him. It didn't work, but it did renew his determination. They started to run again. At their back, out of sight now but not out of earshot, they could hear the groaning of metal that was being subjected to appalling stress as the weight of water pushed at it, searching for weaknesses that it could exploit to find entry. Wailing like a wounded bear, the metal bent and twisted out of shape.

There was only a thin layer of water at their feet, spilling across the floor and barely covering the soles of their boots. But the sounds from behind them were soon to be joined by a trickle of water that spread and covered the floor, rising so that it ran over the toes of their boots as they splashed toward the next level's sec door. If they could just get to it and get the door closed, then it would buy them the time they needed.

They passed the medical facilities and the armory, jumping the discarded boxes that littered the floor, shell casings starting to float past them as the level of water rose. At their backs, the squeal of twisting metal as it was wrenched from the grooves of the automated door frame ripped through their eardrums like knives. It was painful to hear, and painful to think of the consequences should it give before they reached their target.

They skidded around a bend in the corridor, and the sec door came into view. Ryan didn't want to hope, but it seemed like they could reach it before the other door gave way. Then they would only have one level left before reaching the mat-trans unit.

They ran through the open doorway, Ryan turning to

hit the keypad as they did. With an almost exaggerated care he tapped in the code. The door began to slowly grind shut, the long decades since the mechanism had been in use showing in the almost rusty grind of metal in and on concrete.

Nothing he could do to make the door move faster. He should get after Jak and hope for a little bit of luck. He turned and ran, each step getting harder as it splashed in the gathering water.

Behind him, he heard the scream of protesting metal as pressure took its toll and ripped a hole in the gap where metal met metal. It was only a matter of precious time before the rest of the door buckled and bent out of shape. A red glow from the upper level permeated the light above him, and the sirens wailed as the emergency power cut in, the original circuit now shorted. The water rose above his ankles as he hurried through it. He was racing water under pressure, and racing gravity.

Turning a corner, he could see that Jak had already reached the sec doors for the next level, and was waiting, fingers poised over the keypad.

"Hit it," he yelled. "Don't wait—"

The albino youth's red eyes blazed fury. No way was he going to leave Ryan behind. The sec doors were steady but not fast. He sized up the gap between himself and the one-eyed man.

Swiftly keying in the code, Jak set the sec door in motion then ran back toward the one-eyed man, taking some of Ryan's weight as he helped him toward the closing door. The increase in pace ripped a searing hole in Ryan's lungs with every pace, but he gritted his teeth and grunted through the mist of pain. He knew what Jak was risking, and if nothing else he wouldn't let his friend suffer because of him.

The water swirled around their ankles and the door was closing too slowly. They would reach it, which was good, but would it close before the other door gave way?

It was only two-thirds closed when they reached it, and the lights above them flickered and went dark, the siren screaming in their ears. It was swiftly followed by a thunderous crash as the weight of water defeated the other door.

One more level, one more sec door and not enough time.

Ryan pushed himself to the limit. Every fiber of his being was screaming for relief. A dark and secret part of his brain yelled at him to stop and give in to the inevitable. Breath came harder now, his ribs spearing his lungs with every inhalation. His chest was tight and constricted, and it became foggy and dark at the corners of his vision, the mists creeping across the corridor ahead of him.

He didn't feel himself begin to slow, and was only aware of what was creeping over him when his ribs received what felt like a knife thrust. He gasped and turned to see Jak glaring at him as they stumbled toward the final sec door and the last level. It had been the albino teen's elbow in his ribs, not a blade, but the shock had jolted him back to a level of consciousness where the dark recesses of his mind were driven back.

They reached the next level of the redoubt and hurried through the sec door, which had remained open.

They didn't bother to stop and trigger the mechanism. What did it matter now? The water was beginning to rise above their feet, and to their rear they could hear the squealing and moaning of metal on metal as the almost-closed sec door above them was hit by the on-rushing wave.

The fact that it hadn't quite closed might just save them. With part of the water pressure relieved by the available gap, the flow had been temporarily impaired. The lights above cut out and went red, the sirens began to blare.

But the mat-trans comp room was in sight. The water hadn't risen too high, and just maybe the unit would still work. Ryan felt that he was clutching at a distant hope. What if the unit was separately wired, so that escape could be made in just such a circumstance? Surely that was a plan for any eventuality?

They could hear the water start to roar as it came closer. It was beginning to rise to their knees.

Now they were in the comp room. The mat-trans unit was only a couple of yards away, through the anteroom. The water flow was level with the open unit door. If it started to flow into the mat-trans, then it might be too late.

Yelling incoherent frustration, Ryan threw himself forward, his body hitting the edge of the portal into the mat-trans unit with a jarring thud. Jak clambered over him, then turned and pulled at his arms as he pushed himself into the mat-trans.

It was like the hell of the predark religions that he had heard Krysty, Doc and Mildred discuss. The air was filled with a piercing, wailing sound. The whole world was red. And the water was everywhere.

Suddenly it occurred to Ryan that water had stopped rising. Wisps of white mist began to rise from the disks on the floor.

Jak had closed the door and triggered the mat-trans.

They just needed the power to stay on long enough for the jump.

They just needed…

They just…

The mantra in Ryan's brain ceased. With a sickening lurch the world went black once more.

Chapter Nine

The flash of the mat-trans unit as it flared briefly to life made everyone in the control room look away. It crossed J.B.'s mind that if he and Krysty could find some kind of ordnance in the redoubt that they could hide somewhere on their bodies, then they could bide their time and use a moment such as this to make their move. For if there were any moment during which Crabbe was defenseless, and his sec men were distracted, then this was such a moment.

But for now the only thing that concerned him was Ryan's and Jak's condition when they emerged from the mat-trans.

The Armorer started to get to his feet but found himself restrained by a sec man. In a none too subtle manner, the sec man drove the butt of his Kalashnikov between J.B.'s shoulder blades, hitting him from the rear as he tried to move. J.B. yelled as he fell forward, causing Mildred and Doc to scramble to their feet. Mildred helped J.B. up from his facedown position on the floor while Doc faced the sec men who now surrounded them.

"Whoa there," Crabbe yelled. "Don't take them out for nothing."

"He could have been going for you, Baron," McCready growled, more than happy to back up his men.

"Complete nonsense, you annoying little toad, and you know it," Doc snapped before the baron had a chance to say any more. "John Barrymore is merely concerned as to why Ryan and Jak have not emerged from the unit yet, as are the good doctor and myself... as, indeed, should you be, if you have any sense," he added, turning to Crabbe.

"Say, Jock has a point there," he mused. "Why aren't they out yet? Kirsty, you go and check it out," he said slowly, adding, "Not you" to the three companions surrounded by his sec.

Krysty moved cautiously from behind the comp desk, eyeing the baron as she went. She was fearful of what she might find in the mat-trans. Had the jump been successful? She was too well aware of the risks involved at any time. And she'd been keeping an eye on the time as the half hour cut-off time came closer and closer.

With a growing sense of dread for what she might find, Krysty carefully opened the mat-trans door. Inside was dark, shrouded from her by the light that spilled over her shoulder from the room at her back. She could make out little by way of shape in the unit, and there was no movement to give her clue. She wanted to call out Ryan's name, or Jak's, but her tongue was stilled by her own fear. The inside stank of stagnant water and burned cloth. Was it just that, or was there some other smell in there that she dare not put a name to?

The sound a human voice, small weak and mewling, was almost too horrible in such a circumstance. She stepped into the mat-trans, her eyes adjusting to the gloom as if almost by act of will, and she zeroed in on where the noise had come from. Jak was curled into a fetal ball, the edges of his patched camou jacket singed, his hair blackened at the ends. He made another small noise then looked up, his red eyes streaming tears, his head jerking uncontrollably.

As if that weren't bad enough, it was then that she noticed Ryan, who lay almost beside him, unconscious and unmoving.

"Mildred, get in here," she screamed as she rushed to check them both. Despite her sense of fairness and camaraderie, it was Ryan whose stillness pulled at her heart.

Outside, Mildred made to move but found herself constrained by the crossed blasters of two sec men, barring her way.

"Dammit, Crabbe, you want us to carry on your mission or not?" she growled, eyeballing the baron.

"Let her go, boys," he said, signaling her through.

Mildred made her way into the unit and fell to her knees where Krysty was cradling Ryan's head.

"He's breathing," she said tightly. "Check Jak first."

The doctor nodded and turned her attention to the albino teen. Jak was a hardy soul, with the stamina of men twice his size, and despite puking over the floor once again, he was already on his knees. As Mildred checked him over, he told her haltingly what had happened. She could see that both he and Ryan had been soaked through, and as she continued to examine him, she could tell that the water had gone on, rather than into, his body.

Shakily, he rose to his feet and indicated that she should attend to Ryan. Nodding, she switched her attention to the one-eyed man. While Krysty cradled him, and Jak hovered nervously, she checked him over. Jak's initial assessment had proved correct—Ryan had a couple of cracked ribs and some torn ligaments. The pain and strain of pushing himself to get back to the mat-trans had caused him to black out. She'd give him a couple of painkillers from her meager supply and bind his ribs, which would help. The fact he would have to undertake another mission shortly worried her, though.

"Doc, get me some painkillers," she called.

"My dear lady, I would. But I fear that I will not be allowed to bring them to you," Doc called back to her.

"For crying out loud," she growled between her teeth. "Keep him steady here, Krysty." She let the Titian-haired beauty take care of him while she exited the mat-trans.

Doc looked apologetic and shrugged. She could see that he had little choice in his actions, as both he and J.B. were being held at blasterpoint.

"You didn't really think I'd let you pull a little trick like that, did you?" Crabbe grinned.

Mildred couldn't be bothered to argue. "Just let me get some painkillers, for fuck's sake or you won't have a mission to lose us on anyway," she snapped.

There had to have been something about the steel of her tone that persuaded Crabbe she wasn't joking, for he indicated to McCready that she should be allowed to collect items from their gathered belongings.

"Jak, can you help Krysty carry him out?" Mildred asked. She didn't need to add that he should take care: Jak was more aware than any of them what Ryan had been through.

"Sure," the albino teen's voice came from the mat-trans. It was hoarse, but there was an inner strength that inspired confidence. And when he emerged a few moments later, supporting Ryan's feet as Krysty had his torso, he seemed to have fully recovered from the mewling wreck of a few minutes before. They carried the one-eyed man across to the part of the room where they were being contained and where the other three were waiting for them. As soon as they set the man on the floor, Mildred started to work on him, using a disposable syringe to pump him full of hydrocodone, hoping the predark drug had retained its potency, then binding his ribs. He needed time to recover, but she doubted that Crabbe would allow him that. Instead she knew she would have to get him as tightly bound as possible, to avoid further damage, then bring him back to full consciousness and let him know he was in bad shape. The rest was in the hands of fate.

She worked frantically on him, feeling the baron's gaze penetrating her back. She could feel his impatience, and knew that he would be itching to send Krysty and J.B. on their mission.

"Krysty, help me bind this rib," she said.

Although she could almost feel the baron's palpable impatience, Crabbe said nothing to her until she had finished her task. Ryan was now conscious.

"When the hell's one of you motherfuckers gonna tell me what went on there?" he rumbled. "Better make it quick, or else you'll have been patching Brian up for nothing."

"Nothing to interest you," Jak snapped. "Bastard redoubt flooded, looted long before. Nothing but dry shit and empty blasters."

"That right, Brian?" Crabbe asked shrewdly. He could see that Ryan was still a little disoriented as he came around, and would find it hard to back up anything that wasn't the truth, the first thing that would pop into his head.

"'Bout all there is," Ryan stated. "Don't know what else you expect us to find when a place has been opened up. Figure they scavenged the place but never came back 'cause of some kind of landslide. There's nothing there now but water and shorted-out old tech."

Crabbe looked disappointed. If he had any doubts about the veracity of their account, this was negated by the condition in which they had arrived. He would just have to take the bitter pill, ignoring all the while how much morc bitter it had to be for those who had so nearly lost their lives. A person didn't become a baron by showing that level of concern.

"Ah shit," he said in a murmur that was almost to himself, then added in a louder voice, "Guess it's your turn to get going, Kirsty. You, too, J.T. And you'd better start getting some results."

He couldn't realize that they felt exactly the same way as they collected their ordnance and headed for the mat-trans unit—though the kind of result they wanted was very different.

As they walked into the unit, which still stank from the return of Ryan and Jak, they turned wordlessly to watch Mildred take Krysty's position by the comp desk. Her eyes fixed on them in turn. They told J.B. to be careful and Krysty that Ryan was in good hands. It was little enough by way of consolation, but all she could offer.

It didn't make the mat-trans unit any the less cold as Krysty closed the door and they waited for the white mist to rise.

KRYSTY GROANED as she surfaced from the unconsciousness brought about by the jump. She felt terrible. Her limbs ached, her muscles felt like they had been torn out and roughly shoved back into place and she was sure a part of her brain was missing. Her vision was blurry as she opened her eyes, and she could feel that her hair was plastered to her scalp, as though wet.

To her surprise, J.B. was already on his feet. The Armorer was shaking himself, arching his neck and shaking loose the torpor from his limbs. The sight of him, ready to move and already preparing himself, made her push harder. She forced herself to her feet, and could feel her hair begin to relax. Her morale had been boosted by the sense of determination that J.B. exuded.

"You ready?" she asked—a rhetorical question, she thought—as she moved toward the door. He stopped her with a gesture.

"No, wait. There's only two of us, and we don't know what's waiting when we open the door. Best to use a few minutes to be triple red and frosty," he said.

Krysty was taken aback, but after a moment she realized what he was saying. Was it possible that part of the reason Ryan and Jak—and Mildred and Doc before them—had succumbed to such physical rigors could be down to them taking too much notice of the time limit?

She breathed long and hard, taking oxygen into her body. Tinged as it was by the ionization and tang of the ozone left by the jump process, it was still something that she could feel flooding her body with energy and relaxing tensed muscles.

J.B. looked at her, and then at his wrist chron. She checked hers—three minutes of their precious time had ticked by.

"You feeling right?" he asked her.

She nodded, and he studied her face hard before nodding himself.

"Give me cover," he said simply, moving to the door.

She followed, and was in position when he pulled the door open with the soft sucking sound and buried click that was part of the sealed mechanism.

J.B. opened the door enough for them to exit. She swung into position at his back as he slipped out, keeping low. The door gave her cover, but the aperture also allowed her enough of a view of the control room.

It wasn't the view that was the first thing to hit her, even though it was well-lit. The smell was a stench like unwashed humanity, shit and rotting meat. Her hair coiled defensively, and she felt a sinking in the pit of her stomach that told her this wasn't going to be good.

"CLEAR," J.B. SAID in a coughing, choked voice several minutes later. As Krysty moved through the anteroom and into the control room she could see why. If the smell had been bad enough creeping into the mat-trans itself, out here it made it hard to breathe without wanting to gag on the stench.

"Gaia, what the hell has been going on here?" she

whispered as she joined J.B. behind a comp desk that provided them with cover.

"I don't know," he replied haltingly, "but I'll tell you one thing—that smells fresh to me, whatever it is. Not long since it was kicked up."

Krysty nodded. Something that bad was still rotting, which meant that someone or something had been here recently. Chances were that it might still be here. She took the time to survey the room in the same way that the Armorer had on his exit from the mat-trans unit. It was a small room compared to most of its type, with the armaglass grayish now that the light had faded from the inside. Apart from the desk behind which they now crouched, there was precious little else in the room. A table with clear Plexiglas maps and diagrams fixed to the wall above it. To one side was a wall monitor and some old laminated sheets that were pinned to the walls, which had been ignored by whoever had created that unholy stench. There was nothing else.

The room was silent, with no place for anyone else to hide. Nonetheless, Krysty still indicated to J.B. that he should cover her while she went over to the laminates. They might tell her something about the purpose of this redoubt, and give some clue as to what they might find when they left the control room.

As Krysty walked over to the wall, J.B. straightened warily, his eyes fixed on the door to the control room. Krysty was adjacent and to the left. If the door opened, she wouldn't be immediately visible—he would. The Armorer was prepared to draw any fire that might come his way. He decided not to use the M-4000, as the load of barbed fléchettes would spread too wide in such an enclosed space. The last thing he wanted to do was to take out Krysty when he was supposed to be covering her. No, this was job for the mini-Uzi, set on single shot. If the door opened, the first person through would get a gut shot. Any questions would come later.

As that ran through his head, he was aware that the smell and his suspicions about what was causing it were making him edgy. J.B. made a conscious effort to keep it frosty.

Krysty, meanwhile, was scanning the laminates. A lot of what they said made little sense to her. Not because she couldn't read them, but because although they were typed and legible, they used a long-since-disappeared jargon that had no meaning in this world. However, there was still enough that made sense for her to work out the basic meaning.

"Doesn't look that promising," she said over her shoulder to the Armorer. "Looks like this redoubt was linked to the others on Crabbe's list, each one having its own function. This one was about storing basic supplies for the others. Stuff like soap for the showers, cleaning materials, and also all things like replacement beds and tables. On one of the levels here, it looks like there's nothing except a storage for beds and tables. What kind of use is that to us?"

"Dunno, could be worse." J.B. shrugged. "You can fix some decent explosives from the kinds of chemical shit they've got here."

"Yeah? But how long would that take? We've only got—" she checked her wrist chron "—twenty-two minutes."

"Good point. No time for that. Better check to see if

there's an armory here, and if anyone has left us any options. Bastard shame about that chemical shit, though."

J.B. motioned to Krysty to cover him as he took the door out of the control room. She looked across and shook her head. She would take point this time. As he nodded, she moved across and punched the standard numbers into the keypad. The door opened slowly, and as it did she had to resist the temptation to trigger the door shut again. If the stench in the control room had been bad—even if they had managed to control their nausea and were now almost used to it—then the odor that washed over them from the corridor made it seem like nothing.

"Gaia, what kind of mutie, stickie shithead could make something smell like that?" she whispered.

"Or keep living in it," J.B. added. "Listen."

There was movement—scuffling, some crashes, and the sounds of voices that were raised in incoherent babble. It didn't sound angry or alarmed. It didn't sound unfriendly. Why would it? Whoever—whatever—it was didn't know they were there yet. Or so it seemed. But it had a crazy, manic edge that wasn't promising.

Hardly surprising, given the conditions in which they seemed to live.

"Okay, let's move out, but keep real frosty," Krysty said in a choked voice, gagging on the smell. "I can't even imagine what the hell it is we're going to find."

They made their way along the corridor, blasters poised, senses so on edge that it seemed the slightest flickering of shadow would elicit a burst of fire. The smell seeped into every pore.

Now the noises were in the foreground. As they

moved up a level, some of the sounds became clearer. They were getting close to some of the inhabitants of the redoubt, though that didn't mean that the sounds made any more sense than before. They were still gibberish, still incomprehensible.

"What has happened down here?" Krysty whispered. "They sound like a bunch of stupe crazies."

"Yeah, well, if they are, we need to be ready for them," J.B. muttered, flicking the mini-Uzi from single shot to burst.

It was clear that, even though the stench had permeated to the lowest level, the creatures that created it had little use for the control room that constituted that area. They had left well enough alone. The same had to be true of the upper levels that housed the tech that kept the redoubt running, as the air recycler was working, The only light that was lacking was in areas where the fluorescent tubes had blown out. The sec cams were probably still working. The door mechanisms, presumably, were still operational. J.B. made a mental note and filed it away for future use. It would seem that the people—creatures, perhaps, as they seemed almost subhuman on long distance impression—had little use for any of the systems. That much was clear from the condition of the corridors as they ascended.

The floors and walls were smeared with filth. Excrement, blood, food—it all blended into an amorphous mess that was everywhere. Small piles of reeking ordure testified to the fact that the inhabitants of the redoubt had no idea of the purpose of the latrines. They just squatted and dumped as they passed. Layers of the indeterminate filth were on the floor and the bottom of the walls, sticky underfoot. It was impossible for Krysty not to wrinkle her nose as she stepped in it. J.B. grimaced as he felt it underfoot. Coldheart bastards who would run you through before they looked you in the eye he could understand. This, though, was unfathomable.

One thing, though—it showed that whoever lived down here had no grasp of the tech, as the layers of filth on the floor were undisturbed by tracking across them where the sec doors may have been opened or shut. If they did work, then it was a reasonable guess that the crazies—as they had to be—who lived down here didn't know how to use them.

But what kind of creatures were they?

"Heads up," Krysty yelped as something small and fast scuttled across the corridor ahead of them. It scooted from one doorway to another, seeming not to look at them, or even to pose a threat. Nonetheless, they took one side of the corridor apiece, flattening themselves to the walls, blasters raised in the direction of the movement. Exchanging rapid glances, Krysty kept her Smith & Wesson on the corridor ahead while J.B. turned to cover the corridor at their rear. There had been nothing behind them as far as they had known. But the speed at which the creature moved, and the manner in which it had appeared without warning, indicated that these things could move without a prior warning.

Things—that was just it. What the hell were they? This one was no animal they could identify. It didn't look like a stickie, nor did it resemble anything human that Krysty or J.B. could identify. A mutie of some kind, perhaps. And was this one typical of all?

There was only one way to find out. The sounds they had heard may have been gibberish, but that didn't mean that it wouldn't understand them. With gestures, J.B. let Krysty know that he would take the side that the creature had scuttled to. She should take the other, in case it hadn't been alone.

She nodded, and they moved forward with extreme caution. The floor squelched beneath them, but they took little notice. The sense of disgust had been subsumed as their survival skills cut in.

Despite their caution, they moved quickly. To identify and eliminate the threat was a necessity, both for their safety and because they had little time to waste.

Krysty took her room, blaster raised and hammer cocked. She sought the first cover—an old bed—and crouched behind it swiftly. The room was an old dorm, and it was as messy as the corridor outside. The bed linen had rotted through, and the mattress was little better. This was an irony, considering the purpose of the redoubt, but of little interest to her at this moment. What was important was that the beds were raised from the ground, and the space beneath was clear. From this she was able to scope the rest of the dorm, and could see that it was empty. Still wary, she moved from cover, taking each part of the room.

It was clear. She moved to the door and saw J.B. standing in the doorway of the opposite room, the mini-Uzi trained in one corner, away from her view.

"Secured," she said simply.

"Yeah, so is this...kind of," he replied with a note

of puzzlement in his voice. "Come and take a look at this."

Krysty moved across the corridor and joined him. She saw immediately why he was so puzzled.

"J.B., just what the hell is that?" she asked in a tone that more than matched his.

Chapter Ten

"I don't know, but I still want to keep the little bastard in my sights," J.B. said slowly as Krysty entered the room.

"I'll be careful," she said, approaching the creature slowly, "but he's not acting like a threat."

The creature was in the corner of the room, and was cowering under the glare of the Armorer's mini-Uzi. It was a small, stunted creature, a man, of sorts, but one who had been mutated back in the gene pool, with every chance that the pool had then grown smaller with every generation. It had large brown eyes in which the iris was wide and black, making it hard to see anything other than a big, dark orb. More like a dog than a human, it seemed to give it an appealing air. One that was reinforced by the large nose and receding chin, pudgy torso and spindly limbs. It resembled less a human than a cartoon drawn by a man with half his fingers missing. And the way it tilted its head as Krysty approached, as if to try to understand what she was doing, made it seem more like the kind of pet that she had played with as a child in Harmony than a vicious adversary.

Accordingly, she smiled at it. It smiled back—a wide, split-mouth grin that showed rotten stumps of teeth. Its breath was fetid and made her look away in a hurry.

"I think the only problem we're going to have with this critter is if it breathes directly on us," she said, stifling a cough.

J.B. watched her intently. Her hair, a usually reliable indicator of trouble, was still flowing free. There was no way he would have trusted the thing if left to his own choices, but Krysty was pretty reliable.

The woman extended her hand. "Hey, little feller, we don't want to hurt you if you don't want to hurt us," she said in the most unthreatening tone she could muster.

"Krysty, what—"

"It's okay, J.B.," she murmured to him in the same bright tone. "I wouldn't risk it normally, but Gaia knows we don't have much time to play with."

The Armorer shrugged. "Okay, play it your way," he replied in as neutral a tone as he could muster, "but I'll be ready."

"Fine. Now just let the blaster drop and see what he does," she said.

J.B. complied, the nerves in his forearms tingling as he kept on edge ready to pull the muzzle level in an instant. The creature watched them both, its eyes flickering between them.

"Listen, can you understand me?" Krysty asked, looking the creature directly in the eyes when it flicked them in her direction. The creature returned her gaze, smiled another fetid blast and broke into a stream of excited syllables that gabbled out of its mouth in an incoherent burst.

"That'll be a no, then," J.B. said laconically.

"Mebbe he understands us, but we don't understand him," Krysty said cautiously.

"I don't reckon it'd be that simple. Or that we'd be that lucky," J.B. added. "You sure it's a him?"

Krysty was in a better position to see the creature full-length, and as it was naked its shriveled genitalia was in full view. "Yeah, it's male all right," she said. "How many of them do you figure are here?"

"Sounded more than just a couple. You figure we can get laughing boy there to show us around? We don't have much time to waste," he continued, consulting his wrist chron.

"Can only try," Krysty muttered.

"We're going to leave here now," she said brightly. "Want to show us around, little feller?" She stepped back and toward the door, hoping the creature would divine her meaning from her actions, even if he didn't understand the words.

She was surprised, and not unpleasantly, when it broke into more excited gibberish before grabbing at her hand and pulling her toward the door. She was shocked by the feel of its flesh. She had expected it to be spongy and viscous, yet it was dry and firm. Gaia knew that she was sweating more than this little creature.

J.B. stepped back out of the doorway as the creature pulled Krysty towards him. He wanted to keep enough distance for a clear shot.

"Go with it," Krysty said simply as she followed the direction that the creature led her. J.B. shrugged, and still keeping the same disguised vigilance, he followed them.

The creature led them up a level. The smell grew worse, and the filth became more encrusted. It was obvious that these creatures lived more on the upper levels. They could hear them, up a little farther ahead, but none had yet come into view.

They moved toward what had once been the medical facilities and the armory. J.B. expected the worst—a desecration of the ordnance and the complete waste of what they might be able to use. Yet, to his surprise, he could see that the doors to the medical facilities and armory were closed. The crap piled against them suggested that they hadn't been opened for some time. A flutter of hope moved in his chest.

The creature tried to lead Krysty past, too excited to notice at first the way in which she tried to resist his insistent tugging. J.B. slowed and beckoned her back. She pulled against the creature. It had been facing away from her as it pulled, jabbering excitedly at intervals. But now, noticing the resistance, it turned. It looked at her with a furrowing brow that was almost comical, and the tone of its gibbering was curious and hurt that she wouldn't follow at the same pace.

"Look… Want to stop and look…" she said brokenly, indicating the doors they had just passed.

The creature tugged at her hand and jabbered excitedly, waving its free arm in the direction of the next level. Krysty shook her head and pulled away. A low growl escaped from deep in the creature's chest, taking her by surprise.

"Careful," J.B. murmured, raising his blaster so that a flick of the wrist would bring it up in line with the creature's chest.

Krysty backed away to the doors, keeping an eye on the creature. It was silent, watching her intently. As she joined J.B. by the door to the medical facilities, it started to tremble.

J.B. punched in the entry code for the door and it began to open slowly, grinding against the years of accumulated filth that had solidified against it. The mechanism squealed and protested, and the door let light from the medical facilities out into the corridor.

The creature growled again then whimpered as the door revealed the room within. As Krysty and J.B. entered, the whimper rose to a keening wail.

"He's scared," she whispered, amazed. "Why is this closed to them?" she continued, looking around. The room was untouched. It looked exactly the same as it had the moments the nukes had hit.

"I don't know," J.B. replied. "And I don't care. I'm just thinking that if this is untouched..."

He left the thought hanging. Krysty checked her wrist chron. He was right; they should get moving. She followed him as he left the room, door open, and moved to the keypad for the armory door. The code punched in, he waited impatiently for the door to groan and protest as the decades of filth welding it to the floor began to give way. The sound made them wince, but seemed to do little more than entice the creature nearer to them. As the door opened, the light from within spilling out into the corridor, both J.B. and the stunted creature gasped, but for vastly different reasons.

It was as the Armorer had expected—the interior of the armory room was, like the medical facilities, untouched since the time that the nukes began to fall. The walls were lined with racked rifles, SMGs, handblasters and gren launchers. There was a pair of flamethrowers, erect in their stands, the tanks of fuel placed beside them, the shine on the tanks undiminished by decades of lying idle in temperate conditions. Boxes of grens, plas ex and ammunition for the blasters were stacked around the walls, the stencils on their crates as clear as the day they were first marked.

It had been a long time since J. B. Dix had seen such an armory. It would probably be as long again before he saw such a thing.

He stood, awestruck, for a moment. Then with a start he looked down at his wrist chron. Just over half of their allotted time remained. They needed to move, and quickly.

"Krysty," he said hurriedly, turning to her, "if only we could… No, there's no time. We have to look for something small that we can hide on us when Crabbe makes us hand back our own weapons."

He stopped for two reasons—because she wasn't looking at him and because of what she was looking at. The creature had approached the door to the armory, a look of almost comical awe upon its face. It was an echo of the look that the Armorer knew had to have crossed his own face. But not for the same reason, then what?

Before he had time to ponder any longer, the creature let out a small yelp before turning and running off in the direction that it had been leading them.

"What was that all about?" he asked, puzzled.

Krysty shrugged. "Gaia knows. I sure don't. Let's move it, J.B. I've got an uneasy feeling."

J.B. was only too pleased to bow to Krysty's feelings. The sense of not knowing if there was any danger had been getting to him all the while, and he wouldn't be sorry to leave.

"Over there. The gren cases. We should find something small enough to conceal in there," he stated, directing her to the area of the room that held a section of stenciled cases.

As they moved over to the cases and started to open them, they became aware of a sound behind them. The gibbering and yelling that had been ever-present in the background was getting nearer. Fast.

Krysty looked around, but J.B. focused on his task. He was rifling through the cases, looking for a gren that could be used in a confined space without too much risk to their friends. The control room in the redoubt they just left was small. A frag gren would spread too much metal around. A concussion gren would stun anyone in range, without any discernment. It had to be a gas gren. There would be just enough of a time lag for the others to become aware of what was happening and take clean air into their lungs before the gas started to work on Crabbe and his men. Just enough time for them to figure it out, to take advantage of the effects on the baron's sec men, and then get out before it started to seep through their skin. Just enough of an edge of knowledge for them to act and save their lives.

If only he could find the right grens. Feverishly he searched on, aware of the approaching noise. The creature had obviously gone and fetched its friends. Why, J.B. didn't know. Didn't want to guess, if it came to that.

He only knew that if it was going to lead to trouble, then he had to find the right grens, and damn soon.

Krysty was out in the corridor. "J.B., you'd better come out here," she said softly, barely audible over the sounds of the approaching creatures.

"I haven't—" he began.

"No. Now, J.B.," she said emphatically.

There was something about her tone that made him stop his search. With a rising sense of dread, he left the crates and, cradling the mini-Uzi, went out into the corridor to where Krysty was waiting.

"Dark night..." he whispered, not quite sure if he could believe what was in front of his eyes.

"Yeah, I know," Krysty said in a puzzled tone, her hair waving wildly around her shoulders as if unsure of what to feel.

The creatures were on them. There had to have been at least thirty of them, all very like the creature they had first seen, who was at the head of the excited procession—for that was the overwhelming impression that both Krysty and J.B. took from the creatures in front of them. They were almost tumbling over themselves in their excitement as they swarmed down the corridor. They had very little between them to differentiate one from the other. Some had darker hair than others, and in some it was curly rather than straight. But all of them were some shade of brown, and as far as either J.B. or Krysty could tell, they had the same color eyes. Certainly, they all had very similar features and were of the same build and size. There was little difference between females and males, for each had their sexual characteristics reduced by their corrupted genetics. Their gene pool had been small, and had stayed that way for some time.

J.B. carefully brought up his blaster so that it would be easy to rake the crowd.

"Easy, J.B. I don't think they're after us," Krysty said carefully. Yet despite this, she made sure that her blaster was ready.

"Mebbe, but I don't feel like taking any chances," J.B. replied.

However, Krysty was proved right as the creature at the head stopped the crowd with a gesture, still gibbering excitedly. He pointed toward the open doors of the armory and the medical facilities, and then at Krysty and J.B. The other creatures, behind him, made noises that were no longer gibbering, but rather sighs of wonder.

"What the fuck is going on?" J.B. growled.

"I wouldn't swear to it, but I think they've got some kind of idea that this is some kind of sacred place, and we've opened it up for them."

"What? This bunch of inbred muties can think like that?" J.B. asked, astounded.

Krysty shrugged. "Hey, it might be some kind of trace memory that's still there from before they were so inbred. Might not even make sense to them anymore, it's just there."

"So have we violated it?" J.B. questioned.

"Look at them—I think they're kind of pleased," Krysty replied.

J.B. cast an eye over the muties standing in front of them, spreading across the corridor. Krysty seemed to have called it right. The creatures didn't look as though they were going to turn nasty, which was just as well, considering their numbers. He looked back over his shoulder to the open boxes of grens that he had left on the floor of the armory. They didn't have much time, and he just wanted to get back to searching out the ordnance that would give them the edge they needed, then get the hell out before their time was up.

While this passed through his mind and his attention was distracted, he didn't register that the crowd had started to move forward. It was feeling Krysty twitch at his elbow, rather than any vision, that prompted him to turn. As he did, he had no chance to react before the wave of stinking mutie humanity swept over him, pushing him back past the open door of the armory. Before either he or Krysty had the chance to do anything, the creatures had split into two groups that swarmed into the medical facilities and the armory. They started to dismantle the carefully kept inventories of both rooms, scattering the contents with the impatience of a distracted infant rather than any real sense of malice and destruction.

J.B. cursed under his breath as he saw them start to toy with the grens that he had taken from the cases in his search. It wouldn't take much for them to trigger a frag gren, and the havoc it would wreak could be tremendous. Triggering any grens or plas ex in the room could bring down half the redoubt level. And how would the survivors act toward them then, even assuming that he and Krysty would survive.

But before he had a chance to do anything, and even before he and Krysty had a chance to exchange any kind of word, the creature that they had first seen rose head and shoulders above the pack, whooping exultantly. He gestured again, yelling as he did, and the two groups swept from the two rooms. As they passed, they swept Krysty and J.B. off their feet, carrying them away from the armory and the route back to the mat-trans unit.

Yelling to try to make themselves heard to each other above the jubilant noises made by the creatures, and fighting against the hands that gripped them, they found themselves being swept away. Time was running out, and they were no nearer achieving their goal. If anything, they were now further than they had been just a few moments before.

And as they were swept toward the upper levels, the stench grew stronger. They were headed into the belly of the beast, and as they fought against the crowd that carried them along, any chance of getting back to their compatriots seemed to be nothing more than a distant dream.

"THIS WAITING IS really starting to piss me off," McCready said to Ryan, leaning over him. His breath stank of old brew and smoke. His teeth were bared in a mirthless, bloodthirsty grin. "Might just be that I'll get so pissed off and jumpy that my finger might just get a little itchy on the trigger. You know what I'm saying, Brian?"

Ryan smiled faintly. His head was buzzing from the opiate painkillers that Mildred had administered, and although he was aware of the menace in what the sec chief was saying, somehow it didn't seem to really register as a threat.

"Big words. But you're not a big man," he replied.

Crabbe looked over from where he was standing.

"What's going on over there?" he snapped. "What are you doing, Nelson?"

"Nothing, Baron. Just having a few quiet and friendly words with Brian here," he said, ignoring the look of venom he got from Jak. If the albino teen got a chance, then the sec chief would be the first threat he dealt with.

"Good, good," Crabbe said, nodding to himself. "I'm gonna need them all in good condition."

He turned to Mildred. "So what do you reckon Brian's chances are of being right for the next place he has to go to, Millicent?"

Mildred shrugged, keeping her eyes from making contact with the baron, her attention focused on her chron on her wrist.

"I have no idea," she said at length. "If it was down to me, I wouldn't let him do anything for a day or two, just to give that injury a chance to heal. But I don't know why you're asking me, because there's no way that you're going to give him that time. You're not going to give any of us that time."

"Then you'd better start hoping that Kirsty and J.T. find what we're looking for this time out. Then Brian won't have to go back in there," he said, gesturing to the mat-trans unit. "Come to that, none of you will. Now, wouldn't that be just fine?"

"Yeah, sure," Mildred agreed flatly, knowing but unable to say that such an outcome could never happen.

WRITHING AND WRIGGLING beneath them, the creatures made it impossible for either J.B. or Krysty to disentangle themselves from the hands that clutched at them. Their own limbs were pinned and made useless by the constantly changing grip of the small muties that pulled at them.

The upper levels were poorly lit in places. Great chunks of wall and ceiling, including the fluorescent lighting that was contained within, had been pulled down or broken away from the surrounding walls. Cables that carried fiber optic and power lines hung free over gaping holes, and were somehow miraculously intact. Independently of each other, Krysty and J.B. both wondered how these holes, and this damage, had been made. There was no obvious explanation, and it was unlikely that these seemingly harmless little creatures could have done it.

But such speculation was soon swept away, much as they themselves had been physically, by the sight and smell that greeted them as the creatures reached the next level, and came into an area leading off the corridor that had once been used for supply storage. It was now nothing more than a large cave for a group of people who had regressed to the level of precivilization.

The cavelike structure was well-lit, but even so it was large enough for the corners to be shrouded in shadows. Whether this was from lack of light or from the dark matter that gathered there was hard to say. There were even more of the creatures here, some of them seeming to be old. They were lying on something that seemed to be half animal and half vegetable matter, like skins covered in the remains of old rotted fabrics. Around them were piles of rotting, stinking matter that might have been their waste, or may have been their foodstuffs. Again, it was impossible to tell.

As they reached the center of the space, the creatures swarmed over their own bedding as if it wasn't there. J.B. and Krysty found that they were being put down on the ground. There were so many hands on them that it was hard to find their balance, and both went sprawling on the floor. A sticky, viscous mess that was part urine, part feces, and part rotting meat covered those areas of them that they couldn't avoid bringing into contact with the ground, sticking to the palms of their hands as they both tried to save themselves.

Distantly, there was a rumbling and a muffled roar that seemed to come from above and reverberate around the cavelike room. It made the creatures jabber excitedly, and they lifted J.B. and Krysty to their feet, as if their descent and the noise were somehow connected.

That was worrying, as was the way in which their precious time was being snatched from them. They were now on a higher level, without the weapons they had sought and then found, and surrounded by muties who were seemingly friendly, but whose behavior was bizarre. There was no way that J.B. or Krysty could tell how the muties would react if an attempt was made to escape.

It was hard for either of them to keep erect and get a good recce of what was happening around them, the creatures weaving in and out and jostling them in a manner that made it hard for them to take stock. They seemed friendly enough, but there was something about the way in which they were poking and prodding at the Armorer and Krysty that made both of them feel uneasy. The creatures had seemed to be jubilant about the way in which the intruders had unlocked the two rooms that held a deep, primal meaning for them. And yet, now that they had them back in their lair, it was as though the mood was shifting.

Krysty had a nasty feeling that was hardly prescient. Instead, it was based on a memory of something that her mother had once said to her back in Harmony. She had told the young Krysty about the messengers of the gods in predark times—way back before the tech that had come along to wipe out the civilization they had struggled so hard to build—who would be rewarded for their task by being sent to their masters.

She had a feeling that this was what was about to happen to them unless they acted swiftly. She tried to catch J.B.'s eye, but it was impossible under the circumstances. She would have to act independently and hope that he would follow.

She had no idea that he was having more or less the same thoughts. His wasn't based on stories he'd been told, or knowledge of the times before tech advanced enough to catapult them back to the Dark Ages. His fears were based on nothing more than observation.

As he felt the fingers of the creatures prod, poke and pinch from every angle, making him wince with sharp pains that came from his arms, legs and the flesh of his inner thigh—which really galvanized him with its unexpected intrusion of his privacy—he pieced together something that had been at the back of his mind, bothering him since they had first seen the creatures. The supplies that had been laid in for the military before skydark had to have long since been exhausted, as these creatures were the end of a long, long line, and one that hadn't been troubled by outside blood, by the look of it. That meant that the food sustaining them had to come from within. So where did they get it from? And where did they put their dead?

The smell—it had to be that. Shit, blood and rotting meat. The meat had to come from within.

And they were next up on the menu.

"Dark night—Krysty," he yelled, struggling to pull free his hands, which were being pinned by the grasping, groping paws of the creatures as they milled around.

"I hear you," she yelled back, relieved that however he had come to same conclusion, J.B. was in tune with her.

The Armorer wasted no more time with words. There were more important matters. He thanked whatever deities he had ever heard of, and didn't believe in, that the creatures had no idea what blasters were actually for, or what they did. The creature they had initially cornered had been scared, but more of them as people than for the hardware they toted. Or so he hoped.

There was only one way to find out for sure. He wrestled his hands free for long enough to lift the mini-Uzi to the level of his waist. It was still set on rapid-fire. He looked around him desperately, trying to place Krysty so that he wouldn't blast her when cutting himself a swathe. In the confusion, it was hard to locate her, but he could see her head and her flaming red hair above the level of the creatures, even as some of them leaped up and tried to climb up her arms and tresses.

"Fuck!" he exclaimed as he felt sharp teeth bite into

his forearm. At the same time, he felt a gnawing down on his thigh, through the thick material of his combat pants. Spurred on by the pain and shock, he pulled his arms free and aimed the mini-Uzi down into the crowd that jostled around him.

The sharp, staccato burst of two taps on the trigger exploded in the room. At the same time, he heard the boom of Krysty's blaster in the cavernous room.

For the briefest of moments there was a stunned silence from the creatures as they tried to understand what had just happened. But almost before either J.B. or Krysty had a chance to take in the silence, the creatures exploded into sound like a flock of startled birds. Yelling and screaming in a way that was, if possible, even more incoherent than they had been before, they scattered away from the intruders, momentarily terrified at what had happened. As they parted like a sea of crazed flesh, it became apparent that the bursts of SMG fire had claimed three chilled and two with ragged wounds, lying whimpering. Another creature with no head bore testimony to Krysty's own aim. At the far side of the room, two more muties were curiously licking the brain and blood that had splattered on their bodies.

"Come on," Krysty called as she ran for the entrance to the cavern, cursing inwardly at the way in which the stickiness of the floor frustrated her efforts at flight. She had no need to have said anything, as the Armorer was close on her heels, turning as he ran, pivoting so that he covered their backs. It was only a matter of moments before the creatures would be after them.

Most of them, those who had been experimentally licking at the gore spattered over them, raced to their fallen comrades, falling on them with a wolfish fervor. As J.B. hit the exit, the last thing he saw was one of the creatures tearing a chunk from the bloodied ribs of a companion who was injured.

They were out into the corridor and sprinting down the corridor, hitting the dogleg bend before any of the creatures emerged from the cavern. Neither wasted breath on words, nor on looking back. They knew that all the creatures had assembled in the cavern with them, so there was no way that they would encounter any in front of them. All they had to do was to use the advantage of their longer limbs, keep on their feet, and they would reach the mat-trans unit before the little bastards could catch up with them.

Two things that would otherwise have bothered J.B. immensely now no longer seemed to matter. The briefest of glances at his wrist chron as he ran revealed that they would have enough time to make it back before their half hour was up. There was no way that they would get the chance to lose track of time with those little critters at their heels. And they wouldn't be able to stop at the armory and search out the gas grens that he had been so keen to find before they had been interrupted. Vaguely he was aware that this would irritate him later, when he had the chance to reflect on it. Right now, all he wanted to do was to get out. He should have taken the chance, and he would curse himself for it later. Now, survival was all he had on his mind.

Survival that was threatened from another source.

What was that rumbling that he could hear?

"Shit, watch out!" Krysty yelled as she threw herself forward. The rumbling had grown louder as they went lower, past the area where the walls and ceilings of the tunnels were broken and crumbling.

Now they knew why. And they knew because they were caught in the middle of it.

J.B. skidded to a halt, leaning back to avoid a chunk of concrete that flew past his face, so close that he could feel the rush of air as it passed. Dust choked his nostrils, clouded his glasses and stung his eyes. He tumbled, falling backward. Even as he hit the floor with a jarring thud he tried to scramble to his feet. Tears streamed from his eyes as he attained the level, clearing his vision. Not that it made it any easier to believe what he could see in front of him.

A giant white worm, fat and pulsating obscenely, slithered through the hole it had made in the wall. It dropped onto the floor, its dripping ooze blending with the filth on the floor and making it stickier. Was this how it trapped its victims? Or was it simply that it didn't have victims, but was oblivious to their presence and there only by chance?

Right now, that didn't matter; the only thing that was in J.B.'s mind was that the worm stood between Krysty and himself, that he was on the wrong bastard side of the obscenity. On Krysty's side was a clear run to the mat-trans unit. On his side were the creatures, who he could hear in the distance, gaining on him with every moment that he stood, mesmerised by the worm as it writhed on the floor. It turned what he assumed was its head toward him. Eyeless, it was presumably the head only because a mouth opened and closed, seemingly at random, needle-sharp teeth that dripped mucous showing in the pinched maw.

The maw didn't change in the way that it moved, even when the roar of Krysty's Smith & Wesson was swiftly followed by chunks of pulpy white flesh splattering over him as the slug took out where she had—presumably—figured that it had its brain.

The worm didn't drop, as he would have hoped. But being covered in its viscous being while he could hear another ominous rumbling at his rear galvanized the Armorer into action. If the thing had no brain and wouldn't lie down and buy the farm, then he had only one option open to him.

"Krysty, stick to the wall," he yelled before raising the min-Uzi and firing rapid staccato blasts into the worm, chopping up and down in a line so that white flesh and clear, stinking mucous filled the corridor in a fine spray. The maw still opened and closed with little apparent register of what was happening to it, but the purpose of the blasting was soon fulfilled. The blasterfire chopped the worm in two, causing the front end, raised as it was from the ground as the maw moved in the air, to topple and land with a wet splat on the concrete.

Even before the tail end had stopped waving, J.B. was wading through the glop that formed puddles on the already sticky floor, the excrescence swilling around his ankles.

Krysty's face as she reached out to pull him through the mess that was slowing him needed no words. Saving their breath, they kept running, hearing the yelping of the creatures behind them as another of the worms broke through the wall of the corridor. What kind of mutie sickness had led to such abominations as the stunted creatures and the grossly inflated worms couldn't be considered.

The only thing that mattered was to reach the mat-trans.

They kept running, even though the sounds of the creatures receded into the distance as they plumbed the lower levels. The worms had, in their own way, acted as the diversion that Krysty and J.B. needed.

Exhausted, covered in mucous and stinking white flesh that stuck to the patches of shit and blood they had picked up earlier, they reached the control room.

It was so quiet that it seemed impossible to consider that there was so much insanity only a hundred yards or so above them. They didn't dare look back as they threw themselves into the mat-trans unit. Krysty slammed the door shut and hurried to hit the Last Destination button. J.B. checked his wrist chron. The irony was that they had three minutes' grace. After all those obstacles, it was a miracle.

But as the mist began to fill the mat-trans, J.B. regretted the loss of the gas grens and wondered how they would even begin to explain what they had seen.

Chapter Eleven

Mildred was eyeing the hands of her watch with alarm, and trying not to let it show in her face. Three minutes remained before it would be impossible for Krysty and J.B. to return. She had been through this with Ryan and Jak, but it was worse this time around. She figured it had to do with J.B. being one of those who were temporarily—she hoped—lost in the ether. She had little doubt that Ryan shared her feelings, although they were perhaps blunted by the opiates that still coursed through his body. She caught sight of Doc, who was watching her intently. Casting a glance to the side to see if he was being watched, he mouthed the words *"Courage, mon brave"* at her.

The really stupid thing was that when she and Doc had been on their own mission, the thought of how those left behind had been feeling hadn't occurred to her. Nor, she didn't doubt, to Doc. In the heat of battle—which any such expedition was, no matter what—there was no time for reflection.

Right now, there was too much damn time.

Crabbe was eyeing her intently. A brooding silence had descended over the mat-trans control room. McCready's hostility was obvious, and had bred a similar enmity from Jak. That upset Crabbe's plans. His desires depended on their compliance, and to have his sec chief on the edge of opening fire wasn't the best way to get that compliance. As a result, the baron had retreated into himself. Sal, loitering by the doorway, looked like he couldn't wait to get away.

Mildred doubted that she had ever been in a place where the atmosphere was so thick with hostility. It was oppressive, and made the prospect of escape seem all the more remote.

She was wondering if J.B. and Krysty had discovered a weapons stash they could use to tip the balance when the air around them began to crackle with an energy that signaled the return of the travelers.

"Son of a bitch..." she whispered to herself, turning away and closing her eyes as the unit glowed with a phosphorescent flash of brilliant light that seared its way into her retinas even though she had done her best to avoid any direct view. She heard Crabbe gasp as he was taken by surprise.

Maybe this was the chance they were looking for. In that moment when the flash happened, the baron and his men were momentarily disabled. If they could just take advantage of it... They were far more used to the effects of the mat-trans, even though they had never really been on this side of the unit as a jump was made.

As she tried to focus as she opened her eyes, Mildred knew that she was clutching at straws. The afterimage of the flash burned yellow light on all the objects around her, making it hard to distinguish more than a blur of indistinct shapes.

Dammit, there would be no easy way out of this.

Even as the door opened and J.B. and Krysty stumbled out, she was barely able to see what they looked like.

Though she could smell them....

CONSCIOUSNESS WAS slow and almost out of her grasp, but Krysty willed herself back to a level where she was able to pull herself to her feet. A mat-trans jump always made her feel like shit, but this was worse. It was as though some of the pulpy flesh and glop that had shot from the worm, not to mention the slimy crap that had covered the floors and walls of the redoubt, had somehow become absorbed into her very being.

J.B. had to have felt the same. He didn't say anything, but then he didn't have to. The fact that he was puking his guts out all over the floor said everything.

She went across to him, still shaky on her feet, and tried to ask him if he was okay. It was a stupe question anyway, but one rendered impossible by the way that her throat seemed closed and dry, almost choking her on its own thickness. She contented herself with a touch on his shoulder. Just letting him know that they were back safe was, she hoped, enough. He looked up at her, but it was purely a reflex action. His eyes were unfocused, and his jaw was slack and drooling.

Krysty's mind was beginning to return to normal. Three redoubts on the list visited, and no weapons to hide and use against Crabbe. They were running out of time and opportunity.

Gaia, only half the mission completed and all six of them were halfway to buying the farm. They might not need to fight back for their freedom. Their own chilling might buy it for them.

Krysty tried to dismiss such thoughts from her mind. She usually wasn't negative. It wasn't the way she had been brought up back in Harmony, and it wasn't how she had made it this far. But, as she helped J.B. to his feet and opened the door, facing out to the waiting sec men, blasters raised, she couldn't see any way out. Their own weapons—the only edge they had—would be taken from them before they had a chance to protest.

The bastard of it being that they had no energy with which to do anything other than accede to their captors, meek as if they were already beaten.

Maybe they were, this time.

"By the Three Kennedys, what in heaven's name has happened to you!" Doc exclaimed, rising to his feet as Krysty came out of the mat trans, supporting J.B., who was still unsteady on his feet. Doc stood, ignoring the sec man who tried to block his path with the barrel of a blaster. He brushed it away, much to the man's amazement, and went to help Krysty as she guided J.B. to the area where they were being kept between jumps. The sec men surrounded them, blasters triple red as if expecting trouble purely from the fact that Krysty and J.B. were still in possession of their weapons. They had the grace to look embarrassed as Doc shot them a withering glance before turning to Crabbe.

"You fool," he said with venom that he couldn't disguise. "Do you really think that these people pose a threat to you at the moment? You do not understand what undergoing a mat-trans journey can do to the human body. For pity's sake let the good doctor over here so that she can render some assistance, or you will not be able to exploit us as you want for the rest of your cretinous list."

Crabbe should have been enraged by Doc's outburst, yet he was shrewd enough to see the sense in what he was saying. Muttering something barely audible under his breath, he indicated to Mildred that she should leave her station and go to tend to her friends.

Mildred left her post behind the comp desk and rushed to tend to her companions. As she did, it occurred to her that there was a slight change in Crabbe's approach to them. Slight, but perhaps of use.

But that was for later. Right now, she was more concerned with her friends.

"Let me," she said, taking Krysty and turning so that she could look into the eyes of the Titian-haired beauty. They were slightly unfocused, but clear.

"It's not me you should be looking at," Krysty said in a cracked voice. "J.B. is in worse shape."

Mildred was glad that Krysty had told her that. She could see that J.B. was in a worse way, but her innate sense of fairness had compelled her to attend to Krysty first, not wishing to show favoritism to the man she loved.

Ryan rose to his feet and took Krysty by the shoulders. Seeing her and J.B. in this condition was forcing him to push aside the worst effects of the opiates. As he looked into her eyes, she could almost see him willing the fog from his mind.

"What happened out there?" he said in a clearer and more controlled voice than he had been able to use for some time. The steel in his soul told him that now was the time to pull together all the strength he had.

And so, while Krysty started to unravel the almost unbelievable tale, Mildred tended to J.B. She listened to what Krysty had to say, half of her mind appalled by the creatures they had encountered, the other half working analytically to fathom which of the possible substances he had ingested had caused him to react in this way. For, apart from a few contusions, J.B. had suffered no real physical injury. Unlike Jak or Ryan, there were no signs of trauma. And yet he was still disoriented and vague.

"Did you get covered in that shit, too?" she asked when Krysty had finished relating their experience.

Krysty shook her head. Her tresses, even though the danger was now behind them, were still clinging tightly to her skull. "Depends on what you mean. Sure, I've got that stinking shit all over me, but that's just from the floors. The gunk that came from the worm J.B. had to blast his way through—I didn't get any of that on me, but he got covered in it. And he had to wade his way through it, too."

"Did he swallow any of it?" she pressed.

Krysty shook her head. "I couldn't tell you, Mildred. Really. I didn't see much until he'd blasted his way through it. But I tell you what, I'd be really surprised if he didn't get a mouthful of that crap, the way it spurted over him. And he's puked enough up after the jump."

"Goddamn..." she murmured to herself. Deep somewhere within her memory, she recalled that there had been a toad, predark, that had a secretion with hallucinogenic properties as a defense mechanism. She'd seen cases in the hospital where she had served her internship—so long ago in so many ways as to seem almost like an hallucination in itself—of men and women who had tried to get high on toad licking and got it a little wrong, reducing themselves to puking wrecks. It seemed to her like the worm had evolved something similar by way of a defense, and J.B. had been an unwilling partaker.

"Look, if he's ingested something that is some way toxic, there's no telling how long it'll take him to be ready to jump again," she said, directing her comments toward Crabbe. "You can't expect him to go again any time soon."

Crabbe had been watching them with a growing cloud forming over him. His mood, which had been subdued and brooding before Krysty and J.B. arrived back, was now edging into the blackly explosive.

"Who the fuck do you think you are, missy?" he growled. "You don't tell me what to do. You're supposed to find that disk for me in one of these redoubts. There are six. You've covered three and found fuck all. That ain't my problem. Now mebbe that's just the luck of it, and mebbe it's you holding out on me for some reason. Either way, you keep going. You either come clean, or you find the disk in one of the three you got left. It's that simple. You ain't calling the shots here. I am. And you do what the fuck I say."

"That wasn't what you said before," Ryan said coldly.

"Well, mebbe my patience is getting stretched mighty thin," the baron snapped. "Nelson, get their blasters."

Mildred looked up at him. When she spoke, it was in a low and menacing tone, made all the more fearsome by that fact that she was now paying no heed to the situation in which they found themselves.

"Listen, you stupid bastard," she began, "don't you get it? If you don't give us the time to recover before you send us out again, then there's no way that you're going to get what you want out of us. You've been looking for us for a long time, right? You've trailed us, searched for us, and were glad when we fell into your hands, right? Well, if that's the case, why the fuck do you want to throw it all away because you can't stop your fat ass itching long enough for you to scratch it? If you got your brain in gear, you'd realize that there's no way that we can do the job you want us to in the time that you're giving us. Why not send your own sec men in there, then? You think they could do any better than us? You think they could do any worse the way we are right now? Get that brain of yours in action and try to figure it out, for God's sake."

Crabbe stood silent. McCready was half grinning as he retrieved their blasters, expecting his baron to lose control and scream for them all to be chilled, which was something that the sec chief would have taken great pleasure in doing.

But the baron eyed the companions calmly, taking in what Mildred had said and viewing them with a dispassionate eye.

Hell, he figured, Millicent was right. She was on edge from tending to J.T. The man looked a mess, with his eyes showing white and rolling up into his head. Hellfire, even as Crabbe looked at him, his chin rolled forward onto his chest and he puked another thin line of the white glop onto his chest. Brian was trying to pull himself together, but those pills Millicent had given to him—the ones that had made him so spaced—were still running through his system. He was strong, but even so they would have slowed him down. Snowy? Well, he looked okay, but he was sullen and withdrawn. Too on-edge to be anything other than a liability if it came down to it. Jock? He was wired. But then he always was, so it kind of made no difference with him. That was why he needed someone with him who was level-headed. None of them fitted that description right now. Not even Kirsty. Right now, she looked exhausted, as if you could blow on her and knock her down. That was no damn good to him.

Crabbe nodded, almost to himself, and grunted. "Yeah, I guess you got a point," he said at length. "You're halfway through. Take some time out, and remember that the disk is in one of the places on this list—" he took up the laminate that had been lying on the desk "—and if you want to walk out of here and not buy the farm, you'd better find it."

Mildred knew what she would like to do with the laminate, but this time felt it best to hold her tongue. The baron had given them some breathing room, and for that alone she was grateful. But she knew, as did her companions, that there was no way that they would find what he wanted.

Meantime, they should take the opportunity to rest up and recuperate while they had the chance. The time for action would come soon enough.

Uneasy, with no chance to speak among themselves, they hunkered down to try to get some rest. McCready kept his sec men tight on them, and the tiny room seemed even smaller and more oppressive than before. Mildred felt as if the walls and ceiling were closing in on them, and from the looks of the others she knew that they were experiencing similar feelings. Crabbe was a brooding, malevolent presence that was always in the background, waiting....

Time passed slowly, so slowly that it seemed as though the very hands of her wristwatch were slowing with every second.

Mildred tended to J.B. The Armorer had puked all that he had ingested, and the worst of the effects were now beginning to wear off. His eyes were clear, and he was able to focus on as well as speak to Mildred. At first just a few croaks, he was soon able to form simple sentences. She was glad to see him returning to something approaching his normal self, though she doubted the toxin in his system would be fully cleared by the time he was obliged to take up arms again.

For the others, Jak and Doc sat and brooded. Unwilling to speak, unable to do anything to aid their comrades, they both felt—in their own ways—useless. Ryan, too, was feeling that, but as the painkillers subsided, and his mind became less fogged, he began to think about what he could do to lead his friends out of this mess.

Crabbe, keeping a constant vigil, could see these changes. He would give them time, sure, but no more than he would deem necessary.

And so they were cloistered together in an uneasy and unwilling alliance, neither side wishing to be in the room, for their own reasons.

Eventually, it was too much for the baron to bear.

He sighed heavily before crashing his fist into the side of the comp console, swinging his arm to the side so that the edge of his hand dented the metal casing. In the quiet into which the room had sunk, it was a startling sound, breaking the silence with a sudden explosion.

"Enough of this shit, now," he growled. "I want this over and done with. I've waited too long to fuck around."

"Too long to see it done right?" Ryan asked, keeping his tone as level as possible, even though he was seething inside.

"Damn right," Crabbe snapped. "A man don't wait this long and then let someone else yank his chain for him. Not if he's any kind of a man, and that's what I am. I'm baron here, and don't you forget it, Brian. Millicent was right, but fuck it. I want some action."

Mildred sighed. "You're a fool, but you hold all the cards. It's your problem if we don't get you want you want."

"No, missy, it's your problem," he rejoined, "and don't you forget it."

Mildred ignored him and turned to Doc. "You and me again, Jock," she said with heavy emphasis. "You ready for this?"

"No, my dear Doctor, indeed I am not," Doc said sadly, shaking his head, "but our wishes and desires are of no consequence. We shall depart as soon as we have been reimbursed with our defenses," he directed toward the Baron.

Crabbe looked at him blankly.

Doc kissed his teeth. "Our weapons, man," he said shortly. "Come, you cannot expect us to pitch ourselves into the maw of the beast without an adequate means of protection."

Crabbe snorted. "Jock, you are one crazy stupe fucker. But I can't help admire you."

"I could only wish that the feeling were mutual," Doc muttered.

McCready directed his sec men to let Doc and Mildred leave the group and collect their individual ordnance from the stock he was keeping secured on the tarp. Without another word, and without looking back at their companions, they loaded their blasters, checked their weapons with an almost insolent ease, then moved toward the mat-trans door. They didn't look back until they were in the doorway. Doc was in front, with Mildred standing behind him. Doc's hand rested on the door, and he took a slow, searching look around the control room, his gaze raking over everything within, pausing only to linger on Ryan and Jak. Krysty now stood near the comp desk. Doc's gaze, steady and clear as only he could be when his mind was fully focused, met hers.

She knew exactly what he was saying to her. She nodded imperceptibly.

With no indication that he understood that gesture, Doc turned his back on them, his hand still resting on the door. As he pulled it shut, only his bony, gnarled fingers were visible before they, too, relinquished their grip and the door softly sucked and clicked as the airtight seal slotted into place.

Chapter Twelve

Mildred's mind was spinning like a whirlpool that would pull her deeper, making her thoughts all the more difficult and insane to hold together. Fragments of life from her past and maybe even her future whirled inside her skull, there at the periphery of her consciousness but never quite close enough for her to take hold of and fully understand. The thoughts jumbled and flung together before being ripped apart and flung into the deepest recesses and furthest corners of her skull, she felt like her very being was being swept away. If only she could surface, take a deep breath, get some air in her lungs and oxygen in her brain before she went mad...

The physician could hear herself gasping, noisily sucking air into her lungs to the point where she might hyperventilate, even before her eyes had opened. For a moment she didn't know where she was, thought that perhaps she had been dropped into a deep well and her body was reacting to the change in pressure by giving her the bends.

It was only when she felt Doc's hands on her, bony yet strong, lifting her so that was sitting upright, his calm voice urging her to breath slower, more shallowly, that she started to remember where she was and how she had gotten there.

She looked around at the interior of the mat-trans unit. It was like waking into a nightmare. Drowning would have been a preferable option.

"I know," Doc said softly, as though he could see into her mind. "It is, is it not?"

She managed a wry smile. "No time to worry about that now." She let him assist her to her feet. She felt shaky, but the act of standing in itself seemed to buoy her. She frowned and turned to him. "Don't take this wrong, but—"

"You would have expected me to have been mewling and puking on the floor like an infant?"

Her smile broadened. "Well, yeah, Doc. I did."

Doc sucked his teeth in rumination. "I must confess, I would agree with you. But I actually feel rather well. It is as though the act of a second jump so soon has pushed me beyond the usual barriers. Perhaps there is a point at which the body exceeds its own pain barriers and comes full circle?"

"That's not a thing I ever came across in all my years in medicine, but that was a long time ago, and there isn't anything that would surprise me now, Doc." She shrugged.

"Good," he said brightly. "I think it is always rather splendid not to be too blasé at life. After all, you never know what it may throw at you. Shall we ready ourselves to exit this shell?"

Millie grinned. "Sure," she said. "I'll take point."

"Then I shall deem it an honor to provide adequate cover, my dear Doctor."

Without another word, he moved into position as she made for the unit door. The walls of the mat-trans were opaque, but any excess of movement from outside could at the very least be detected, particularly as the lighting on the other side of the walls was strong, and the inside of the unit was now dark. However, they were only too well aware that the flash of intense light that greeted their arrival would have alerted anyone who happened to be in the control room.

Mildred took a deep breath as she took a grip on the door. Her fingers tensed slightly around the grip and trigger of her Czech-made ZKR target pistol. Not the most prolific of weapons, but with her eye more deadly than any SMG with a spray 'n' pray finger on the trigger, it became a tool of instant chilling.

Always assuming she got out of the mat-trans in one piece and was able to use her talents....

Doc stood at her back, ready to grasp the door and use it as cover. The LeMat grasped in his bony fist was exactly the kind of weapon that was the antithesis of her own approach. But no matter. With it, Doc could more than do a job.

She nodded shortly, her beaded plaits bobbing as she pulled back the door and shot out, keeping low and secure in the knowledge that Doc was covering her back. The desks in the control room offered her some vestige of shelter, and she rushed forward to cover. Coming up to scope the area, she whistled softly.

It was, frankly, a miracle that the mat-trans had acted as a receiver to the signals sent from Crabbe's redoubt. The equipment had been well and truly trashed at some point, and it was little short of astounding that anything was working. As it was, the few winking lights were desultory in the banks of dead comp banks. Many of them had the panels ripped from them, their electronic entrails spread across their surfaces, trailing to the floor.

It was silent in the control room, but there was an air of menace that suggested danger might not be too far away.

"Clear," she said simply, coming up to her full height and lowering the ZKR, "but keep it frosty, Doc."

The old man stepped from the mat-trans, taking a long look around him as he joined her. "Someone, it would seem, was less than keen on the idea of predark tech surviving," he said softly. "And whilst I cannot disagree with their sentiments, the manner in which they have realized those sentiments could well give us warning."

"Uh-huh… Can you feel it, Doc?"

"The savagery?" he questioned. Then, when she had nodded, he added, "I can indeed. There is an uneasy feeling here… It's… Lived in, is, I suppose, the phrase for which I search. Not down here. No, they've finished with here. But not, perhaps, with the parts of the redoubt that may be of some use to them."

"That's exactly how I read it, Doc," Mildred agreed. "In which case we'd better watch ourselves. We've got—" she checked her wrist chron "—twenty-seven minutes to scout and get the hell out."

"Then let us not waste any more time," Doc agreed.

The access door to the corridor was open, and a swift recce ensured that they were able to move into it with no danger. In truth, there was nothing to suggest danger as they moved up a level. The corridors were clear, with the rooms on either side of the concrete run open. Inside, the room had been looted and trashed, but in what appeared to be a more constructive manner than the mat-trans control room. That bore the hallmarks of a savage burst of temperament. These rooms had been turned over in a much more methodical fashion. Pulled out and looted for anything of value, and then left.

There had been no wanton destruction. The rooms were trashed, but anything that couldn't have concealed something of worth had been left. The lighting above them and in the interior rooms had been left alone. The air con and purification system still worked.

Coldhearts, bandits in search of loot—had they found it and then gone?

A prickling at the base of her neck told Mildred that this wasn't the case. There was someone still here, somewhere, waiting for them. For she had little doubt that whoever they were, they knew that they had visitors. Looking up, she could see the blank fish-eye lens of the sec cams for the corridor. If the lighting and air systems were operational, she had no doubt that the cameras were also operable. So if they had half a brain, all they had to do was sit, watch, and wait....

As they moved up another level, she turned to Doc, indicating the sec cams with an inclination of the eyes. His nod was barely noticeable, though she could tell from the gleam in his eye that he had been ahead of her in working it out.

They were now coming up to the level where the armory was situated. From the size of the trashed dorm room, she knew that this was a small redoubt. Its purpose was alien to her, and she had no concern about finding out. What she did work out was that the armory would be correspondingly small. Therefore it was more likely to have been stripped to the bone, rather than merely cherry-picked. And the medical facilities? Normally that would have been her primary concern. On this trip, and with their current imperatives, it barely registered.

This was a time for focus.

She indicated to Doc that he should keep point while she looked into the armory. He agreed, and stood against the wall, the LeMat grasped in both fists, head swaying side to side to take in where they had come from as much as where they were headed. He knew of old that most redoubts had maintenance shafts that bypassed the corridors. The idea that anyone would have the knowledge, or indeed inclination, to use these was remote. The sense of fear, however, lingered on. There was something here to out them on edge, and to ignore such an instinct was foolish.

The door to the armory was open. Not damaged, or rendered in any way. Merely open, in a way that suggested it had been looted methodically.

Mildred sighed as she stepped through the door and took a look around. Her instinct hadn't failed her on this. The room had been stripped bare, with not even any discarded boxes or jammed ordnance to show that it had ever been stocked. She cursed under her breath and stepped back out, meeting Doc's questioning glance with a resigned shrug.

"No matter," he said in a tone that gave lie to his words. "There may yet be something left in this godforsaken place."

"Yeah, try to sound like you mean it, Doc."

"May as well check the medical facilities while we are here, dear lady," Doc added. "Who knows, we may be able to overdose the good baron on headache pills."

She shook her head and laughed, seeing the twinkle in his eye. "Yeah, why not."

Yet when she entered the medical room, through doors that were once more already gaping, she cursed, louder, this time, before coming back out.

"Son of a bitch! Whoever they were, they were thorough, I'll give them that. There's jackshit left in there, too."

"They had some knowledge, then," Doc stated. "It takes that, and perhaps some intelligence, to want to clear out both. Indeed, to know what they could use the meds for."

"That's what worries me," Mildred replied, her eyes traveling up to where the sec cams were located in the ceiling. "If they're that bastard smart, and they decided to hang around..."

"Then they'll be watching, and wondering just how we got here," Doc finished. "Funny, is it not, how we're assuming they're still here."

"I know they are. I can feel the fuckers," she said flatly.

Doc looked her in the eye, a vulpine grin spreading across his face. "Then why do we not find out? After all, we have—" he checked his chron "—at least twenty minutes in which to go apeshit crazy. Perhaps we will strike lucky. If they are here, then that which they have plundered cannot be too far away. If we take them off guard, then there may be something we can use."

Mildred was taken aback. What Doc was suggesting was almost like voluntarily putting a down payment on buying the farm, knowing that the settling of the account wasn't far away. Yet he might just be right. If the feelings they had were down to the proximity of some coldhearts, and they were being observed, then nothing in their behavior so far would prepare their observers for an all-out attack.

And if all they could feel was the residual presence of people long gone?

Then they'd feel pretty stupid. But that was all. And that wasn't so bad.

"How many levels you reckon there are here?" Mildred asked.

Doc squinted, as if in deep thought. "It is not big—about the size of the one we have come from, I would say. Maybe another two levels before we hit the surface, which means that if they're here, then they are not far away."

Mildred's face split into a leering grin. "Let's get them, then."

They set off suddenly, picking up pace as they hurried up the corridor floor, trusting that their sudden turn of speed would carry them into a fray before their potential enemies had a chance to consider their own actions.

It was insane. They were running headlong into a firefight that might not even be there, and for what reason?

Reason: a very good word. It crossed Mildred's mind that the effects of two mat-trans jumps so close together might have resulted in what she would, at any other time, consider derangement.

But right now, she didn't care. Crabbe and his sec boss, McCready, and the way in which they had treated the companions since their capture, had done nothing more than rile her up to the point where she just wanted to kick ass. Regardless of whatever the consequences might be.

Damn, she was getting as crazy as Doc.

They had made it up to the next level before there was any indication of life. Until then, there had existed nothing more than the fragile whisper of instinct, murmuring fear in their ears if not their hearts. But now there was something more tangible.

"Hear that?" Doc gasped.

"Uh-huh," Mildred grunted, unwilling to waste her breath for the fight that was to come.

For their unseen and only suspected enemy had now become tangible, out of hiding and on the offensive themselves. In the distance they could hear the sound of feet pounding on the floor of the corridor. As hard as it was to differentiate between the thudding footfalls, Mildred was sure that there were more than five pairs of feet. She could pick out rhythms with an ear long born of experience. But how many more than five she couldn't tell. Did it matter? Whatever happened, they were more than two-to-one in odds. The feet were the only clue, as their enemy approached in silence. No giving themselves away by voices.

Coldhearts maybe, then, but not stupid.

She should have kept that in mind.

"Ready?" she gasped as they continued to run.

"Not really," Doc replied with a manic cackle.

They were approaching the dogleg in the corridor that would lead them up to the next level, and from the sound of the footsteps that were pounding toward them, their enemy was about to meet them head-on at the point where the dogleg took an angle.

"Now," Mildred snapped when they were within a few yards of the bend. At the command, Doc stopped and flung himself against the wall, dropping to one knee and hugging the wall, raising the LeMat so that it was muzzle up to any approaching danger. Mildred took the wall nearest to her, pressing flat against it so that she was ready to spin around the angle and start blasting when Doc gave the word. She held the ZKR muzzle upward, breathing in tight, controlled pants that took oxygen into her lungs. She could hear her heart pounding in her ears, feel it thudding against her ribs.

And she could still feel and hear it, even after she should have been throwing herself into action. The sound of approaching footsteps had reached a crescendo. By rights, the coldhearts should have passed them by now, and yet…

Then the sound ceased.

She looked over at Doc, her face telling a story that didn't need words. His answering expression told likewise.

"Nothing," he said simply, breaking the silence.

"What?" She was incredulous.

Doc shrugged. "No sign."

"What the fuck have those bastards been doing?" she muttered almost to herself. She came around so that she could see the corridor beyond, just as Doc.

It was deserted, without any indication that anyone had ever been running down it.

"They can't fuck with us like this, we don't have the time for games," she said angrily.

"Wait," Doc cautioned. "Do not be too hasty. I suspect that they may not be as stupid as we supposed."

But his words were wasted. Mildred was in no mood to be jerked around by people she hadn't even seen. Every logical and rational process that usually ran through her head was thrown out, jettisoned by the red mist of anger. Maybe Doc had been right with his notion that the successive jumps had affected them in some way, physiologically or psychologically. Certainly, there was a part of her that knew what she was doing was crazy. But for the most part she just didn't care.

She strode out into the corridor, ZKR held steady in both hands, pivoting from side to side to cover any enemy that may lurk. Where, she couldn't say, as there were no rooms leading off this section of the corridor in which the phantoms behind the footsteps could have concealed themselves. In fact, there was nowhere that they could have gone. And it was a hell of a lot of corridor for them to have retreated up—and unheard, at that—before Doc would have been unable to see them.

Doc hurried to catch her up. He was casting anxious glances around him, and was cradling his LeMat like it was a security blanket.

"My dear Doctor," he said in urgent tones, "I think you are being a trifle hasty over this. We are opening ourselves to any possible attack. We're exposed here," he said hurriedly. "I think it may be best if we try to get back to the mat-trans. This could take up too much time."

"I don't get it," she muttered, almost ignoring Doc. "We heard the bastards, and there's nowhere that they could be hiding. Nothing on the sides, nowhere ahead that I can see—oh shit!" she suddenly exclaimed, flinging out her right arm so that it caught Doc across the chest and pushed him back. "Back, for God's sake, back."

The old man was on his heels, stumbling backward and falling as her actions caught him completely off guard. It was only as he fell that he realized what had caused her outburst, and by then it was far too late. As she turned, Mildred found herself entangled in Doc's flailing limbs. Despite her best efforts, she found herself becoming entwined with him, and falling as his momentum carried her down.

They hit the concrete floor with a bone-jarring crunch, but that was nothing compared to the hubris that Mildred felt as the net fell gracefully from the ceiling and covered both Doc and herself.

"Don't move," she whispered, her fingers exploring behind her to try to feel the type of net. She was facedown, and it was difficult. "Doc—"

"No need," he cut in. His own fingers had grasped the netting and were feeling for any weaknesses. It didn't seem likely that there would be an easy way out. They were covered from head to foot and beyond. The netting didn't feel like the kind of rough twine that was usually encountered. This had been taken from within the redoubt, and was of a man-made plastic fiber. Even with the blades, it would take some time to cut through it. And he doubted very much that they had that kind of time.

"I fear, dear lady, that we are trapped. It would take some time for me to cut us free, even if I had the tools. We must face the fact that we are, perhaps, stranded."

Mildred could feel tears pricking at her eyes—not of sorrow or pain, but of frustration and anger. How could she have been so stupid as to let this happen? She shifted her weight, hoping to be able to turn around so that she could, at least, see whatever fate was about to befall them. But as she moved, all she succeeded in doing was pulling the net tighter around them.

And now there were footsteps again. Four pairs of footfalls, approaching at leisure and with an ease that led her to a deeper frustration. She wriggled onto her back and lifted her head so that she, like Doc, could see the four men that approached them.

All four were lean, the leanness that comes from battle rather than hunger. They were dressed in an assortment of old military camou, presumably looted from the redoubt, and all of it looked as though it had seen some action. They were armed with SMGs and handblasters, though the latter were in unsecured holsters, and the former were carried at ease. They walked in a loose formation—one on front, one at the rear, and the middle two fanned out on either side. At least it gave all of them a clear view of their captives. Any attempt to fight back might claim one of them, but would be Pyrrhic. All were unshaved, and dirty in a way that meant that Mildred and Doc could smell them before they could pick out details by sight.

The leader, who wore an eyepatch over the same

eye as the absent Ryan, was smoking a cigar that had also presumably been looted, but had perhaps not been stored too well. It was he who brought his men to a halt a few yards away.

"You know, I always wondered if that little trap would work," he said to no one in particular, gazing up at the ceiling where empty grappling hooks had been drilled into the concrete. "The weird thing is that I always figured the enemy would be coming down, not coming up." He fixed his gaze on the prone warriors. "Just as well we figured out how to use that loudspeaker and vid system they had down here. Might not have seen you coming, otherwise. 'Course," he continued, hunkering down so that he could get a closer squint at Mildred and Doc, "that ain't the real question, is it? The real question is, how the fuck did you two get down there in the first place? 'Cause you sure as hell didn't come past us. And as far as I know—any of us, come to that—there ain't no other way in."

He paused, as if waiting for them to answer. But both Doc and Mildred opted for silence. So he sniffed and stood.

"Okay, so you want it to be like that. Didn't really expect you to spill it just like that. Not if I'm being truthful with you. In fact, if I'm going to keep on being truthful, it might just get a little painful for you until you do tell. The boys here are gonna let you loose. Don't try and be smart 'cause we'll just shoot through them to chill you if you're trouble. And they know we will. It's how we survive."

As he spoke, he casually leveled the SMG and turned to them. The man at the rear moved up, adopting a similar stance, while the two men who had been on the flanks walked toward Doc and Mildred. There was something about the way all of them carried themselves, and the manner in which they moved, that suggested he wasn't bluffing. Without having to communicate, the trapped companions decoded that their only option was to roll with things and wait for an opening.

They patiently let the two coldhearts free them, carefully unwrapping the netting and pushing it to one side of the corridor, ready to be reset at their leisure. Doc and Mildred were gestured to their feet, and ushered the way they had originally been headed. Not a word was said by their captors.

It was only when they were up another level that they saw how organized their opponents could be. The level on which the rooms and the offices of the old redoubt had been reorganized showed that a lot of thought had been put into the way the coldhearts had chosen to live. They may be stonecold chillers, but they couldn't be underestimated in any other way.

Beds, kitchen equipment and clothing had been carried up to this level. The old uses of the rooms could no longer be defined as the whole level had been converted into a multipurpose living area. The armory had been moved wholesale into one of the rooms, and the supply stores had been jammed into a couple of others. The only things they couldn't have moved were the latrines and showers. And it didn't smell like they were too fussy about the latter.

There were seven other men that they could see, and half a dozen women who also stopped their own tasks to look around as Doc and Mildred were led into the room.

"Where the blind norad did they come from?" one of the women asked.

"That's what I intend to find out," the one-eyed man replied in a tone that was ominous in its matter-of-fact flatness. "Bring them around and sit them here," he continued, pushing a table out of the way and pulling two chairs into the gap he had made.

Mildred and Doc allowed themselves to be directed into the chairs, biding their time. There was nothing they could do as yet, but that didn't stop either of them scanning the space around them for the slightest opportunity.

"Down," barked one of the men holding a blaster on them. He spoke like he had a mouth full of stones. Looking at his teeth, it was possible that he had chewed them good and hard before spitting them out. But it didn't really matter. What was important that he stood back from them, as did his compatriots. These were men schooled in hard knocks. They knew how to keep their asses covered, which didn't bode well for Mildred and Doc. But for now they did as they were bid.

"Take a good look at these two," the one-eyed man said to the inhabitants of the room, "they could be our way out of here."

"Your way out?" Mildred asked carefully, looking around as the men and women in the room slowly gathered, studying her and Doc in a curious and detached manner that reminded her with an eerie sensation of the way she had stared at lab rats during her medical training.

"Let's not get too curious now." He grinned coldly. "We're the ones asking the questions here. See, it's almost impossible to get in the front way. And even if you did, chances are that you wouldn't have much chance of getting past all those old vid cams that still work. We keep a close eye on those and the ones to the outside, see. So you'd have to have come from down below to get in. Fact of the matter is that we know you did. Of course we do. That's how we saw you, on one of those old vid cams. Thing is, what I can't figure is how."

Mildred was sure that he was going to ask them about the mat-trans. She would stonewall for as long as possible if it meant giving away the secret, but maybe they could use that fact to get back down there in time to somehow shake these bastards off and make the jump before their time had elapsed. She was weighing these odds when Doc threw a curve ball into the room.

"So," he said with an intimation of calm that Mildred didn't feel, "you are aware of the tunnels that were built in and around these old bases then."

"See, Jeb? I told you, didn't I? I knew these fuckers could never have been built with only one way in and out. That would have been too stupe."

The coldheart with the mouth of marbles was plainly excited by the prospect, and couldn't contain his exuberance. The savagery with which the one-eyed man turned on him was both a clue to the nature of these people and the atmosphere he was endeavoring to build in the interrogation. "Shut the fuck up, Maddock," he replied. "We don't know that for sure..." His voice faltered. Not much, but just enough to catch Doc's gimlet attention.

"I think you should listen to your friend Maddock, Jeb," he said. "Just because you have not found it does not mean that it is not there. After all, how else would we have gotten in here? Ask yourself that."

Mildred suppressed a smile. She had to hand it to Doc. If they had any suspicions about the mat-trans unit, this would force their hand while at the same time reinforcing the idea that the man Maddock's obsessions with the tunnels were well-founded.

The one-eyed man Jeb looked around at the people in the room. They were staring intently, their attention divided equally between their captives and their leader.

"Okay," he said with just the slightest tremor of hesitancy in his voice. "Suppose there are tunnels—"

"How else would we have gained an entry?" Doc slipped in smoothly.

"If there are," Jeb emphasized, "then how come we haven't found them in the time we've been here?"

"And why is it so important that you find them?" Doc prompted, sensing he had his man cornered. Jeb needed to keep face with his people, and Doc would give him no room to maneuver.

The one-eyed man stared grimly around him. The faces that stared back at him were hardened by battle, fatigue and by the rigors of a bandit life. They would, Doc thought, have been happy enough to have ended up in such a place as this redoubt. Certainly, they had taken advantage of the resources they had found within, albeit adapting them to their own mode of life. Yet there was something about them now, as they looked to their leader, which was contrary to the way they should have been—an almost keening sense of despair that seemed to sing off their very being.

It made Doc's heart sing, too, albeit in a very different key. There was a weakness here that he might just be able to turn to their advantage. And he knew that Mildred trusted him enough to let him run with it, even though she may be wondering what he would do.

The one-eyed man took a deep breath. "We need to find another way of getting out of this place. It's a fine and dandy place, sure enough, and we've got us enough weapons here to win a war with a decent-size ville. But it wouldn't be a good idea for us to go out the way we came in. Don't matter why. Now we all know there must be some way out. Maddock's right about that. No way would those predark bastards build somewhere that they could get their asses trapped in. But they were smart, and they hid it well so that only they would know about it. Which would be okay for us, except that those fuckers have been feeding the worms for too long to be any good at telling us their little secret."

Doc smiled. It was expansive and leering. It spoke of an arcane knowledge that might be shared…for a price, of course.

"Precisely. Except that now, my friend, you have us in your hands. And for whatever reason that you cannot tell, we seem to hold the key to that old secret. Which makes us a valued item to you, does it not?"

Careful, Doc, Mildred thought. Don't overplay your hand.

Jeb's eye reminded her of Ryan's. Although a single orb, it seemed to burn with a greater intensity than the stare of a normal, twin-eyed man. It bore into Doc, and for a moment she wondered if Jeb had seen through him. Certainly, his next words were edged with caution.

"You came from somewhere," he said carefully, "and you can bet your ass you won't be going back there in any kind of a hurry if you're screwing with us. You telling me, old man, that Maddock is right, and there's a way out of here from more than just the big door?"

Doc allowed himself the smallest of smiles. He knew at this moment that he had them hooked, and all he needed to do was to play them in like a prize pike on a hook.

"There is, indeed, another way to exit this mausoleum," he said at length. "As your friend suspected, the old ones from before the nukecaust would not allow themselves to be trapped…as, I suspect, you feel you are. Tell me, why are you so afraid to use the entrance that you know?" he asked.

Jeb's eye narrowed. If anything, it made it seem as though his glare was even more fiery and sharp than before. "I wouldn't ask too many questions like that, if I was you. You might not get to ask too many more."

"And you might not find out how to escape from here," Doc snapped in a tone that made Mildred wince. He was pushing, maybe too hard. Jeb's initial reaction—snatching at his SMG so that it was leveled at the old man's chest—certainly indicated this.

But Doc was smarter and cooler than Mildred reckoned. For once he was in full and total control of his faculties. This was a coldly calculated mood. He stared down the barrel of the SMG, keeping his voice as hard and level as his gaze when he addressed the coldheart leader.

"So, a slight misunderstanding with whoever waits at the gates for you, eh? Well, it can happen to the best of us. It's happening now."

"Don't fuck with me, old man. If you ain't afraid of dying, then your bitch might be," the one-eyed coldheart whispered, shifting the aim of the SMG so that it was leveled at Mildred. She kept her face as impassive as possible, but she was sure, as she looked around, that everyone in the room could see that her heart was pounding visibly against her rib cage. Their faces were tense and expectant. Doc had been right about one thing—there was something or someone out the front of the redoubt who was pinning these people in. For all the riches of ordnance and supplies they had found, they were as imprisoned as surely as if someone had put bars around them.

Let's just hope that Doc's guessed the rest of it right, she thought as she felt cold sweat prickle at her hairline and in the small of her back.

To her amazement, Doc actually laughed. She could feel the sharp intake of breath from the assembled watchers, and could see her own life flashing at the periphery of her vision.

"My dear man," Doc said, sighing, "I meant that it was happening to us. Are we not in the same situation as yourselves? Chilling my friend will do you no good. You do that, and I would rather buy the farm myself than speak. It would be a poor piece of judgment on your part. And if I am any judge of a man, then I do not think you are a man for poor judgment."

Her vision of her past life receded. She could see the flicker of doubt on Jeb's face.

Damn, but Doc was good when he was on form.

"So you're gonna tell me, then?" the one-eyed man questioned.

Doc grinned slyly. "I'll do more than that. I'll show you."

The surprise on the faces of the assembled throng was so forceful that it was almost laughable. Not that Mildred was laughing. She was too busy being astounded by Doc's assertion. What the fuck was he playing at?

"How you gonna do that, old man?" Jeb growled suspiciously, unconsciously echoing Mildred's thoughts.

"Hellfire, Jeb, what does it matter?" Maddock exploded, unable any longer to contain the excitement he felt at Doc's revelation. "We're gonna get out. Ain't that all that matters?"

"Mebbe," the onc-eyed man said slowly. "We'll see… Just what are you gonna show us, old man? And how do we know you ain't gonna use it as an excuse to get the hell out, leaving us here?"

Doc shook his head with an equal slowness. "I would not underestimate you, my dear sir. I look around at your people, and at the way you have thoroughly plundered this place, and I can see that you have an observant eye. There are, after all, two of us." He gestured at himself and Mildred. "It does not take a genius to work out that you will hold one of us prisoner while the other shows you the egress you may use."

Jeb eyed him suspiciously. "Don't try and be a smart-ass bastard," he snarled. "Don't use big words you know I won't understand just to look big. I can still work out what you mean. And I'm smart enough to know that you can still show us a way out even if I blast your fucking toes off first for being such a smartass. You get me?"

If Doc was taken aback by the cold venom of the words, he didn't let it show. Instead he said calmly, "You must excuse my verbosity. My tendency to let my mouth get carried away with itself. I only meant to say that I credit you with the foresight to have planned to hold one of us hostage. And indeed, you would be a fine judge of character, as Mildred and I would not be parted." He swept an arm around the room. "In truth, I do not care who waits for you or why. I can see that you have comradeship. As do Mildred and myself. Further, I would suggest that one of your men accompanies me at close quarters, so that he may be able to relay the route to you all. Perhaps your friend Maddock? After all, he has always been convinced that this route exists."

It was a smart move. Mildred could see from the way that Maddock was almost frothing at the mouth with excitement that he wouldn't let Jeb refuse—not without one hell of a fight. And, looking around at the rest of the assembled coldheart crew, she could see that any such refusal would make them restive. They wanted to get out of the redoubt, and although they accepted Jeb as their leader, he would be endangering the respect they held for him if he backed down on this one.

Thing was, how the hell was Doc going to pull this off?

She was soon to find out.

"Okay," the one-eyed man nodded, his tone grim. "You and Maddock, stranger. We keep your friend here. See that you don't fuck with us, okay?"

"That, my dear sir, is perfectly fine by me." Doc shrugged. He gave Mildred the briefest of looks, and an even briefer wink. "Shall we get going then?" he directed at the excitable Maddock.

The young coldheart looked at his one-eyed leader, almost as if needing the assurance that this could go ahead. Jeb nodded, and the young man beckoned Doc to him.

"I'm gonna keep this on you," he said, gesturing with his SMG, "just in case you might get any smart ideas."

"That, my dear sir, is the last thing on my mind. Indeed, may I further suggest that we are accompanied by another man, as there will be a moment when you find yourself at a disadvantage." Then, noticing that Maddock was trying to hide his puzzlement, he added, "There is the way into the tunnels to think about."

Jeb gestured to another of the coldhearts to join them, and with the two men covering him, Doc left the room, with Mildred's wondering glance following him.

At the back of her mind, she knew that the time left to them before the automatic return function on the mat-trans ceased was getting shorter and shorter.

Doc had better have a good idea of what he was doing.

Chapter Thirteen

Doc walked in front of the two men, moving as swiftly as he dared, but trying at the same time to make his motion look easy and relaxed. Like Mildred, he was only too well aware of time left before the LD button ceased to work. But to arouse suspicion at this point would be to invite disaster.

Doc led them down the corridor and past the dogleg that would allow them to take the incline to the next level down, past the point where they had been captured. The netting in which they had been entangled still lay to one side of the corridor, a reminder that these people weren't as stupid as their ragged appearance and coarse manners might lead him to assume. He would have to play this one carefully.

But he already had his plan mapped out in his mind. Chance, he mused, was a strange and fickle beast. It was a preternatural sense of how tricky these coldhearts may be that had first seeded in his mind the idea that was now—he hoped—to bear fruit. It was seeing that they had gathered their ordnance in the one room. It was the need to have kept an eye out behind him because of the maintenance vents and shafts that he knew peppered every redoubt. It was the realization that the coldheart band didn't realize what the mat-trans unit could do. All of these things had come together in his head.

Now he could only hope that the layout of a redoubt and its maintenance shafts was a generalized phenomenon.

He came to a halt in the corridor.

"Why have we stopped?" asked the coldheart who as accompanying Doc and Maddock.

The man was looking around.

"That's a damn good question, old man, 'cause I sure as shit can't see anything that looks like a tunnel," Maddock said.

Doc smiled knowingly and shook his head. "Well, you would not, would you? It could hardly be a concealed route if it was out in the open. Otherwise you would have spotted it before, would you have not?"

"I guess..." Maddock looked at his coldheart companion and shrugged.

"Anyway," Doc added, looking around, "it is not actually out here. That would be just silly."

Beckoning to them to follow, he headed for the empty medical facilities. "This way, gentlemen. No tricks, I promise," he added, seeing their suspicious looks.

Once inside, and aware that the two armed men at his back were on a hair trigger, his gaze frantically raked over the room. It should be...

Ah, yes.... There, in the corner of the room, barely visible behind what would once have been the medic's workstation was a grille set into the wall, six inches from the ground. If he was correct, then it would lead into a series of rising and falling shafts that were angled around the inside of the redoubt structure, allowing access to the inner workings should anything need repair.

There were such grilles in only a few rooms. In others, there were access routes set into such pieces of equipment as air-conditioning units, allowing them to be swung free if the need to effect repairs became a necessity.

Which, of course, now gave them a use that was quite different to that originally intended. Especially since the coldheart crew was smart enough to store their plundered ordnance in a room that was kept temperate.

"Help me move this," Doc said, moving to the workstation. Maddock hesitated for a moment unsure as to whether this was a trick. But, as he saw the grille become more visible, and with a nervous glance to see that his companion was covering him, he moved across to help Doc heave the workstation clear.

"This leads to the outside?" Maddock questioned. "How the hell can it do that? Not big enough to get anything through. What about all the crap these predark bastards used to carry around with them? All the shit we got from here, for a start. And then from the armory—"

Doc gasped as he dropped his end of the workstation. "For heaven's sake, young man, will you please be quiet. The whole point about these exits was that they were intended for emergencies. In such an eventuality, do you really think they would want to pack up the whole camp and move on out? No, it was the barest essentials and then out as soon as damn well possible. And as such, it would not require much space. And of course, if it was as big as you seem to think, then it would hardly be a secret, would it? No wonder you never tumbled to it, even though you had the right idea. Now, do you want to go first, or shall I lead the way?"

Doc tagged the question on to the end of his speech with no little deliberation. He could see that the young man was eyeing the enclosed space with some trepidation. Of course Doc knew it would make more sense for him to go first, but he wanted the notion to come from his captor.

"You'd better go first," Maddock said, unable to quite keep the wavering note from his voice.

Just as I wanted, Doc thought. But the words that he used came out as "If you insist..."

The old man dropped to his hands and knees and crawled into the confined space, maneuvering himself into the narrow tunnel that allowed maintenance. It was lit at irregular intervals by red strip lighting. Boxed-in cabling and old panels peppered the four sides of the tunnel. There was just enough space for the bony and angular Doc to turn and look over his shoulder as he advanced. For the bulkier more muscular young Maddock there was barely the room to keep moving ahead, with no looking back. As he moved along the tunnel, Doc could hear Maddock grunt as he squeezed himself into the tight angle, wheezing out instructions to the coldheart left behind to wait and keep the open space covered.

And then he was at Doc's tail, following as the old

man crawled along the narrow space until he reached the first junction where the maintenance shafts crossed.

Now it would get tricky. Doc had to work out how to double back to the room where the ordnance was kept, while at the same time keeping Maddock from being suspicious.

The first junction came up. The tunnel along which they crawled was opened up on the left by one that ran for a short distance before running into a dead end that was vertically dissected by another tunnel, this one equipped with ladders. Doc was unsure which way to proceed. The quickest way to get back to their destination would be to go up. But if he did, would the man at his rear find that suspicious, seeing as Doc and Mildred had originally come from down below?

Perhaps he would be overexplaining, and certainly wasting time that he really couldn't spare, but if he was to make this work in the optimum time then perhaps it would be as well to take a short detour.

Reaching out and pulling himself up on the rungs of the ladder until he was able to drag his legs free so that they hung down enough to place his feet on lower ladder rungs, Doc started to descend. He looked up to see the face of Maddock staring down at him, eyeing him with suspicion.

"Why are you going that way? Surface is up," he snapped.

"And we came up from a lower level when you first detected us," Doc said smoothly. "Think about it. These tunnels are on every level, so that they can be accessed from those very levels. We climbed down to the lowest level to explore from the base up. But the way the tunnels run, it is sometimes quicker to take a tunnel down to hit a straight run up."

It was a lie, but Doc hoped that his honeyed tone and the grain of sense on what he said would be enough to carry the words. He was also banking on the look of discomfort on the young man's face. Maddock was finding the tunnels a little claustrophobic. Doc couldn't say that he blamed him. However, the time traveler had found himself in—literally—tighter corners, and was sure of his superior capability when it came to keeping his nerve.

He knew he had won the battle when Maddock said, "Okay, that makes sense to me."

"Good." Doc nodded, meaning it in more ways than the young man would ever realize. "Then I suggest you trust me while we are in here, and I will take us the shortest route out. Even if it may not necessarily seem that way."

Then, without waiting for the young man to answer, he descended to the next maintenance shaft entrance, sliding himself in and moving along, listening to the clanging of Maddock's feet on the ladder rungs behind him. Knowing he couldn't be seen, he allowed himself a vulpine grin of triumph before proceeding.

Having won the man's dependence, if not his total confidence, it was now time and a sense of direction that was his major enemy.

Face set grim, Doc began to crawl along the maintenance shaft. His mind was working overtime. As always in times of great stress, there was a part of him that was geared toward protection—part of his mind would gladly descend him into madness as a kind of refuge. Inside that secluded and sylvan glade, the outside world didn't matter. He was safe, no matter what happened to the physical shell he inhabited. With the claustrophobic confines, the man at his rear, and the knowledge that Mildred was relying on him mixed in with the pressure of a severe time limit, there was a part of Doc that wanted little more than to escape to his refuge. But the greater part of him didn't want to let his companion down, and leave her to a fate over which she had no control. As well, he owed it to Ryan, Jak, J.B. and Krysty for the times they had hauled his bacon from the fire. The fate of all of them rested on his shoulders, especially as he had a plan that, if carried through, would give them a fighting chance against Crabbe and his men.

If only he could hold his sanity together until the first part was realized.

Sweat spangled his brow, both from the heat that permeated the tight tunnel and from the inner tensions that racked him. It was, if only anyone could have realized it, a heroic struggle of titanic proportions. And one he was determined to win, if only he could work out where he was going.

That was how to do it—focus. As he led Maddock up, through, down and along the maintenance shafts, moving at a pace that had the man behind him struggling to keep up and wondering why it was necessary to move in such a space at such a speed, Doc concentrated on trying to keep his mind running along the straight lines of maintenance tunnels.

Redoubts all followed similar patterns of design. They might differ in size, but these were little more than expansions and contractions of the same model. Therefore, the maintenance shafts that were in them would follow a similar ideal. Doc was aware of how one of these had run in a redoubt that he had been confined in many years—centuries in some senses—before. Allowing for the similarities between the old bases, then it was pretty obvious that the shafts worked on a grid principle. Doc visualized such a thing as it would appear on paper—like a map viewed on a table—and then transposed this into three dimensions. All the while he kept moving, using this visualization process to keep him focused and in motion.

It was working. With a renewed vigor and purpose he took junction after junction, moving down one ladder to access a shaft that would take him up two. He knew which way he was moving, and he was convinced that he was right.

Up one ladder and along a shaft—about halfway along, he could see light spilling through a grille. Faintly, he could hear voices. They were too indistinct for him to make out any individuals, but the distant sound could only mean one thing. There was only one place in the whole of the redoubt that was inhabited. He had reached his destination.

"Not far now," he called over his shoulder, adding, "Be careful, it may be a little tricky getting out if you have not tried this before."

He cursed himself. He was talking crap. But how else to cover any of these faint sounds reaching the man behind him?

"You sure we're there?" Maddock asked, his voice

querulous, his breath short. "Seems like we've been going up, not down."

"The tunnels lead to the surface, of course they go up," Doc snapped. "Didn't I say that we entered at a low level for a purpose?"

"Guess so," Maddock murmured, "it's just that this is real confusing."

As I would hope, Doc answered, but only to himself. Out loud, he said, "Not to worry, you'll soon be out of here. It is confining, I know. Why do you think I have been moving so swiftly? I like this about as much as you do."

He was now at the grille, and he angled his body as much as possible to block any light or shadow that may have given the man behind him a clue as to their real destination.

Now he could see that he was where he had intended to be. The grille was set high in the room, behind the air-conditioning unit. There was a small grille space around the unit, which was built, in this particular redoubt, so that it protruded into the room. Through this lattice he could see that the room was packed tight with the looted ordnance. And, as he had been certain, some of the crates of handblasters, ammo and grens had been left open, just as they had been split to view the contents. It was the latter that took his interest. These were the key to salvation, immediate and long-term.

Doc paused and took in a deep breath, his eyes flicking over the rear of the air-conditioning unit as he did so. It was hinged, and the locking mechanism worked from both inside and out, as he had gambled that it would. If he could open it, thrust himself out, keep his balance and then take hold of a gren… It was a lot to ask of himself, but he could see through the open door the man Jeb, standing menacingly with his blaster trained on a figure out of sight that had to surely be the good Dr. Wyeth.

It wasn't a case of "if," but rather of "must." But first he had to dispose of the man at his rear, incapacitate him before he had a chance to raise any alarm. Very well, then.

Doc turned so that he was almost on his back, raising himself slightly so that he could see Maddock staring questioningly at him.

"The damn thing is stiff. The lock will not give," he said pleadingly. "This can happen. These places are so old, and at this level they are prone to the elements. Perhaps you could try to squeeze past me, lend some more muscle to the catch?"

Maddock looked for a moment as though he was suspicious, but that passed. Either Doc's acting skills were better than he would have ever suspected, or Maddock was just keen to get out of the tunnel confines. For he tried to move forward, muttering, "I don't know if—"

"Let me move out of the way," Doc murmured, making as though to create space. Yet in so doing, he raised his left leg as far as possible. To Maddock, it looked as though it was an attempt to move out of his way. As he moved closer, Doc brought the heel of his boot crashing down onto the point of the young man's jaw with all the force that he could muster. Maddock grunted, his head snapping back and smashing against the wall of the shaft with a clang that resounded along its length. Doc cursed the noise, hoping that it wouldn't travel through the concrete and into the rooms beyond. He had to move quickly. Pulling his leg back again, he smashed it back into Maddock's jaw. To Doc's advantage, the young man was jammed against the shaft, unable to move, even though he had to have been reeling from the impact. His eyes were glassy, and blood flowed freely from his mouth.

One more blow should do it. Doc crashed home his boot once more, and watched with satisfaction as Maddock's eyes rolled up into his head and he slumped back awkwardly against the shaft wall.

Now there was no time to lose. Doc wriggled around, reaching out to loosen the catch as he did so. He pushed the air-conditioning unit outward, flinging himself through the gap. He landed on his hands, pain jarring in his wrists, but he used it to spur himself onward, rolling so that he was able to gain his feet. He knew where the gren crates were situated, and blindly thrust out a hand to grasp at the contents. It was only when he was on his feet and facing the door to the room beyond that he could see that his entry had shocked the people beyond. They were staring in from their positions, as if frozen—even Mildred, although the ghost of a smile hovered over her lips, as though knowing that she should have expected as much from him.

The exceptions to this tableau were the three men who had advanced to the doorway, SMGs raised. One of them was the one-eyed Jeb.

"Whatever you are thinking of doing, I wouldn't if I were you," Doc said, grinning. "You are not a stupid man, are you? Of course you could fire on me. Between the three of you, I would be reduced to a pulp of flesh and bone in no time. But then, of course, I would detonate these grens. I have no way of knowing if they are gas, fragmentation, concussion or merely explosive. But that does not really matter, does it? If they do not set off everything else you have crammed in here, then your ricocheting fire most certainly would. There is an old game I used to play, and the phrase used was stalemate."

Jeb had no idea what game Doc was talking about, and the word made no sense as a sound. But one look at the situation made Doc's meaning clear.

"And you think I'm just gonna let you walk out of there?" he questioned. "Make it that easy for you?"

"I don't see as how you have any option," Doc countered.

Jeb turned and pointed his blaster directly at Mildred. "You want to walk out of here on your own?"

Doc leered his most manic of grins. "My dear, dear man, do you really think you can blackmail me like that? If you fire on Mildred, I will simply detonate that which I hold. And then we will all go together. Look into my eyes and doubt whether I would actually do it."

He held the one-eyed man's gaze until Jeb looked away.

"Bastard. What do you want?"

"For myself and my friend to make our way out of here, back the way we came. And if you let us leave, then perhaps we will leave you some indication of how you, too, could get your people out of here. Never let it be said that Theophilus Tanner was ever anything less than generous."

"Generous enough to chill one of our own," Jeb countered.

"Ah, is that what concerns you? Have no fear, I did not harm the young man. Much. A slight headache, but he is in the shaft, and merely unconscious. I could not harm him. After all, if not for his obsession with tunnels out of here, I would still be your prisoner."

"So he was wrong."

Doc shrugged. "Unfortunately…for you, that is. But not for Mildred and myself. Still, if you follow us, you may yet effect an escape. However, I do not have the time to bandy words. My patience wears thin, and I may become a trifle unpredictable."

Doc had his eyes fixed on Jeb, his best manic grin communicating to the one-eyed man that he meant every word. He couldn't see the reaction of the others in the outer room, but Mildred could. They were nervous, and looking to their leader to make the right move. The question was, what would he consider that to be? It would look like tough leadership to call Doc's bluff, but if he did, then he would be faced with no choice other than to fire and risk blowing them to hell and back. If he allowed Doc and Mildred to make a break, then at least he would keep them in one piece and give them a fighting chance of finding an alternate way out.

And the one-eyed man knew it. From the way that his shoulders seemed to sag under the pressure, he could feel the eyes of everyone in the room boring into his back.

"Okay," he snarled. "I don't like it, but I ain't gonna blow us up just 'cause you're crazy. You get a way out."

"And you, my dear sir, may have one for yourself if you pay attention. Now listen very carefully, as I shall say this only once. Allow Mildred to gather our weapons and go to the door."

He waited while this was done. Then, when Mildred was at the door, he called, "Check the corridor, my dear, and tell me if it is clear." She nodded. "Very good. Wait for me."

Keeping one eye on the men who still faced him, blasters poised even though they dare not fire, he transferred both grens he was clutching to one hand, then risked a brief glance at the boxes around him. Now he could see which were the frag grens, which the concussion, which the gas. He knew which he wanted, and used his free hand to gather four of the small grens, which he stashed in the pocket of his frock coat. Then he regained his initial position and flashed a mad grin at Jeb and his men.

"Now, if you will let me by, gentlemen," he said, moving to the doorway. "Notice that I have my thumbs on the detonators. One round from any of you, and even with my chilling breath I will trigger these little beauties. Believe me." Of course he counted on their not knowing that grens didn't have detonators.

They moved aside to let him pass and join a tense Mildred.

When he reached her, he said, "Now, you will no doubt follow us. I would not expect anything less. But be warned. You play a dangerous game. Too close, and you will get a gren in the face. It will bring down the walls around you, and then you will never be able to find your way out."

As he spoke, he gestured Mildred to go. She needed no second bidding, and he was shortly on her heels as they pounded down the corridor, headed for the lowest level of the redoubt and the mat-trans unit.

Doc was mindful of the man he had left behind when entering the maintenance shaft, and as they neared the dogleg to take them past the medical facilities he juggled the grens into one hand, pulling the LeMat from where he had stashed it in his belt when Mildred had returned it to him. As they hit the turn he raised it and fired ahead of him. He was firing blind, but trusting to the fact that the guard would have heard them approach and, without knowing the situation, would step into the corridor from the medical facilities.

He was right. The man had no idea what was going on, but was nonetheless curious enough to step out, his blaster raised in anticipation of trouble, like the fighter he was. What he didn't expect was the hot metal fired from the scattergun barrel of the LeMat. Although Doc had fired blind, his racing mind had told him that there was a good chance that the shot would spread out over the distance to cover the whole corridor. It wouldn't land a lethal blow, but one that was disabling enough to prevent the man firing on them.

So it proved. Covering the length of his body, the stinging metal blinded him in agony, the blows in his chest and gut causing him to twist and fall forward. As he did so, Doc loosed a .44 round, the large projectile hitting the man on the top of his head as it dipped down, splintering his skull and spreading the brain and bone shards across the floor and walls, his body skewing sideways as the downward fall and the forward momentum of the round played off each other.

Mildred jumped over the falling corpse, nearly skidding on the gore that spread beneath their feet. She risked a look back as they skittered forward, their momentum almost carrying them beyond the speed their feet could keep. There was no one on sight, but she could hear yelling voices spurred by the sound of the blaster.

They were in sight of the mat-trans control room. Her lungs felt as though they were about to burst. In the white heat of anger she wondered why Doc hadn't just thrown one of the grens up the corridor. Almost immediately she realized that this would risk a fault line on the tunnel that could bring it down in front of them.

So it was down to their speed.

The coldhearts were just too far behind to have them in sight. She was certain that, having seen the corpse of their compatriot, they would have no hesitation in firing on sight now, regardless of any consequences.

They reached the chamber's anteroom and flung themselves across the room toward the unit. Doc stumbled and fell as he was on the threshold. One of the grens he held dropped from his grasp and rolled across the floor. For a brief moment time seemed to stand still as they watched it. But the pin stayed in and it hit the far wall out of their vision as they spilled into the unit.

Mildred hauled herself up and threw her weight against the door, closing it, then quickly went to the panel and punched the LD button.

Almost as she did, the first volley of fire from the coldhearts hit the armaglass as they reached the mat-trans unit. It sounded deafening inside, and she winced and ducked, even though the armaglass would hold. For the mist started to rise…

Mildred turned and sank to the floor, panting heavily. Doc was looking at her and laughing breathlessly, holding his chron in one hand and a pair of grens in the other.

"Twenty seconds," he gasped. "Twenty moments between ourselves and separation from our companions. And two chances to salvation."

He was still laughing as the darkness overtook her.

Chapter Fourteen

Krysty sucked in her breath as the glare from the mat-trans unit made her shut her eyes. Still, the after-image from the flash burned into her eyelids. The pain from the intense light flashed through her mind, but still couldn't erase the question that burned even brighter: had Doc and Mildred made it back in time? The fact that the return trip had been made suggested that something or someone was in there. As she knew from her last foray with J.B., however, there was no guarantee that it would be her companions.

Crabbe swore loudly, once more too late to avert his eyes from the brilliant light. As Krysty opened hers, blurry though her vision was and dotted with dancing lights, she could see the baron rubbing furiously with the backs of his hands, his body now turned away. In truth, she was the only one who had been quick enough to avert her full gaze, and she could now see that there was a window of opportunity when the unit had been operated. The sec men and Sal the mechanic were as disabled as their baron. If only her friends were in a position to take advantage. Ryan, Jak and J.B. had the awareness to turn away, but no ordnance with which to take advantage.

That was the challenge that all of them in the room faced in their last jumps—time was running out.

The afterglow of the flash was dying away and there was no sign of any movement from within the mat-trans. She wanted to run from behind the desk and wrench open the unit door. The effects of a second jump so soon after the first could be devastating. If Doc and Mildred were in the mat-trans, what kind of condition would they be in? Yet if she made a move before the baron was recovered, who would stay his trigger-happy sec chief?

So she stayed in position, even though every fiber of her being wanted to head for the mat-trans. And the seconds ticked on, increasing her concern with each moment, still with no sign of Doc or Mildred.

MILDRED FELT HERSELF being pulled inside out and then tugged the right way in from the feet up. Her mind felt as though it had been scrambled, wound up tight like an elastic band, then let free to spin wild until straight once more.

She opened her eyes to see Doc staring at her. His eyes were bright and clear. "How are you feeling?" he asked simply.

She pulled a face. "Weird.… I should feel like shit, but actually I feel okay."

He nodded. "Strange, isn't it? But while I feel this lucid, perhaps it would be as well to discuss strategy, lest I get lost before we have a chance to act." His voice was low and soft, but carried to her across the mat-trans unit with an authority she wouldn't have expected at this juncture.

"Here, take this," he continued, producing one of the grens that he had stowed in his pocket and tossing it at her. She caught it with alacrity, and a grin flashed across his features. "Our reactions are surprisingly sharp, are they not, given the circumstances? Still, stow that one away somewhere it cannot be found. If our previous return is anything to go by, the arrogant fool McCready will not bother to do more than get his men to strip us of what he knows we have. It will need considered use, but it is something." With which he gestured her to hurry as he stowed away the gren he had been carrying as they'd run to the chamber, secreting it so that it nestled safely with the gas gren that he also held.

Mildred secreted away her gren similarly, and only just in time, as the door softly clicked as someone tried to open it from the outside. Oddly, the door swung open.

KRYSTY HELD HER BREATH as she looked into the darkened interior of the mat-trans unit. She had been determined to reach the mat-trans before any of Crabbe's men, and had started to move before the baron had given the order, staring down the sec man who tried to step in front of her before Crabbe signaled him to let her go. But nonetheless she noted that the baron was at her heels as she reached the unit, determined not to miss anything.

In truth, she didn't know what to expect herself. It was with no little sigh of relief that she saw Doc and Mildred slumped on either side of the mat-trans resting against the walls, and apparently unconscious. Yet there was something about the ease with which they stirred when they sensed—perhaps—her entrance that made her wonder. They seemed to come around almost too easily.

As she helped them out, one at a time, and led them to where the others sat waiting under the glare of McCready's sec men, it seemed to her that they needed less help than before. And the way in which they relayed their incredible story of what they had found, and how they had managed to effect their escape, was almost too crisp. There was little sign of the fatigue that had beset all of them the first time around. Why this should be was baffling to her. But more than that, she had the feeling that they were concealing something. It wouldn't have been obvious to anyone who didn't know them. Certainly, Crabbe and his men seemed oblivious. Even Ryan, Jak and J.B. showed no outward sign of notice. But Krysty felt her pulse quicken. Instinct told her that there was something they were holding in reserve, something that could only be to their friends' good, and the detriment of the baron and his men.

Which if nothing else, she figured, meant that there was hope.

That was all she needed.

Crabbe listened with interest at the beginning of their narrative, but soon found himself becoming bored. Although their companions found Doc and Mildred's story riveting, for the baron it began to pall as soon as he realized that there was, for him, no point to it.

"Fuck's sake," he said, exasperated, "what good does this do for me? Sure, you outwitted a bunch of stupes who's got themselves in shit and in a trap. So fucking what? You still ain't found my disk. And time is running out for you."

"My dear sir," Doc said mildly, "I would suggest that it is running out for you as much as it is for us. Perhaps more. You may do what you wish with us when we have traversed all the bases on your list. But where will you be if the disk you seek does not turn up at either of the last two locations? We may, perhaps, have bought the farm, but at least we will not be back where we started with naught to show for our endeavors." There was an authority and insistence about his tone that silenced the baron even before he had a chance to begin the blustering that any of them would have expected. Doc paused for moment to see if his words had hit home, then continued. "Very well, then. I suggest you waste little time in furthering the cause. Perhaps you should dispatch the next party."

Krysty looked at Mildred, and particularly Doc, with a puzzlement that she did her best to kept hidden. Ryan and Jak were next out, and although the albino teen seemed fully recovered, Ryan was still obviously drugged by the painkillers Mildred had pumped into him only an hour or so before. And there were his ribs. Ryan was a hard man and could bear pain. But cracked ribs would hurt and, more importantly, would impede his progress and possibly compromise his safety. She knew that Jak would look out for him, but there was no knowing what they would find out there.

If Doc's attitude over this wasn't bizarre enough, the next words to come out of his mouth made it even more confounding. For as Ryan rose to join Jak, who was already on his feet and eyeballing the sec man who stood guard over their ordnance, Doc said, "Wait. Ryan is carrying an injury that could cause him a great problem. Allow me to go in his place."

Krysty was baffled. She knew what Doc was like after a jump, and she knew that two so close together would...well, what? Was Doc completely crazed and this was why he was offering to put his body through it so soon? But if that was the case, then why hadn't Mildred objected?

Krysty may have been able to keep her feelings muted, but the expressions of shock held by both Ryan and J.B. told their own story. Only Jak, with his usual stone visage, was able to keep his face a mask.

"No, Doc, I can't allow that," Ryan said, shaking his head. "I can't ask you to do anything I wouldn't do myself, or to take my place."

"But you are not asking, I am offering," Doc implored. "Think again."

"No." Ryan was adamant. "Don't think I don't appreciate what you're offering me here, Doc, but me and Jak'll be fine."

He hauled himself to his feet and went over to join Jak in picking out their weapons from the pile that was gathered on the tarp. Doc watched him go with an evident distress.

Crabbe chuckled. "You're a brave man, Jock, I'll give you that. Not the smartest stickie in the swamp, I'll grant, but still got a whole lot of balls. You all have. Brian included, though I guess I'm worried about him for different reasons to you. He fucks up 'cause of that rib, it don't do me no good."

"I'll be fine, shithead," Ryan growled. His words were greeted with the cock of blaster safety catches.

He looked around to see that McCready had directed his men to draw direct beads on Mildred, Doc, J.B. and Krysty.

"Just in case you might be getting any ideas, Brian," the squat sec chief said softly, his sibilants carrying an air of expectation. Ryan knew that he'd just love it if he was given the excuse to open fire.

But the one-eyed man wasn't going to give it to him. A crooked grin crossed his features. "Not that easy," he mouthed at the sec chief. Then, out loud, he said to Jak, "Come on, let's go."

The albino youth nodded without a word and joined Ryan in the short trudge to the mat-trans unit. They passed within a couple of yards of the baron, close enough to reach out and choke the life from the bastard, who looked on with a smug expression. If only there hadn't been so many blasters trained on their companions…

Ryan held himself erect as they entered the unit, but as he closed the door on the tableau outside, the mask slipped and he allowed the pain to crease his features.

"Ryan—" Jak breathed.

The one-eyed man shook his head as he settled on the floor of the mat-trans with Jak's assistance. "It's going to be a hard ride, Jak. I don't know if I can do much right now. You might have to carry me if the going gets rough."

"No problem. Never."

Ryan believed him, but he was still uneasy about facing the unknown in such pain.

There was no knowing what they faced, but he knew that whatever it was, he was nowhere near ready for it.

COMING UP FAST, as if he had been immersed in a sea that was thick, dark and choking, the viscera of the inky depths forcing its way into his nose and mouth, insinuating itself into every passage and snaking toward his lungs, the sludge making him choke as it slipped over his tongue and down his gullet, searing his sinuses as it filled his nostrils and forced its way upward and then down. Despite every struggle, despite every effort he might make, it would drown him, no matter how much he thrashed and fought against the rising tide. Finally, with the desperation born of one last cry against the night before all was lost, he opened his mouth and filled his lungs with the wine-dark sea, giving all to vent one last scream of frustration, anger and desperation.

And opened his eye to find himself yelling incoherently as he thrashed around on the floor of the mat-trans unit.

Jak stood over him, looking down. Looking puzzled, too, which was unusual for the albino teen, as his face was usually unreadable.

Ryan felt about as puzzled as Jak appeared. He stopped yelling, the sound dying away to an embarrassing silence.

"What was that about?" Ryan said in a softly puzzled voice, almost to himself.

"About ask you same question," Jak commented.

Ryan pulled himself up to a sitting position. He frowned. His ribs actually felt a little better than before the jump, even though he had moved gingerly, expecting the opposite to be true. Carefully, he stood. Nothing. He prodded at his rib cage experimentally.

"Feel good?" Jak asked. Ryan nodded, and the albino

youth chewed on his lip. "Yeah, triple weird. Jump usually makes puke. Not this time. Feel okay."

Ryan was still feeling across his injured torso. "Strangest fucking jump dream I've ever had, and there have been a few. Like I was drowning. But now I wake up and it doesn't feel like I've cracked a rib. It's sore, but..."

"Like being born," Jak stated. Ryan looked at him, puzzled.

"Dream drowning. No. In womb, waiting be born. Like what we are during jump."

Ryan shook his head. "Mebbe. Tell you what, I don't really give a shit right now. Felt weird, but not as weird as this rib being okay now. Mebbe that's why Doc was so normal when he came back with Mildred."

"Won't matter if Crabbe chills all." Jak spit pithily. "Find weapons before too late." He fingered the hem of his patched camou jacket as he spoke. He felt naked without it, the glittering metal shards sewn into it concealing the places where his beloved knives were kept. If only there was some way he could hold on to one or two of them when they returned. But even then, it wouldn't be enough against the sec men's blasters, not if his friends remained unarmed.

Ryan grinned and clapped him on the shoulder. "It matters, Jak. Crabbe and that coldheart scumsucker McCready think we're getting weaker as we jump. They won't be expecting much of a fight. Good. Let the bastards underestimate us. Even better, now that we feel stronger, we can try to take advantage of whatever we find here. We can face off whatever's outside that door a whole lot better."

"Mebbe." Jak shrugged.

Ryan laughed, a low, growling chuckle in his throat. "Shit, Jak, we can take on anything that gets thrown at us now. I've got a good feeling about this, like we've just pulled ourselves out of the shit and can smell the sweet air."

"Better get going," Jak said simply.

Ryan nodded, and without wasting any more time on words, the two men prepared to leave the mat-trans. Blasters and other weaponry checked, they exited using the procedure that had, for a time, become second nature to them.

Once he was out of the mat-trans and into the anteroom, Ryan saw that the control room was in semi-darkness, with much of the overhead lighting not functioning. There was a patina of dust and grime over the consoles and the wall-mounted tables, which still carried maps and papers in the disarray with which they had been discarded when skydark hit. Whoever had been here had wanted to get out in a hurry. And by the look of it, no one had been here since. The dust and grime suggested that parts of the automated system had also ceased to function effectively, an impression that was only confirmed by the staleness of the air they were breathing.

Without a word the two men exchanged looks. Ryan nodded shortly, and Jak moved to the control room door. He keyed the sec code to open it and stood back as it shuddered to life, opening slowly with the stiffness of a mechanism that had been too long out of use.

Light flooded in from the corridor outside, but the quality of air remained the same. There was the same musty and stale aftertaste to it that suggested that it had been recycled with a decreasing frequency. It was breathable, as no oxygen had ever been extracted from it, but age hadn't flavored it with any sweetness.

"No one here, and not been ages," Jak commented. "Should be safe."

"Still, keep it frosty," Ryan said, moving ahead of the albino youth and out into the corridor, his trusty SIG-Sauer loose in his grasp. His eye scanned in either direction. The corridor was empty, and like the control room, a patina of dirt covered the walls and floor, smearing dust and grime over the lighting. Webs of dust and dirt had formed in the curves of the corridor's wall and ceiling. The floor was undisturbed. Any footprints or tracks would have shown in the dust.

"Come on," Ryan said, beckoning to Jak to follow as he headed toward the curve of the corridor that would take them on an upward path.

The albino teen fell in behind him.

There was a quiet that hung like a pall over the redoubt as they ascended to the next level. Jak kept his attention focused, keeping an ear out for anything that may betray the presence of another living creature. Yet his instincts, working on a more subconscious level, spoke to him of the lack of life.

"We might just get lucky here," Ryan whispered. Even as he did, it struck him as absurd that he was keeping his voice low. What need was there for him to do that? The redoubt was deserted, of that he had little doubt. Yet there was something about the sepulchral silence of the corridor stretching in front of and behind them that caused him to speak quietly despite himself.

"Lucky?" Jak responded, puzzled.

Ryan nodded. In response to Jak's normal tone, he endeavored to raise his own voice. It rang in his ears and the empty space of the corridor.

"Yeah, lucky. Think about it. This place has been deserted, since the dawn of skydark, by the looks of things. It looks like whoever was here got the hell out in a hurry. If they didn't clear up after themselves in all the little things, chances are that they weren't too bothered to hang around for a major evacuation, either. And it sure as hell doesn't look and feel like anyone else has been down here since. So what are the chances of the armory having been moved out, or looted at some point since? And if that's the case, then chances are that there's some weapons there that we can use."

"Have to be small," Jak mused. "Something can hide from prying eyes."

Ryan nodded. "Grens. Small enough to not be seen. They'll only be looking to take back our own blasters and blades. Shit, they haven't looked for anything else so far."

Jak's face broke into a crooked and humorless grin. "Yeah. Bastards are shit sec men, but no chance slip shit past yet."

Ryan's grin matched Jak's. "Mebbe that's all about to change, eh?"

The two companions continued their climb to the level where the medical facilities and armory would be kept. They didn't bother to waste time, as they saw it, looking in any of the other rooms that they passed. Some doors were closed and would remain so for the rest of time. Others were open, the briefest glimpse as they passed showing that there was nothing inside but the debris of a hasty evacuation. In one dorm, clothes, bedding and magazines lay strewed across the mattresses and on the floors, hastily tipped over as belongings were grabbed before the long gone inhabitants had run for…what? Most likely their own hastened demise.

This mute testament to the panic of the nukecaust went unremarked as the friends headed for their goal with the determination of those bent on vengeance. They were intent on getting the weapons they needed to gain the upper hand in the unspoken battle with Crabbe, and to do it with the maximum amount of time to spare.

In a redoubt such as this, deserted and with nothing that could deflect them from their course, it should have been a simple matter to achieve their goal.

At least, that was how Ryan saw it as they reached the level on which the armory was housed. Ahead of them was a door that had been closed for well over a hundred years. The one-eyed man exchanged a glance with Jak. From the level of grime and dust that was gathered on the corridor floor in front of them, the armory was as intact as it had been when predark military stalked the corridors.

Ryan looked at his wrist chron. It had taken them no time at all to secure the area and move from the mat-trans unit to this level. They had plenty of time to take a leisurely look around to see what was inside, take their pick of the ordnance that had been stored there since skydark and return to the mat-trans with ample time to spare. Ryan grinned and motioned Jak to the armory entrance.

With a brief nod, Jak stepped forward and keyed in the code that would open the armory after so long.

With a squeal of protest, the door began to open. They had a brief, tantalizing glimpse of the ordnance within before all hell broke loose.

ALL WAS SILENT in the mat-trans control room. Krysty was huddled over a comp desk, not wanting to look up and so catch the eye of the baron. Crabbe, for his part, was pacing the floor, muttering to himself. Sal, lurking in the background, was trying as much as any man could to render himself invisible. He didn't want to catch the eye of his baron. Far too often over the years he had felt the force of Crabbe's anger, even when he had been achieving the kind of near miracles that any other would have rewarded him for. Crabbe demanded high standards of himself, and was driven by an overwhelming ambition. He expected the same of all others that served under him, expected it even if they didn't share that ambition.

McCready didn't have that ambition, but he could fake it. And he had for a long time. When the baron became old and lost his grip on his ville, then he would be ready to pounce. Meantime, he would play the loyal lieutenant and say "yes sir" and "no sir" when Crabbe demanded.

For now he would keep his men with their blasters trained on the outlanders. It was a no-brainer that the old man would want them chilled at the end of the mission. He didn't give a shit about the disk the old man kept going on about. If he got it from the two missions that were left, then he would be difficult. If he didn't, the disappointment would drag him down to such a level that maybe—just maybe—the time would be here sooner than he could have hoped.

He looked at his men, and then at the three outlanders as they sat at his feet. As it should be, he figured. Jock and J.T. were sitting quietly. The old bastard had a smug look about him, and it was bugging McCready. He wanted to shake down the old geezer before the one-eyed fucker and Snowy came back. They were the worst ones. Mean streak in the pair of them, and they looked like they could handle themselves more than the others. Millicent was a tough bitch, but at the end of the day that's all she was. She was looking around, sizing things up, and trying to look for some kind of opening. He'd trust her as far as he could throw her. No, not even that far. It was like she was trying to communicate with Kirsty. Not that the mutie bitch wanted to look up. Running scared or holding secrets. Weird. He was sure there was something going on. Come to that, he was less than happy when he looked at J.T. Under the lighting, the way he was sitting, the light was reflecting off his glasses and shielding his eyes. It was impossible to read him. McCready didn't like that.

Maybe he should do something before the one-eyed freak and his bastard dwarf sidekick came back.

J.B. WAS OBSERVING the sec chief, knowing that the way he had tilted his head would make it impossible for the man to know that he was being watched. He figured that the sec chief was getting jumpy. Whatever might go down, the squat man was liable to be a loose cannon, a danger to the baron as much as to J.B. and his companions—and that made him a liability that would need dealing with as soon as possible.

Both Mildred and Doc harbored their own thoughts, kept their secret clutched tight to them as there was no way that they could share it with Krysty and J.B., much as they wanted. There was a moment when they would have to act. Without this action, they were doomed. If not from Crabbe, then from his sec man. But how to judge that moment?

The air was tight with the tension between them, so tight that it was almost impossible to breathe.

The question was, would it crack before Ryan and Jak returned?

Chapter Fifteen

For a moment they got a glimpse of what lay within the redoubt. It was, as they had hoped, a fully stocked and untouched armory. More than that, the quality and range of the weaponry showed that this was more than just an ancillary base. The racks of rifles and SMGs, the open cabinets of handblasters and the crates of grens and ammo—this was only to be expected. But there were strange-looking blasters, as well, that were of an odd design and a strange white metal. The barrels ended in molded shapes that would allow for no conventional ammo. They looked like the kind of pulse and laser rifles that Jak and Ryan had seen before, and which they thought were a rare commodity. There were also strange weapons that were like flame-throwers but were of a different hue. They had base packs like flame throwers, but the nozzled handsets ended in dishes with protruding antennas.

It was a treasure trove, the likes of which would have astounded J.B.

But there was no chance for them to really take it in. Even less of a chance for them to select anything that they could take back and use against the baron and his hateful henchmen.

For their vision was suddenly restricted by the way in which the lighting around them cut out for a second, to be replaced a strobing red light that was accompanied by a Klaxon that sounded at a deafening volume. Even as it started, a Plexiglas screen descended from the ceiling, sealing the contents of the armory forever beyond their grasp.

Ryan looked up and around. The hair on the back of his neck began to prickle. There was more to this than just an alarm.

Jak grabbed his arm and tugged. The sirens were so loud that it would have been pointless to waste words on speech. Ryan had instinctively stepped back from the Plexiglas screen as it had fallen, and now he looked around in the direction that Jak's movement indicated. It was hard to make out anything in the strobing light: a dark, crimson slash of red followed by a blinking of the blackest night that gave his eye no chance to adjust to the contrast and the bleeding of the spectrum.

As such, it took a fraction of a second before he understood what it was that the albino teen was trying to bring to his attention. And when he did comprehend, he knew that the fraction of a second was something that he could no longer allow himself. There would be no time if this was the shape of what was coming their way.

Knowing that, like Jak, it would waste time and breath to try to yell above the blaring siren, Ryan simply turned and began to run, beckoning to his companion that he should follow. In truth, Jak needed no second bidding as he took one look at the bizarre mechanical creatures that were fast approaching through the alternating red and black, the strobe effect rendering their progress strangely jerky and unreal. He had never seen anything like them before, and he was damn sure that, like Ryan, he had no desire to stick around to see what they were like up close. His every instinct was screaming at him that these were stone-cold chillers, whatever they were.

If Krysty had been with them, she could have told him that they were likely to be the automated remnants of soldiers who had once served at the base. During her brief and bizarre encounter with the man who called himself the Thunder Rider she had seen such machines. The last insane descendant of a megarich and powerful predark family, he had lived among the remains of his ancestors' wealth and privilege, including military tech that had taken the family servants and housed their brains in machines that would never wear out or buy the farm. Perhaps such bizarre experiments were what had happened to some of the soldiers stationed in the redoubt.

Right then, it didn't matter. All that mattered was that these bizarre creatures, remnants of a time long since past, had been drawn out of the shadows and into life by the intrusion of Jak and Ryan. And for whatever reason they had been released from a point between the armory and the level that housed the mat-trans unit, in effect cutting off the duo from their effective escape route.

Looking back over his shoulder as he ran, Ryan could see that the machines were gaining on them. It was like a nightmare—you kept running, you looked back and saw them at your rear, and then for a moment the world went black. Then, when the light returned, poor as it was, you could see that they had gotten closer, as though leaping in time as well as space. The strobing actually made it impossible to judge just how close they were, or how fast their progress was. All Ryan could see was that these inhuman monsters, already seeming to move in an even more alien manner because of the disorienting light, were gaining on them far too quickly for his liking.

He fired the SIG-Sauer over his shoulder as he ran, hardly even bothering to sight. There were five, maybe six of them—it was hard to tell with the way in which the lights were messing with his vision—and although they weren't large they kept in a close formation, moving almost abreast across the width of the corridor. Even the wildest of shots was likely to hit something, and Ryan was no wild shot, albeit on the run and firing over his shoulder without anything more than a glance.

He was pretty sure that the SIG-Sauer wouldn't be powerful enough to penetrate the metal shells of their mechanical pursuers. The white spark of light as the slug hit the casing of one of the creatures showed this to be true. A ricochet couldn't be heard above the blaring sirens. Even though its progress was momentarily slowed as the impact knocked it back and sideways, it did little more than gain the companions an extra yard of distance on that mechanism alone. Knocked back and out of line, it soon righted itself and continued as though nothing had happened, moving at the same pace as the others, but just a little to their rear.

Jak turned and fired in the same way. The heavier ordnance of his Magnum blaster should make some kind of difference. The recoil from firing over his shoulder and while on the move caused him to stumble momentarily. Ryan almost broke step, instinctively moving toward Jak to halt his fall, should it happen.

But there was little chance of that. Jak was far too fleet and sure of foot, and he compensated in less than the blink of an eye. He also grinned, hungry with the fire of battle in his belly. The heavier gauge slug had hit one of the creatures full-on, denting the middle of its armor plate and sending it spinning around, its momentum causing an increasing orbit that cannoned it into some of the others, knocking them in turn from their forward momentum.

The pair gained some time and some valuable distance: not much, but enough for them to hit a bend in the corridor and lose the machines from their sight for a moment. A moment that could be of the utmost importance, for they had a double problem. The first was that they needed to get some kind of cover, find some kind of angle from which they could turn the situation around, so that instead of being pursued they could round on their attackers from some kind of relative safety and then blow the bastards to pieces.

The second problem was that they were being driven away from the mat-trans unit, with the clock ticking and this obstacle barring their path. They had to knock it out if they were to stand any chance of getting out of the redoubt. Already it had become as simple as that: they had to get out. The armory with its treasure trove, hidden and preserved behind the Plexiglas screen, was now something that Ryan tried to put out of his mind. Whatever they may have been able to plunder from it and take back was now lost to them.

It would be all they could do to get out in one piece.

As this flashed through his mind, he kept his eye out for anywhere that would give them cover for attack. The sirens were disorienting, their alternating screech seeming to run in rhythm with the strobe, making it hard to think without his train of thought being interrupted. That would be the point of them, he guessed. Couldn't be much else. The trouble was that it made it hard for him to see where they could find cover. Everything around him seemed to be red and black shadow, fading in and out of vision. If he tried to stare too hard into the flashing abyss, he found himself becoming mesmerized by the insistent light pulses, his gait faltering.

It was Jak's hand, tight around his forearm, that once again brought him out of his reverie and showed him a solution. The albino teen had been keeping his eyes wide open, his own natural albinism meaning that his vision was less affected by the reduction in light. As to the mesmeric effects of the strobe, it had long since been proved that it took a lot to make Jak Lauren lose his focus.

With two quick gestures, he indicated to Ryan that they should use the rooms on either side of the corridor to mount an ambush. There would be no time to recce either room; they would have to burst through the closed doors and hope for the best.

Without even the time for this thought to take full shape in his mind, Ryan briefly nodded and took two strides, launching a foot at the door on his side of the corridor. In the blare of sound around them, it was strangely noiseless as it crashed open. The room beyond was also flashing red and black—the whole redoubt, it seemed, had hit this kind of emergency state—and so it was almost impossible for him to see inside the room with any kind of clarity. It didn't matter. SIG-Sauer raised and cocked, he followed his own forward momentum as it carried him into the room. He swept the interior with his arm. If anything had dared to move, it would have got blasted before he could even register exactly what it might be.

The room was empty. Without pausing for breath, he pivoted and closed the door until it was almost shut. He got the briefest glimpse of a door doing likewise on the other side of the corridor and knew that Jak, too, had found his room empty. He couldn't hear them above the sound of the siren, but he knew that their mechanical pursuers had to be closing on them. Whatever kind of sensory equipment they had, he hoped that they wouldn't have registered what had just taken place, and that they wouldn't be able, likewise, to sense that the rooms on either side were occupied by life as they rolled past.

Moments later, through the gap in the door, he could see a blur as the mechanized sec passed by. Were they on wheel, tracks or feet of some kind? It was impossible to tell. Would it make a difference to how they could be defeated? Probably not, he thought.

With a yell that was to psyche himself, seeing as it wouldn't be heard above the clamor of the Klaxon, Ryan pulled open the door and swung out into the corridor, adopting a two-footed stance that would enable him to steady himself and take careful aim in the minimum possible time. From the corner of his eye he could see Jak do the same, almost in exact parallel. The albino youth's stance was looser, but then he had more recoil to absorb from his heavier weapon.

The machines were a few yards in front, with their backs to the two companions. Neither Ryan nor Jak could be certain, but it was a bet worth taking that they would be unable to turn that quickly. Their backs were exposed, and it was unlikely that they could return fire.

Just as well, considering that Ryan knew his SIG-Sauer wasn't effective against their metal plate. He would have to pick his shots with care. Jak's Magnum blaster could do more raw damage, but the SIG-Sauer needed to be used as a precision tool.

Despite the situation, he felt calmer now. They were more in control of the situation, and he knew that they thrived in situations like this.

The first volley of fire was loud, even with the sirens going off around them. The boom of the Colt Python resounded, cutting through the blare of the Klaxon and momentarily deafening Ryan as he stood beside the albino teen. His own weapon sounded like a popgun next to it—or would have done if it had been in any way audible above the other sounds.

The machines were hit by a hail of fire as Jak and Ryan fired repeatedly. The one-eyed man aimed low. He could just about see in the red shadows that the lower backs of the machines had exposed panels that looked like connectors: to what, he neither knew nor cared. All that mattered was that the rear of their pursuers had a weak spot that might just allow him to place a shell that would have some effect. And he was pretty sure that he did. Showers of spark and fire, white in the red and black glare, rose from two of the machines, causing them to suddenly move in erratic orbits around each other, crashing into the others and sending them spinning in their own orbits.

As they pivoted like targets in old predark fairground attractions, Jak's Magnum slugs hammered into them. The heavy-caliber ammo smashed the plating that would otherwise have protected them. Two exploded, their innards spilling out as the power units combusted. The pieces showered over the corridor, skidding across the floor and making Ryan and Jak move quickly out of the way of their trajectories.

The machines that weren't damaged beyond repair and movement by the hail of fire that let up only instantly while both men reloaded their blasters soon found that they were scuppered by their own allies. The rogue and damaged machines caused as much if not more damage than the blasterfire than had precipitated the carnage. Whirling and combusting, they became the engines of their own destruction.

By the time this had occurred, Ryan and Jak had already turned and were on the move toward the lower levels of the redoubt and their route back to their companions. Satisfied that the machines were no longer a threat they felt safe in turning their backs. And yet, as they ran, they both had the feeling that the machines wouldn't be the only danger that would beset them before they could find a way back.

Ryan could feel the pounding of his heart against his damaged ribs as he ran. Almost unconsciously he started to take shorter breaths, trying to save his ribs from strain. Sure, he had felt better after the jump, but he was still carrying the injury, and the strange boost given him by the second jump was now wearing thin with the exertion.

Jak could sense, rather than see, that Ryan was slowing, and he adjusted his pace accordingly. He wasn't going to leave the one-eyed man in his wake. They would get through this together, and he was sure that there was something to get through just ahead of them. With the sirens and lights like this, a few automated sec machines wouldn't be the sum total of the defenses they had triggered.

They careered around a bend past the armory. Not sparing it a glance, they skittered along the corridor, their feet weirdly silent beneath the noise of the sirens. It could be that the sirens were more than a mere alarm. Their very presence masked so much other sound that it would be a simple matter for any other attack mechanisms to be launched without coming to Ryan's and Jak's notice until it was too late.

So it was only with a modicum of surprise that they saw the sec door between two sections of corridor start to grind down in front of them. The noise of the long-immobile mechanism was drowned out, but from the way that the dust fell in a black rain through the flickering red light, it was obvious that the door had been dormant for a long time, and wasn't falling with the intended speed. Was it just the strobe that made it seem as though the door was actually shuddering, or was it that the mechanism was stilted enough to make the motion as grinding as it appeared?

They could only hope so. They were still about a hundred yards from the door, and even though it was falling with an almost painful slowness it was going to be a tight call. There were flickers of movement on the other side of the door, but the black sheet of metal that descended made it almost impossible to make out what might lay in wait for them.

There would be time for that when they were past the door. Whatever it might be, it wouldn't matter if they found themselves trapped on this side, cut off from the mat-trans unit.

The door was now only a couple of yards from the floor; they were more than a couple of yards from the shrinking aperture. There was only one thing to do. Jak launched himself forward, hitting the ground belly-first and skidding over the floor so that he shot beneath the shrinking gap, rolling as he did so that he would come up facing whatever awaited them, blaster in hand and ready to act.

It was only when he came to his feet that he felt, rather than saw, that Ryan wasn't beside him.

The one-eyed man saw Jak launch himself across the floor and under the gap, and he knew that this was the only option that was open to him. Yet he was filled with trepidation. Hitting the floor like that with his ribs as they were was a greater risk than facing whatever was on the other side of the lowering door. In combat, he felt confident. Of the stabbing he could feel with each footfall, each breath, he wasn't so sure.

There was no choice in the matter. Jak was already down and under with the door lowering at what now seemed to be an incredibly fast rate. He knew that it was all perception, and that the door was moving at the same rate as it had a few moments earlier. But this shift told him that he had to throw caution to the wind and get down on his belly. It was only later that it would hit him as odd that the door was coming down from the ceiling, rather than in a vertical manner as was the norm. This was obviously no ordinary sec door.

Only later because, at that moment, the whole of his being was shuddering with the incredible pain that came in conjunction with his contact to the floor. His ribs felt as though they were crushed beneath the weight of his torso as he hit the deck, and rather than skid and slide as Jak had done, he jackknifed and doubled-up in agony, rolling at a much slower speed. That was crucial. He found himself too slow to beat the unrelenting momentum of the door. By the time he reached it, the metal was too low for him to slide under and he found himself bouncing back off it. His body was too thick and muscular to slide and squeeze into the narrowing gap, and he rolled back.

When he opened his eye, which he'd squeezed shut in almost unbearable pain, he found that he was now stranded on the wrong side of the sec door. He opened that eye in time to see the last vestige of light from the other side of the door disappear behind the bland, dark metal.

Wincing at the knives of pain that shot across his ribs as he hauled himself to his feet, Ryan wondered how he could break through the door. And he wondered what Jak was facing on the other side.

But all such speculation was driven from his mind as the low rumbling at his back became felt, rather than merely audible, below the sirens and the strobe. He turned to face the source of the noise.

"Fireblast!" he gasped, despite the pain the exclamation caused.

Jak stood square on to the enemy that now faced him. Aware that he was alone, he felt a pang of relief. If he was going to have to face this, then he would rather do it alone. Ryan was struggling, and Jak knew deep inside that whatever he intended, his devotion to his comrade would have divided his attention.

The thing that was in front of him would demand everything he had.

It was unlike anything he had seen before, and yet had a sinuous familiarity. He had heard Doc talk of the strange machines made by the whitecoats in the days before skydark, yet he had never really been able to grasp some of what the old man had said. Now, he felt that it was all too clear. The gently writhing creature in front of him—no, not creature, for it was certainly a machine despite the uncanny reptilian manner in which it swayed—was like a snake, raised on its belly so that the head was poised ready to dart forward and attack.

Jak looked the creature up and down. It was hard to see in the strobing red and black, but it seemed to have no obvious weak spots. In fact, it seemed to be made from one continuous and living piece of metal.

But there was no such thing that he had ever seen, and from his rudimentary knowledge he was certain that such a thing couldn't exist. If it was metal, it couldn't move like that without being ribbed or jointed in some way. It was just a matter of finding those joins. It had to be some kind of fake skin covering it that made it look seamless and sinuous.

If it was metallic, and ribbed or jointed, then his blaster would be no good. Jak holstered the Colt Python and palmed a leaf-bladed knife in each hand.

It was then that he realized that the thing worked on the principle of motion detection. For as he moved, his elbows shimmered in sharp darting angles away from his body—and the head of the creature, previously poised and immobile, jerked suddenly in each direction.

He stopped, suddenly, motionless and alert, studying that which was his prey. It was as still. It seemed strange that there were two such small oases of calm in the midst of the flashing light and two-note roar. They both seemed to stand apart from their surroundings. Jak watched carefully, his own breathing reduced to a shallow draw that was barely noticeable.

And then he moved, a sudden kinetic blur of action, taking strides that combined with leaps and hops to make his movements erratic and hard to follow. If the machine did what he suspected, he would have to make damn sure that he was hard to follow.

The blazing light, crackle of heat and choking sprays of concrete dust that followed in his wake showed that he had been correct. The bastard mechanism was fitted with a laser that pulsed bursts of energy at the areas where Jak had been but a fraction of a second before. It intended to blast him from the face of the redoubt, but he proving just a little too quick.

But from the heat he could feel in the heels of his combat boots as he moved, a little too quick wouldn't be quick enough for much longer. The heat was becoming more painful with each burst. It was getting the range and sight of him.

He wasn't one for fancy theorizing, but it was pretty obvious by now that this redoubt had been some kind of research base. He'd never seen things like this before, and hoped that he'd get out of here and never see things like it again. Perhaps that was why the armory had been wired. The advanced test stuff was stored there, and by using these mechanical creatures to protect it they were also testing them at the same time.

It might have seemed odd that this was calmly running through the front of his mind as he kept just a millisecond ahead of the laser fired by the mechanical snake. Odd only if you weren't Jak Lauren. Operating on instinct and trusting that very asset was what kept him alive. And the best way to tap into that was not to muddle it by worrying about your problem. Think about something else and let the back of the brain sort out a solution.

It would have to be bastard quick, though. He could feel the blisters forming as his heels burned.

It flickered across his mind—would Ryan get past the sheet metal sec door?

"FIREBLAST AND FUCK IT," the one-eyed man breathed, wincing at the strain on his ribs as he did. The low rumbling that had cut through the siren's wail now revealed its source: a bottom-heavy, squat flatbed on tracks that were made for a more porous and yielding surface than the concrete floor. The metal caterpillar was scoring the floor, making a noise disproportionate to its size. Ryan had expected some kind of big version of what they had just faced. Not this....

The tracks had been deceptive. The wag was wide, but the blaster mounted on it wasn't the kind of cannon he had expected. It was smaller, and seemed dwarfed by the width of the flatbed. It didn't, in fact, look like it could do much harm at all.

But it wouldn't be on something that wide and heavy-duty without a reason. Why?

He stood immobile, waiting. In an echo of what Jak was just discovering, he came to the same conclusion about the redoubt's purpose—hidden on the document Crabbe possessed, but that kind of duplicity figured—and also to the possibility of the machine having a motion detector.

He was four-square to the sec door, facing the strange wag. For what seemed an eternity but was probably only a heartbeat he waited—then it began. A dull throbbing low in his gut, a slow pulse that he couldn't hear so much as feel, and sensations of nausea and a spinning head.

He snorted, tried to shake his head to clear it, feeling like he was going to pass out. The tiny blaster mounted on the flatbed started to glow green at the tip. The metal frame and the caterpillar tracks on which it was mounted seemed to shimmer in front of his eyes, though the walls and floor around stayed still.

That was it—vibration and sonics. Doc had once said something about the whitecoats having such weapons, and there had been suggestions of this from the technomads who had come to their aid in the past.

The nozzle was pointed right at him. He knew he had to get the hell out of the way, and quick. But it seemed that the vibration was deep in his bones now, making the gristle and tendon between the joints seize up and refuse to obey the commands of his nervous system. Muscles seemed to shake and vibrate as if he'd been in a fight followed by an all-night run across rocky terrain. His ribs felt as if they were being pried apart. The sound from the tiny blaster was now so immense that it blotted out the sirens. There was nothing except the low, slow oscillation from the flatbed. It wasn't so much that he could hear as it that it enveloped him, forming a barrier against all other sound, growing greater with each wave, like an ocean crashing on the shore, moving in and taking over as the tide washed over the rocks. He was the rock, and he was about to be obliterated.

But he was in front of the sec door; the barrier that barred his way. Maybe…

He was as good as chilled unless he moved now. There was only the one chance. Eye screwed tight in concentration, his breath rasping in protesting lungs as the oscillation seemed to be interfering with his natural rhythms, slowing them to its own pace, Ryan focused all the strength he could muster into one last, sudden and violent act. If he couldn't make his protesting body act counter to the obscenely slow pulse, then he'd board the last train west. He thought of Krysty, J.B., Mildred and Doc; of Jak, on the other side of the door. He thought of all they had been through and all they would continue to go through together…if he could just do this one thing.

Maybe it was these thoughts and emotions that spurred him on. Maybe it was nothing more than the desire to survive, to carry on. It didn't matter, ultimately. All that mattered was that when the moment came, he was able to throw himself to one side. At least, that was his intent. His musculature was suffering heavily from the sonic interference, and his leap to the side was in truth nothing more than a collapse and crawl toward the far wall.

But it was enough. The pulse grew so intense that, even out of the direct line, it made him vomit as his stomach was turned inside out. He felt as though his eardrums were being ruptured by rusty blades.

If he could have looked around, other than sightlessly at the floor, he would have seen the black metal sheeting of the sec door wobble, seem to melt, and then implode with a roar that drowned the sirens that, as the pulse suddenly ceased, momentarily returned to his ears.

JAK'S SPEED WAS increasing as he leaped from spot to spot, just ahead of the laser from the snakelike machine, partly because increasing his speed was the only way to avoid getting himself fried. It was also partly because he had some idea of a plan. The machine was made to move like a reptile, but it wasn't flesh and blood. It was metal and machinery. As such, it was jointed. And he had been watching, seeing how it moved, and was sure that he knew where the joints were on the sinuous body. There was a section where, he was almost certain from his rudimentary knowledge of mechanics, the metal heart had to be contained. All he had to do was to get in a position to strike, and he knew that he could drive his knives into the belly of the beast and blow out its circuits.

He was making a wider arc with each jump. Soon he would have the speed and range to run up the wall and somersault in the air. The machine would find it hard to bend its head section back on itself. If he was quick enough, he could beat the arc it would take and get in underneath its range, landing exactly where he needed to thrust his own metal into the heart of the creature, an alien metal that could slay the mechanical dragon.

He was fast enough now and one step away from using the wall as a springboard. Yet all the while he was aware of a deep throbbing pulse that resounded down his spine. It was as he turned, pivoted and thrust off the wall with one foot that he could see the sec door behind the snake machine. It looked as though it was melting from the middle outward, turning to liquid that pulsed in time with the vibration down his spine. The very center was now beginning to glow.

Jak's instinct for danger kicked in, and he blew out the idea of tackling the snake machine. It was right in line with the glowing center of the door, and there was no way he was going to get caught up in anything that might erupt. He sailed through the air, underneath the arc of the creature's head as it tried to fry him with its laser. All it succeeded in doing was to send up a shower of sparks as it cut into the straggling tail of its own body. Its balance disturbed, it toppled as it tried to turn, the laser scoring across the ceiling and bringing down a shower of debris. It was falling backward as the sec door exploded in a shower of molten metal, splashing out the center over the snake, while more solid fragments shaken loose by the sonic wave were flung down the corridor, their sharp edges and high velocity driving them into and through the mechanical snake, severing portions of the body and rendering it into a useless heap of junk on the corridor floor.

Jak had landed on the far side, hugging the wall and keeping down as much as he possibly could. The violence of the sonic ripple made him feel like vomiting, and his ears felt like they would burst, but he opened his mouth to try to equalize the pressure. Before he had a chance to really register pain and shock, the wave had passed.

Hurriedly, still feeling uncertain on his feet, he straightened. Ryan had come through the hole where the sec door used to be, looking as unsteady as Jak felt, his face set in a grim mask of determination. He mouthed something that Jak couldn't hear as his ears were still singing with the vibration. He figured he knew what it was, though. Looking back, he could see a flatbed truck on tracks, with a tiny blaster that looked far too small for such a trailer. That had to have been what caused the explosion.

For sure, he didn't want to stick around to see what else it could do.

As he turned, he could feel the vibrations in the ground as it started to move forward. A quick glance told him how slow it was. It wasn't made to move on rubble, and that was to their advantage. It also needed time to build up the power necessary for another blast like the last. The nozzle of the tiny blaster was showing a faint green tinge that grew brighter with an encouraging slowness.

Ryan was already ahead of him as Jak turned back to the remains of the mechanical snakelike creature. The head that had risen above him and looked so dangerous was now nothing more than a heap of inert junk—but inert junk with a small and easily concealable weapon in its midst.

Keeping one eye on the rumbling flatbed, Jak leaned over the snake machine and started to detach the laser from its mounting in the end of the mechanism. He hoped that the weapon would have its own power source, and not be wired into the machine.

He got lucky. The head of the machine was obviously designed to carry any number of interchangeable weapons. That much was clear from the ease with which he detached his objective. The fact that it had been a laser mounted in the head was simply down to a quirk of fate when skydark hit the unlucky military and whitecoats who had been based here.

Lucky for Jak, though. He could see that the laser had its own small power cell built in as he detached the clipped circuit boards that wired it into the snake. He wanted to try it out and fire on the flatbed. It might serve a dual purpose and knock out the thing that was winding up toward pursuing them. But then he thought again. The power that the tiny blaster had unleashed might be even more destructive if just released by fire. Better that they outrun the bastard thing.

He angled the laser up and fired it into the ceiling. A crackle of power, and then a hail of dust brought down a small section of the ceiling on and around the flatbed as it rumbled slowly but inexorably forward.

Jak turned after Ryan and began running. He figured that the machine at their rear would have trouble following at anything approaching the speed they could run. And if it took time to build power, then even if it could tail them, it was of no real immediate danger.

Still, it wouldn't be wise to hang around. He sprinted after Ryan, catching the one-eyed man with ease. Ryan was running awkwardly, hunched over to one side. Jak knew that he had added more damage to his ribs, and as he ran he took hold of Ryan, supporting his weight and taking it off the sore side of his body. It was far from graceful but it was effective, and Ryan's pace picked up even as Jak slowed.

They were still vigilant for any further dangers, but it seemed as though the redoubt had flung at them all it had to offer. Despite the rumbling that grew more distant at their backs, but was still ominous, and the constant blare of the siren in time with the strobe, there was nothing else to bar their passage.

They reached the mat-trans anteroom, the strain of the run making both of them slow despite the desperate urging of their wills.

The unit stood in front of them, and at their back there was the low thrum of vibration as the sonic blaster began to build power. They threw themselves toward the mat-trans: Ryan collapsed on the floor, sprawled across the disks, while Jak slammed the door and hit the LD button. He hadn't had a chance to check his wrist chron, but he fervently hoped that they hadn't exceeded their time as the white mist began to rise in small columns.

"Hurry, you bastard," Ryan hissed to the floor as he felt the low, slow thrum build in intensity. The rumbling of the tracks was audible now as the flatbed truck approached the corridor outside.

The low, sickening fluttering of the sonic wave grew in his gut, making him want to puke, even as the wave of darkness from the mat-trans jump began to sweep over him.

As it did, he looked up to see Jak grinning triumphantly, brandishing the laser.

Fireblast! Let it be in time....

Chapter Sixteen

Heat. That was the overwhelming impression of everyone in the room as the seconds ticked slowly past. Krysty and Mildred were able to look to their wrist chrons with some degree of stealth, but for Doc and J.B. it was a no go. They were being covered by McCready's men with an eagle eye that grew ever more jumpy as time went on. The companions were exhausted because of the mat-trans jumps and the action they had encountered in the past few hours. The sec men, Crabbe and his mechanic didn't have that excuse. Nonetheless, they found that their nerves were ground to a fine edge, singing with the tension of waiting.

The room was small. As a control room, it had been designed to hold only three or four people at a time. There were twice that number within its narrow confines. Sure, there was air-conditioning in the room, as the redoubt was in full working order, but even with the best air filter and cold air mechanisms, it was still too many people rammed into too small a space for such a long stretch. As well, the number of jumps had only added to the stifling atmosphere, as each flash of light was accompanied by a correspondingly large release of heat that had nowhere to go other than to be absorbed by the people who were contained within the confines of the room.

The tension of waiting was written large on all of them, albeit for vastly differing reasons. The friends were anxious that Ryan and Jak return, and in one piece. Crabbe was anxious that they return, and this time bearing the disk that he so craved. Sal was just anxious. The mechanic was proud of his work, but he wasn't a brave man. He knew that the baron was volatile. He also figured that McCready was even more volatile than his supposed boss. And it didn't take a genius to work out that the sec chief was just itching to send the outlanders on the last train west, maybe even the baron too. It could, from his point of view, chill two rank old birds with the one blast. And where would that leave Sal, then? Now there was a question that the mechanic didn't want to have answered in any kind of a hurry.

As for the sec chief and his men, beads of sweat dripped into sore and red-rimmed eyes as the sec men maintained their vigilance. Each one of them was aware that their chief was ambitious, and although it wasn't openly spoken of, they all knew that there would be a time when he would push for power, and it would be politic to be on his side. So they were all determined to do their best for him.

But the heat, the strain of not sleeping and having to stay vigilant when they ached in every fiber, and the knowledge that even unarmed these coldhearts they guarded had a reputation that made them something to be feared.... That lay heavy on them.

That and the fact that their chief was starting to show signs of impatience and a desire to get things moving. The muscles in his jaw twitched as though he was barely restraining muttering to himself, and each of his men was acutely aware of the way in which his eyes flickered between the baron and the captives.

When the mat-trans disgorged its cargo, then things were okay for a while. It was the interminable wait in between that was stretching them so tight that they might just…

Snap?

It was a sudden and disturbing flash of light that made them all jolt. Fingers on trigger guards instinctively tightened in a way that would have tapped bursts of rapid-fire under any other circumstances.

For a moment there was complete silence and no movement in the room. Krysty looked over to where Mildred, J.B. and Doc were seated. She could see that they were trying to keep it from their faces, but each was wondering if Ryan and Jak had made it back in one piece—and perhaps whether they had found some ordnance that could be used against their captors.

Then Crabbe yelled, as though woken from a reverie with a start. At his command, McCready beckoned two of the sec men to go to the mat-trans. With a shock, Krysty realized that less than the stipulated half hour limit had gone by. Did it mean that they had found something they could use, or—infinitely worse—that they had encountered a peril that had forced them to cut short their search? Did it mean that there may only be one person in the mat-trans?

She made to move, but felt the arm of the baron as it moved across her chest, barring her way. She looked at him, and there was coldness in his eyes.

"You stay where you are missy…and you," he

barked, pointing with his free hand at Mildred as she made to move. "Cover the bitch," he continued. "I ain't taking no chances with these outlanders."

Krysty felt the tension in his arm lessen as she moved back, stopped straining forward. But even so, she felt a burning desire to push past the baron as the sec men pulled open the mat-trans door.

Inside it was dark now that the initial flash had faded, and for a moment there was no detectable movement, nor any audible sound. Her heart leaped to her throat as she wondered if there was anyone in there at all. Was it possible that the unit had somehow triggered itself, leaving Ryan and Jak stranded?

And then there was the sound of footfalls, and Ryan and Jak stepped into the light. Both were disheveled and showing obvious contusions. And Ryan was walking awkwardly, suggesting that his ribs were causing him more than a little discomfort. Yet both men were stoic as they emerged into the room, handing over their weapons to the sec men before calmly making their way to where the others were seated. Ryan resisted a small grin as he saw how that infuriated McCready, who wanted them to be suffering. Even though his ribs were starting to feel as though a horde of mutie buffalo had been dancing on them, Ryan refused to let any sign of discomfort consciously show. Without a word they seated themselves. Anyone who didn't know them wouldn't realize a thing, but to those who did, there were clues. The body language was just a little more relaxed than it might have been, and there was something about the way that Jak looked all of them in the eye by turn, with something that would have been taken by a stranger as a slight nervous muscle twitch. But to those who knew his usually stonelike features, it was more than that.

It was the closest to a wink that the albino youth would ever get.

For each of them, it signaled that there was hope. How or what, they couldn't tell, but there was no denying that the signal meant that either Jak or Ryan—maybe even both—had somehow managed to find, and conceal a weapon.

They took their place among their companions and said nothing. Ryan grimaced as he seated himself, the pain from his ribs making him catch his breath.

"Well?" Crabbe exploded eventually, unable to contain himself any longer. "What the fuck happened to you out there? You look like shit, so it must have been something spectacular," he added, taking them in with a raking glance.

"Thanks for that," Ryan commented wryly, the effect spoiled a little by the stabbing pain that made him wince as he spoke. "You'd never believe me if I told you."

"Try me," the baron said coldly, his face set in stone. "Don't fuck with me and hold back, Brian. It wouldn't be a good idea."

Ryan shook his head. "You keep saying that, but I tell you, considering what we've just seen, there isn't much of anything that could be worse. Chill me now, fat boy, I really don't care. But you might not get what you're after if you do."

"Now you know that holding out on me would be triple stupe—" Crabbe began. But Jak cut him off.

"No disk, but getting close. Must be."

"Why do you say that?" Crabbe questioned, his brow knitting with the effort to understand.

"One redoubt left. Each got more weird shit tech. Should have figured before. They run in order," Jak commented, waving a pointed finger at the laminated list that the baron treated as a holy relic.

Crabbe looked at it afresh. Suddenly, it seemed to him that something very obvious had been going on under his nose all along, and he had been blind. "Of course," he breathed slowly.

Ryan tried to turn the grin that spread across his face into a grimace, which, considering the pain he was in wasn't too hard. That had never occurred to him. The cunning of the albino teen was something that never ceased to catch him off guard. Looking across, he could see that Krysty was trying to keep a similar expression from her face. Had she, he wondered, caught on to the fact that he and Jak had returned with a hidden weapon? If he had figured right, then Doc and Mildred also had something hidden.

One redoubt left. One trip to be made. Krysty and J.B. needed to make it. And Jak's subterfuge was exactly what could ensure that.

"I don't get it," McCready snarled. "What's Snowy going on about?"

Crabbe shot him a pitying look. "I don't guess that you wouldn't get it," he said in a condescending manner. "It's really simple. The list was arranged in a certain order for a reason. The places we've sent them to have grown in importance as they've worked their way down the list. So it's pretty fucking obvious, even to a stupe like you, that the last one on the list is the most important. And where else would you hide the disk except in the most important place? See? Fucking obvious."

Mildred and Doc, without exchanging a word, were thinking the same thing. Jak was some kind of genius to get inside the baron's mind and twist it his way. Without that kind of thinking, the old man would be on the verge of boiling over. But now he was looking almost triumphant, as though he could smell success. It was almost in his hand.

J.B., on the other hand, was just thinking that some people were born stupe and were bound to buy the farm that way, no matter what they did in between, and that Crabbe was one of those people.

"Okay, Snowy, Brian," Crabbe began with a newfound enthusiasm in his voice, "if Kirsty and J.T. are going to be the ones to get the motherlode, then they'd better have an idea of what they're going face. I want to know what happened from the time that bastard flashed until it did it again," he said, indicating the mat-trans unit.

Ryan looked at Jak. "You want to tell it?" The albino teen shook his head. "Okay then, here goes…"

And so Ryan began. He related what had happened at the redoubt, from the moment that they had exited the mat-trans, through to the discovery of the armory. From the corner of his eye, he could see J.B.'s eyes almost glaze over behind his glasses at the thought of such an untouched and expansive armory. If nothing else, there was one man in the room who could appreciate the treasures that they had been forced to leave behind. Although it had to be said that the fact that it was so well protected and alarmed seemed to bring home the immensity of what they had found to Crabbe and McCready, the latter cursing audibly at the thought of what he could do with such a haul.

But any thought of what had been left behind was lost when Ryan began to describe the machines that had been triggered by the alarm. As he spoke, he could see a distant look spread across Krysty's features, followed by an almost involuntary shudder as she recalled similar things that she had seen. The rest of the companions had encountered similar types of machines, and so found it less hard to comprehend than the baron and his sec chief. The guards remained impassive, guarded in so many senses of the word. Crabbe was almost slack-jawed with amazement, and McCready was frankly disbelieving.

"Bullshit." He spit. "They're making it up, Baron. Trying to fool you. Mebbe they've already got this fucking disk you want and they want to keep it from you."

"My dear sir, I can vouch for the veracity of my friend's words. I have seen many things, and I can tell you that whitecoat scum of the predark age had many such obscene devices."

"Shut the fuck up, Jock, I wasn't asking you," McCready snapped. He leveled the barrel of his blaster directly into Doc's face. The old man stood calmly, but inside he was certain that his misery was about to end.

If only the sec chief had known how close to the truth he had inadvertently come. The friends kept their counsel, but hoped that this wouldn't spur the baron into another train of thought.

No worries on that score. Any doubts that might have been sown by the words of the sec chief were immediately obliterated by an unlikely source of excitement—the mechanic, Sal.

"Bullshit yourself," he exploded angrily in the face of the sec chief. "You're always saying what I do is shit, but who got this going and enabled these bastards to make the trip? It was me, and the skills I learned from the old days. These things are possible and given enough time to study it I could bring back that kind of glory. You're just shitting yourself because you're worried that this kind of tech could make you useless and pointless. And who the fuck could you bully then, you stupe shithead?

"Baron," he continued, turning to a startled Crabbe and carrying on before a furious but stunned McCready had a chance to bite back, "you've got to let me go there and study it. I know I could rebuild anything I found."

For a moment it looked as though the baron was seriously considering this option. Then, at length, he said, shaking his head, "No, I can't see that. Not yet. Mebbe once we've got the disk and started to learn from it. These things they talk about, they ain't going nowhere. Just be patient. You get there in the end, Sal. Look at what's happened to me—all that time, and now it's within my grasp."

"But will you let me?" Sal implored, an almost messianic gleam in his eyes.

"In due time," the baron said simply. But there was something in his tone that the mechanic recognized, and he seemed to be satisfied. It was just another reason why Ryan and his people knew that they had to stop Crabbe.

There was a moment's silence before the baron looked at the laminated list in his hand with something approaching reverence.

"Let's do this," he said quietly. "Give Kirsty and J.T. their weapons, McCready. It's time for them to get going."

Without a word, J.B. rose to his feet under the watchful eye of the sec, while Krysty moved to join him. The briefest of looks passed between them as they moved close to each other. Brief, but enough for both of them to know that when the Armorer and Krysty returned it would be time for action.

It was only when they were in the mat-trans unit, and the door had clicked shut on the world beyond that Krysty and J.B. dared to speak.

"Think there's anything in that, and we'll find it tougher going?" the Armorer asked.

Krysty shook her head. "Jak was just shitting Crabbe. I don't think there's any reason to any of this. I would have said they were just maintenance redoubts from the look I had at that list. But mebbe some of them were storage facilities, too, and that's why they had that weird shit."

J.B. grinned crookedly as the mist began to form. "Yeah, well, let's hope we find a nice little storage facility for heavy-duty blasters this time around."

They were the last words she remembered as the darkness closed in around her.

WHEN THE DARKNESS ebbed away to be replaced by a foul light and an equally foul taste in her mouth, Krysty knew that they had arrived at their destination. She was sprawled facedown on the floor, and she fully expected the taste in her mouth to be echoed by a leaden feeling in her limbs. Yet as she tried to drag herself to her feet, she realized that she felt very differently. There was almost a springiness to her as she clambered to her feet, and she looked over to see that J.B. was similarly affected.

"Weird, huh?" she said. "Wonder if there are any other surprises waiting for us out there?"

"Nothing like last time, I hope," the Armorer answered wryly as he moved to the redoubt door. "Take it like last time, okay?"

Krysty nodded, and as he opened the door onto the anteroom beyond, they fell into the roles that they had established for themselves on the last jump. And, as it had been that time, it was a simple task to secure the anteroom as it was empty, and the control room showed no sign of having been in use since skydark.

"So far, so good," J.B. murmured as they recced the corridor before heading out. The rooms were cold and dry, despite the temperate conditions maintained automatically. It was a different kind of cold, one that came from years of emptiness and lack of use.

"Looks like it might be an easy ride," J.B. observed.

"Don't speak too soon," Krysty retorted. "Wish Crabbe could see this, though. It shoots holes right through his belief."

"Hey, he only has that 'cause of Jak…and that's Jak's

way of ensuring the rest of us stay away from buying the farm before we get back."

"I know," she admitted. "It's just that Crabbe is really bugging me."

"Don't let him," J.B. said in a matter-of-fact tone as they moved along the corridor, scoping out the empty rooms as they went. "The way I figure it, both Millie and Doc, and Jak and Ryan managed to get some kind of weapon they could hide away on their last jump. I figure if we can do the same, and we get surprise on our side, then we can wipe out that scumsucker McCready before Crabbe even knows what's going on."

"You figure him for the real danger?" she asked as she kicked open another door onto an empty room.

"Dark night, the baron is a fat fuck with a temper, but he's got no real ordnance. McCready is the man with the blaster. And he's boss of the men with the other blasters. I've seen the way he looks at the baron when he thinks Crabbe isn't looking. And I've seen the way his men obey him. I know who they'd be with if it came to a straight decision."

"Yeah, guess I'd have to go with you on that," Krysty admitted. Her hair was twitching at the ends, but she couldn't figure out why. The place seemed deserted.

"J.B.," she said quietly, "is it me, or do you reckon this place is just a little too quiet?"

"Not sure if you could call anything too quiet after some of the shit we've all been through," J.B. mused. "Feels to me like it's empty down here, and there doesn't seem to be too much sign of life. Why? You starting to feel something?"

Krysty shook her head. "I don't know," she said

slowly. "There's something that doesn't feel right, but I'm not really sure."

J.B. grinned and racked his mini-Uzi. "Just have to keep it triple red. And blast first, ask later, right?"

"Sounds okay to me," she agreed.

They moved along the deserted corridor until they were beginning to move up to the next level. Unlike some of the redoubts in this sector that were on the baron's list, there seemed to be nothing wrong with this one. The corridors were free of dust and dirt, and the air was fresh and clean. All of the maintenance systems were working fine, and it gave the redoubt the strange feeling of being a place where the previous inhabitants had just left temporarily, and would be back in a moment.

When they reached the next level, it became apparent that something wasn't right. The sec doors to the dorm areas were closed, and they showed no signs of being forced or even of having any wear. But when they opened them, they could see that the beds within had been disturbed, and there were clothes on the floors.

"Someone left in a hurry and never came back," J.B. murmured.

"Don't be so sure," Krysty returned. She could feel her scalp prickling as her hair started to coil, though for the moment she couldn't identify the feeling of unease that was causing this. She walked to the bed nearest to where she was standing, on the threshold to the room. Bending, she reached down and touched the sheet and blanket that were rumpled in the middle of the mattress. She had only half expected it to be cold, so even though it was a shock to find it still warm, it didn't make her jump.

"I don't think we're as alone as we thought," she said softly. "Though where the hell anyone else is hiding down here I don't know."

J.B. joined her, looking down at the bed as though expecting it to yield some secrets to him.

"It hasn't been empty that long by the feel of it," she continued. "Though where they are… I mean, I can feel that there must be someone using this place, but I don't feel like they're here."

"Mebbe they're not," J.B. said. "Could be they're out on a hunt or recce of some kind. Whatever, we'd better be real careful."

They left the dorm and, making certain that their blasters were ready to fire at the slightest twitch of a trigger finger, they explored the level they were on in more depth. There were two other dorm rooms, both of which showed signs of life. There was some soiled laundry on the floors, but not enough to suggest that these people—whomever they may be—lived like animals. Indeed, to judge by the shower and latrine blocks that they then explored, the people who used this redoubt as a domicile were about as civilized as it was possible to get in the Deathlands. They showed every sign of keeping the redoubt as a clean, well-maintained residence.

That showed a certain intelligence, if nothing else—keep the place in good condition and don't destroy the haven you have found. It was an intelligence that could make them very dangerous indeed.

Krysty and J.B. continued their recce and moved up to the next level. The kitchens, food stores and dining area showed signs of use. The stores were depleted, but not needlessly decimated, and there were cuts of meat in the deep-freeze area that weren't wrapped in plastic, and had obviously been chilled in recent times. The kitchen area was a little dirty, as though not recently cleaned, but had obviously been rearranged and washed down at some point. In short, it probably resembled the way it would have looked in predark times when it was a working military base. The original food stocks had been partially used, but showed signs of being eked out with care and caution, another sign of an obvious intelligence at work.

"These people use this as a base. They're not just muties, stupes, stickies, crazies or looters," J.B. stated. "Dangerous."

"Probably out doing whatever it is they do. And from the look of the meat in the freezer, they can do it well," Krysty added.

"Then we'd better be ready for them when they come back," J.B. said softly. "Let's see what they've done to the armory."

Ultracautious and on triple-red alert, they continued their exploration by moving toward the armory and the medical facilities. They found a selective use of the facilities that told them a lot about the type of people who had made the redoubt home.

In the medical room, things like bandages were in heavy use. Dressings for wounds were sorely depleted. Yet the more complex meds, and the ready-filled hypos of antibiotics and painkillers that Mildred had taught them about, and which had been so useful to them, were untouched, as were the facilities for minor surgery that all such redoubts carried.

The armory told a similar story. The handblasters and SMGs had been freely looted, as had the ammo for such things. Among the stock of rifles, too, there had been some heavy use. Yet even here, the stock depletion hadn't been random and unchecked. The boxes from which they had been taken were stacked carefully to one side, seemingly to keep a record of what had been used. Those boxes that hadn't been opened had been separated from the others with an equal care. And yet they had stayed away from the boxes of grens. Again, a careful separation had taken place, as frag grens had been moved to sit beside the boxes of ammo. Some of them were now empty, with one half-full and open on the floor. The flamethrowers had been left in their racks, untouched.

"Very selective, aren't they?" Krysty commented, eyeing the ordnance that they had used as much as that which they had ignored.

"Go for what you know, and don't trust the tech you can't take apart," J.B. mused, scratching his forehead under the brim of his fedora. "That would explain why the mat-trans had been left alone."

"And why it felt so empty down there," Krysty added. The way in which her occasional doomie sense had been bugging her was now a little more explainable. And it gave them more of a clue as to the kind of people they would have to expect when they returned from wherever they had gone.

"I'd bet you every piece of ordnance in here that they've got no idea how this place works. They're just thankful that it does. Which, I'm hoping, means that they also don't know how to work all the automatic sec shit, and watch the cams. So mebbe, when they get back, they won't have any indication that we're here. That'll give us the drop over them, at least. If we're still here, that is. Just a bit of luck and we can be away before they get back."

Krysty pursed her lips and nodded. "Yeah, sounds reasonable. Guess we'd better recce the rest of the place while we still can."

The Armorer nodded, and they wasted no time in covering the rest of the redoubt. There was a vehicle bay that was large enough for two wags, both of which were gone. Oil and gas stains on the concrete showed that they were in some kind of regular use, and cans of gas were stored by the predark reservoirs that were built in to the bay, bespeaking of a regular use and an outside source of gas.

Question was, where did it come from and how had they acquired it?

A quick recce of the rest of the areas showed that the sec camera area had been left well alone, while what had once been the mess room for the predark military staff was in regular use. One thing for sure—these people had been happy to use the facilities, and if they had ever questioned how it kept itself ticking over they had opted not to delve too deeply. They also felt secure enough to never leave a guard behind when they left their base.

J.B. looked at his wrist chron. Only ten minutes of their allotted thirty had been used, and they had secured the area.

"Figure we shouldn't hang around here too long. Let's get ourselves some ordnance and get out of here."

"Yeah..." There was something in Krysty's tone and the way she gazed around the mess room that made J.B. turn back as he headed for the door.

"What?" he asked.

She shrugged. "It's strange, really. It just struck me that these people are using the redoubt and living the kind of life that Crabbe is looking for. They've found their own small piece of the motherlode that he's obsessed with, and they're making some kind of use of it. That's just what he'd like to do, except the stupe fat bastard is still caught up in his own little power games."

"These people might be, too. We haven't seen them, and hopefully we won't. So let's just get going."

She shrugged. "Yeah, guess you're right. It's just that I've gotten a little curious."

"Fair enough, but we don't have time for that right now," J.B. said.

Krysty knew he was right: there was no telling what the inhabitants of the redoubt might be like. They lived in a civilized fashion when they were inside the redoubt, but there was no way of knowing what they were like when they were outside. Or what they would be like when they came back to find that their safe haven had been invaded from the inside.

She followed J.B. to the armory, where they surveyed its contents.

"Too much choice." J.B. grinned. "Where do we start?"

"Something small, easily hidden," Krysty commented. "We need to get it past McCready's men when they take our blasters from us."

"You reckon?" J.B. queried. "Think about it. We're the last ones to go out, and the last to come back. Do we really need to hide it?"

"Come out blasting, you mean?" And when he nodded, she added, "Then why do we need anything else? Couldn't we just use our own ordnance? Come to that, if we're the last ones to go out and come back, then why shouldn't they just blast the fuck out of us when they open the mat-trans door?"

"Because they'll think we have the disk, and Crabbe isn't going to risk damaging it," J.B. stated. "So we'll have a chance to start blasting before they take the weapons from us."

"Yeah, and if we do that, then they take out the others before they have a chance to use whatever they've got," Krysty argued. "Think about it, J.B. We come out meek, make out we've found the disk, let them take our blasters and let their guard down, then hit them with whatever we've taken from here. That means they get taken by surprise, and our people get a chance to ready whatever it is they've hidden away."

J.B. sniffed. "You put it that way, guess I can't argue," he agreed.

He was about to move toward the grens, having already figured like Doc and Mildred before him that a gas gren would be a good start, when Krysty stopped him.

"Wait," she said suddenly. He looked at her quizzically, though he could see that her hair had suddenly tightened on her scalp, curling protectively around her neck even as he stared. He waited for her to continue.

"There's something really wrong here," she said.

"What?"

She shook her head. "I don't know… I just know that something isn't right."

His face set. "Okay then. We have some time to play with, but let's forget that. I don't know what the fuck is going on here, or how these people live, and I don't care. Let's grab some weapons and get out."

With which he turned away from her and reached toward the grens. A box of gas grens lay behind an already open box of frag grens, and his hand snaked toward it.

"No!" Krysty began as the dread feeling in the back of her head took shape. She suddenly realized that it was as much instinct as doomie feeling that was fueling this dread. She had seen something that hadn't registered, but now…

"Dark night!" J.B. cursed, mentally calling himself every kind of a stupe that he could as he realized what he had done. In taking the crate of gas grens to open it, he had triggered a trap.

Maybe these people weren't quite the technically ignorant stupes they had supposed, he thought. Or maybe they were just suspicious of one another, regardless of the seeming harmony that their living conditions suggested. Whatever was behind it didn't matter. All that did was that the closed crate of grens was empty—he could tell this by how light it was to his touch—and now it seemed to have triggered a light beam that shot across to the door, triggering its closure mechanism.

The sec door slid across swiftly, its mechanism undimmed by the passing decades, and although Krysty flung herself full length, reaching out to try to jam it at the last by thrusting the barrel of her handblaster into the ever smaller gap, she found that she was just a fraction of a second too late.

J.B. ran across to the door, thumping the panel around the keypad in frustration. He keyed in every default sec code, but even as he did so he was aware that it wasn't likely to work. He turned and looked at Krysty, who was picking herself up from the floor, her face a mirror of the frustration and anger that he was feeling.

There was nothing they could do now but wait, and pray that their captors wouldn't be gone for long. If it was more than—they both checked their chrons—eighteen minutes, then they were screwed. There would be no way they could return to Crabbe, and whatever happened they would be stuck in this place.

The fact that they were in an armory, and so it was unlikely that their captors would come in blasting was of little consolation.

All they could do was wait.

THE WAITING WAS driving Crabbe to the point of madness. The baron was pacing up and down, his mood swinging violently between elation and frustration. Mildred watched him and recognized the symptoms of a man on the verge of a breakdown. She could also see that McCready, although not a man who had the medical training but nonetheless a man of great cunning, was able to make a similar diagnosis. The time would soon be coming when he would make his move. Maybe that would be a good thing. In the confusion it could be easier for them to use the weapons that they had been able to conceal. She was sure that Ryan and Jak were carrying, just as she and Doc were.

"MAKE YOURSELF comfortable. There's no knowing how long we'll have to wait, so we might as well rest and be ready for them." Krysty sighed in a resigned tone as she settled on the floor.

"I can't." J.B. shook his head in frustration as he paced. He was on edge, and there was no way he was going to be able to keep it frosty. He blamed himself entirely. How could he be such a stupe? It wasn't the thought of having to enter into a firefight that bothered him. He could do that with his eyes shut and still outshoot most men. No, it was the thought that they were running out of time and could be stuck here that was bothering him. He could remember vaguely the map they had seen of the redoubt locations. Which one this was, he had no idea. They would be stranded unless they could shoot their way out in—he checked the chron again—just over ten minutes. The hands seemed to move with an infinite slowness as he looked at the face, and yet they were still too bastard fast for his liking.

It would need one hell of a change in luck. But maybe, having suffered so much bad in the past few hours, they were due such a change.

No sooner had that thought crossed his mind than he heard voices and footsteps approaching, muffled by the thickness of the door separating them from the corridor outside, but nonetheless plainly audible.

Ten minutes. Hurry, you bastards.

Krysty was now on her feet, her blaster held down by her side, partly concealed behind her thigh, but her hand tensed around the butt. J.B. nodded to her as he stepped back to stand beside her, bringing up the mini-Uzi so that the barrel was parallel to the floor at waist level.

The voices outside grew clearer.

"How did they get in here?"

"The tech… Always knew that it all must work, or else we wouldn't be able to live down here. Mebbe they come from somewhere like this and they've figured out the shit that we haven't."

"Dangerous, then."

Three voices. The footsteps were too indistinct to make out. Maybe just the three, maybe one or two others that weren't speaking. They'd only know when the sec door was opened. J.B. kept his gaze level and focused on the sec door.

The voices and footsteps ceased, and the door began to slide open. As it did, it seemed that the corridor beyond was deserted. J.B.'s lips quirked into the shadow of a grin. They weren't that stupe, obviously.

"Okay, you come out with your blasters lowered, and no harm will come to you," yelled one of the three—at least—men in the corridor.

"You think we're crazy?" Krysty replied calmly. "Why would we make ourselves defenseless and then come out?"

"Because you haven't got any way out, and you can't stay there indefinitely," the voice replied.

"That's true. But then again, we stay here and you can't fire on us without blowing yourselves to hell. See this?" J.B. had an idea as he spoke, and bent to reach behind him for where the box of frag grens lay partly opened. He grabbed one and tossed it into the corridor without pulling the pin. There were momentary sounds of panicked movement as the gren hit the concrete and rolled out of J.B.'s view.

"You see that?" he continued before anyone outside had a chance to take action. "That was just a warning. I've got a whole box of these at my feet. Next one comes out without the pin unless you back off."

"Do that and you'll blast the fuck out of all of us," said another of the disembodied voices, this one from the opposite side of the corridor to the first.

So they had split into two groups. The bad news was that it meant both sides of the corridor were covered. The good news was that it divided their forces. Krysty looked at her chron and gestured to J.B., showing him her wrist.

Eight minutes. They had to move quickly now.

"What have we got to lose?" J.B. said hurriedly. "You're going to chill us anyway, right?"

"Who says we're gonna do that?" The third voice made itself heard. It was to the left of the doorway, leading back toward the upper levels. That made only one on the side that they needed to take. More importantly, this voice had an authority that the other two lacked. This was top man in the group. The way in which J.B. addressed him played up to this.

"Why else corner us like this? If you call your men off, then mebbe we can talk about this. You look like you run this place pretty well. Mebbe we can come to an agreement of some kind."

The voice gave a harsh, barking laugh. "Nice try. But I'm not in charge here. None of us are. We work together."

"You don't trust one another, though," Krysty stated. "Why else lay the trap?"

"Because we don't understand all this predark shit. We can use some of it, sure, but that don't mean we get it. But someone might. So we're a little cautious… And guess what, we were right. 'Cause you're here, right?"

"Right," J.B. said, glancing at his chron. Just over five minutes. If they had time, then maybe they could stall until they could come up with some kind of plan. But time was the one thing that they didn't have. He looked at Krysty and shrugged, mouthing "Trust me" at her as he suddenly took her arm and threw her to one side of the doorway, so that she twisted and hit the wall square with her back, gasping as the air was momentarily driven from her lungs. She looked bewildered and then shocked as she watched J.B. and realized what he was about to do.

The Armorer took one of the frag grens from the open box, pulled the pin, and then flicked his wrist as he leaned toward the open doorway. The spin on the gren took it out through the gap at an angle, moving in the air as it did so. It hit the far wall and bounced, the spin causing it to cannon off the wall at a corresponding angle so that it fell beyond the open doorway and into the area where two of the voices had been standing. There was a momentarily jumble of confused and panicked voices before they were obliterated by the noise of the gren exploding. J.B. had already flung himself down, opening his mouth to equalize the pressure change brought about by the explosion. He could only hope that Krysty's reactions were quick enough for her to do the same.

He was taking one hell of a risk, he knew, but a calculated one. The armory was behind thick walls, and he had angled the gren's trajectory as much as possible so that it would explode in an area where little, if any, of the shrapnel would blow in through the doorway. It was still possible that he could trigger off the ordnance around him, but highly unlikely.

If he had called it right…

A sudden and engulfing silence swept over him momentarily. It seemed as though the whole world had gone silent, including himself. His central nervous system, which he could hear even at the most extreme of moments, was seemingly stunned into silence. The pressure was like being suddenly immersed in a tank of water and thrust down several fathoms, only to surface again with a gasp of shock as the pressure suddenly returned some kind of equilibrium.

He gasped for air, felt his jaw ache with the shock wave, and his hearing return, if bottom-end heavy and lacking in anything that would register above a muffled roar. From experience, he knew that this would soon pass. The important thing was that he was still there. Looking across the room, through the clouds of choking concrete dust that were billowing in from the open doorway, he could see that Krysty was still also alive.

The Titian-haired beauty had dragged herself to her feet, shaking the dust from her tightly coiled hair and the sense back into her head.

They were still there. That was the most important thing. The detonation hadn't penetrated the walls, and no shrapnel from the gren had leaked back into the armory and triggered a domino-effect explosion.

J.B. felt as if he were moving in slow motion as he hurried to grab Krysty by the arm. She was still slightly dazed from the blast, her eyes not quite in focus. That was okay. He felt like she looked. It didn't matter. He knew her well enough by now to know that she could recover on the run. He tried to speak, but found that he couldn't hear the words inside his own head, let alone expect her to hear them. So he yelled. It was still muffled and distant to him—to Krysty, too, most likely—but at least she seemed to be able to understand him.

"Move out…check corridor…back to chamber…blast anyone following…" He nodded vigorously, feeling absurd as he did so, but hoping that this would somehow emphasize his message.

He need not have worried. Krysty was already nodding with an equal vigor, checking her blaster and moving to the doorway. She pointed in the direction of the corridor leading back to the mat-trans. J.B. nodded briefly and gestured his intent in the opposite direction. At his signal, she moved out into the corridor, blaster held in front of her, while he did likewise to cover the opposite direction.

There had only been one man on the mat-trans side of the doorway. They had figured that, and Krysty could now see that they had been correct. He had tried to turn away from the blast but had found nowhere to seek cover. As a result, he had been hit from the back by the frag shrapnel, which had ripped into him from top of the head to the feet. All that remained was a bloody pulp shaped like a human. She prodded him with her foot, turning him over to reveal that his front was almost untouched, apart from a gout of blood that had been forced up his throat and had dribbled down his chin, and an expression of complete surprise.

She turned to face back down the corridor, where J.B. was looking. They assumed there had been three men: It was hard to tell now, as all that remained were bloodied mounds of flesh and bone in some vague semblance of shape. The remainder of what had once constituted human beings was spread across the walls, floor and ceiling.

They would present no problem. It was their companions, alerted by the blast and now bearing down with a noise that was audible even through the roaring fog that was J.B.'s and Krysty's returning hearing, who would present a real threat.

J.B. gestured to her that they should move. She began to run, turning on her heel every few steps to look back. J.B. was close on her heels, spending some of the time running backward, watching for the approaching enemy.

Time was of the essence now, not just because they had an unknown number of potential assailants at their backs, but also because they were running out of time before the automatic return timer would run out, and they would be either stranded here or at the mercy of a random jump.

That the enemy was gaining on them was of little doubt. Even with impaired hearing, they could tell that the rest of the coldhearts who called the redoubt home were closing on them. The anger in their yelling voices increased as they stumbled on the remains of their friends. J.B. and Krysty had reached a bend in the corridor, and it gave them an edge as they descended toward the mat-trans. The bend covered them and allowed them to race forward without having to check over their shoulders.

That they had misjudged was made obvious by the sudden hail of blasterfire that showered them with concrete chips as the whining ordnance rained around them. The coldhearts were either firing blind at the corner or their anger had blunted their aim. It didn't matter which. It gave Krysty and J.B. a warning that should have been their chilling.

Instead it alerted them to the fact that they needed to stop for a moment. To go on would have been obeying the imperative of time, but would only have led to their own premature deaths. Instead they acted as one, falling back to the angle of the bend that would allow them the most cover as the enemy approached.

As they advanced, the men—they could only assume they were all men, and in truth it didn't matter—kept firing wildly. Their anger made them careless, and that was all the edge the more experienced companions needed. The wild firing echoed around the confined space of the corridor, loud even to Krysty's and J.B.'s ringing ears, providing the perfect cover as it chipped away at the walls, sending up a covering cloud of dust.

The two companions didn't have to look at each

other. They knew that they just needed to keep focused on the onrushing enemy. Wild and unthinking in their surprise and anger, they were rushing headlong to their own doom, even though they seemed to be completely unaware of it.

J.B. and Krysty kept their focus tight on the bend in the corridor. The overhead fluorescent lighting cut through the dust, its even glare making the use of shadows to track the enemy impossible. It would have to be split-second timing....

"Now," J.B. yelled, even though he knew Krysty didn't need him to tell her—indeed, it was doubtful that she could even hear him in the sudden explosion of sound as he tapped the mini-Uzi. That didn't matter. All that mattered was that his chattering roar of fire was punctuated by rapid rounds from her Smith & Wesson blaster, stilled only momentarily as she paused to reload.

The enemy—were they really that, or just men who were responding to intrusion and attack much as they would have done under similar circumstances—came rushing. Too fired up to think straight, too angry to react with any speed, they came into the hail of fire. There weren't many of them, but more than enough to have cut J.B. and Krysty to ribbons given half a chance, which was denied to them by the calm under pressure of people who had seen more combat, and could keep anger under control.

As soon as the last man hit the ground and they were sure that there were no others in his wake, the two companions were once more on their toes, now running unhindered toward the mat-trans.

They entered the unit and slammed the door shut, J.B. checking his wrist chron as Krysty hit the LD button.

"Thirty bastard seconds," he rasped, his face cracking into a grin. "Plenty of time."

Krysty sank down the wall, gasping for breath as the air started to crackle and the mist began to slowly gather in wisps around them.

"Nothing to take back," she wheezed.

"No worries," J.B. said in return, holding up his mini-Uzi while he racked another load. "Just have to come out blasting. Surprise the bastards." He grinned at the unspoken question her expression threw at him. "Don't reckon Ryan would expect anything less."

It was the last thing he said before the inevitable darkness overwhelmed them once again.

Chapter Seventeen

The one-eyed man was keeping that single orb focused on the baron. Crabbe was a man who was being almost driven to distraction by the prospect of both grasping and losing his dream. Grasping it if J.B. and Krysty returned with the disk—which, of course, Ryan knew they couldn't—and having to finally realize his wildest fantasies, which had in all probability never entered the realms of being practically mapped. Paradoxically, he was face-to-face with the idea of his dreams being finally dashed. While he had been searching for the companions, and planning how to get to the mysterious places of dreams that the laminated sheet represented, he had been able to nurse the secret dream to his breast and take comfort from its possibility.

Not now. Neither was an option. There would only be the cold hard fact. Ryan knew which way it would go, but for Crabbe the double edge to the sword was that he was facing the fact that whichever way it went, it would never be like the fantasy.

And he was cracking under the strain of that realization. Pacing up and down, muttering to himself, casting glances at Mildred and at his own men, he was a baron who was no longer in control of himself—and so, by extension, of his people.

There would have been those who would have wondered why Ryan was watching the baron when McCready was the one with the blaster in his hand. The sec chief was waiting for the moment to mount his own coup. He had the men and the blasters. He was the real threat in that sense. Ryan didn't like the sec chief, any more than the squat man liked him. But he knew a natural fighter when he saw one. McCready was such. The one-eyed man knew that he would be watching the baron with similar thoughts racing through his mind. To watch him and then react would be, for Ryan, to put himself at a disadvantage, a fraction of a second behind.

Screw that. To do that would be to invite your own chilling. The man a fraction of a second behind was the one who bought the farm. But to watch the baron just as McCready was doing, and then to react at the same time, or perhaps that fraction before—that was to be the winner.

Ryan trusted his own skill and experience. He believed he could make that judgment just that moment before the sec chief decided to act.

And if he couldn't, he was damn sure that Jak was doing exactly the same thing. Just as he felt certain that Doc was watching the sec chief who stood almost directly in front of him. Just as he knew that Mildred was using her position to watch the overall picture, ignoring the pacing and angst-riddled baron.

The tension in the room was tighter than a drum. It would take just the slightest thing to make it snap.

Like the sudden flare of light from the mat-trans unit, momentarily blinding them as it signaled the return—he could only hope—of J.B. and Krysty.

And then there was silence and stillness. Crabbe

watched the door with an intensity that was almost frightening. Ryan watched him with something that was equal, but different in intent. The baron couldn't take the strain much longer, and neither could his sec chief. The longer that the unit stayed still and silent, then the more likely it grew that the eventual explosion of violence would be cathartic and final.

It was just a matter of time...

INSIDE THE MAT-TRANS, Krysty and J.B. were coming around. The Armorer took off his battered fedora and rubbed his scalp vigorously, as though that might, in some way, make him recover with a greater speed. Krysty stood and shook herself with the kind of shiver that usually presaged a portent of dread. That was fine. It mirrored how she felt. She turned to the unit door, expecting it to open. If things went to the pattern established by the previous five jumps, then someonc would come for them if they waited long enough. One of their own, with armed sec on their ass. That was the last thing she wanted. J.B., too, she was certain. That would just contain them in the confines of the mat-trans walls and make it easy to pick them off. And it would keep them from firing for fear of hitting one of their own.

No, the only way to tackle this would be to move quicker than those on the outside and come out firing. She was almost willing herself to shake off the nausea and torpor of the jump.

J.B. was doing much the same. He felt like he'd left half his guts back in the other redoubt. But there was no time to worry about being at the top of his game right now. Speed was the essence. He looked across at Krysty as he racked the mini-Uzi. She chambered a round in her blaster and gave him the briefest of nods.

Neither of them was really ready, but it had to be now.

"DON'T JUST STAND there, get them out. They must have the disk. Don't let them just sit there," Crabbe yelled, gesticulating wildly toward his sec men and the three prisoners. Mildred, close by, instinctively stepped to one side, distancing herself.

That would make the already jumpy McCready move, if nothing else did, Ryan figured. With a flicker of the eye, he was able to take in almost from the periphery of his vision that the sec chief was momentarily distracted and wasn't watching them. He reached out, his iron grip closing around the calf of the sec chief, squeezing for the muscle. It was a simple maneuver to cause him so much pain that he would yell and lose focus while paralyzing the muscle momentarily and make him topple. What would happen then was another matter.

McCready fell backward, yelling in surprise and pain, his SMG angling upward and arcing a spray of fire into the control room, bringing down dust and debris while blasting out some of the lighting, plunging the room into a semigloom. There were confused shouts from his men, unsure of what to do. Should they concentrate on the prisoners, or was this the chance they should take to rid themselves of the baron?

The loudest shout came from Crabbe, unable to take in what was happening around him. Even more so, as he caught sight of the mat-trans door opening. The disk was within his grasp, and now for this to happen! He held out his arms in unthinking imprecation to the salvation he expected from the mat-trans.

It was salvation of another sort that greeted him. Steeling themselves despite the dizziness and gnawing nausea that beset them, J.B. and Krysty emerged from the redoubt with blasters blazing. The first volley was intended to go over the heads of their enemies while giving them the chance to take in their bearings.

Without even pausing to take in what J.B. and Krysty were up to, Doc had decided to act. The gas gren that he had kept secreted in his frock coat pocket was swiftly palmed, the pin pulled and the deadly package rolled across the room.

"Gas," Doc yelled as he loosed the gren, knowing that the one word would be enough for his companions to take the appropriate measures—that was if they could hear him over the chaos.

Jak was about to contribute his own hidden surprise for the baron and his men—or, to be more accurate, the sec chief and his acolytes. As smoothly as Doc had palmed the gren, it was nothing compared to way in which the lithe albino teen produced the laser from the place in which he had hidden it. The power pack was the only thing that gave him concern, but he kept a firm grip on it to keep it connected. Using one hand for that, and keeping the nozzle mechanism of the weapon in the other, he aimed the beam of light it was emitting toward the two men who were standing guard over the captured ordnance. Still confused about the sudden explosion of events, and torn about who to aid—the baron or their own sec chief—they were frozen for just a fraction of a second. It wasn't much, but it was long enough for Jak to achieve his aim. Both men yelled in sudden shock and anger as the red beam of the laser cut across their bodies, burning a searing line across their chests. More importantly, it cut diagonally across the two men, taking them at the shoulder down to the elbow on one, and then the forearm and wrist of the other. Even if they could have gathered what remained of their senses enough to raise their weapons and fire while the heat of the laser began to cook their internal organs, the fact that their tendons, muscles and nerves had been severed by the intense heat of the beam was enough to render their upper limbs useless. They fell away from the weapons they guarded, both of them screaming in incoherent high voices raised by pain.

Krysty and J.B. fanned out so that they would be a harder target. At the same time, they focused their fire on the doorway to the control room.

Terrified by what was going down, and seeking only to escape a fight in which he had no interest or wish to take part, Sal had found himself running right into the onrushing sec men who had been stationed in the redoubt corridor. The first rounds of blasterfire had brought them running, and now those closest to the control room had reached the doorway. The mechanic ran straight into them and frantically tried to scrabble past them. They, in turn, had tried to push him back so that they could pass, and in consequence had done little more than push him back into the hail of fire that had been intended for them. Sal, who had only ever wanted to be able to continue his work in peace, bought the farm in a hail of bullets.

His lifeless body, for a second kept upright by the force of the rounds that poured through it, was an obstruction that prevented the sec men in front of him from firing on Krysty and J.B. for that moment when they were exposed. By the time that it had fallen, the two companions had taken cover, and it was the sec men who were now exposed, those following at their backs doing little more than forcing them into the room and the burst of bullets that greeted them.

While that was going on, Mildred had acted to take out the baron, even though she was unarmed and had moved away from him at that moment when she judged that McCready was ready to blast him. But now she could see that the sec chief had other concerns as he grappled with Ryan, the one-eyed man rising to his feet even as the sec chief sank, so that the two of them came face-to-face, gritted teeth and steely gazes fixed on each other.

That left both of them unaware of and undefended against the baron. Crabbe, aware that his carefully constructed and plotted world was suddenly falling around his ears, was determined to extract some kind of vengeance. Whether he suspected that his sec chief was plotting against him and that now was the time to act—and surely he could not have remained baron for so long without some kind of insight—or whether he had decided that Ryan had outlived his usefulness and was the catalyst for the disaster now befalling him, and as such worthy only of chilling was immaterial. Perhaps it was both, and he had decided to chill two birds with the one slug. Either way, he was drawing a bead on them while both, immersed in their own struggle, were unaware of the hot metal that awaited them.

Mildred had to act. Crabbe wasn't looking at her, and she used that to her advantage. Two steps, a swing, and with the full force of her weight behind it she slashed the straight edge of her hand toward the area just behind the baron's ear. He had to have sensed it, perhaps felt the draft of the approaching blow, as he tried to turn and duck. But too late. The blow caught him in the soft tissue area at the base of the skull. Before he had a chance to turn his blaster on Mildred, the light went out in his eyes, which rolled up into his head as, with a soft grunt, he slumped to the ground.

In the midst of the chaos, Doc and Jak were now on their feet, pushing past the still-writhing corpses of the laser-carved sec men, and had gathered the tarp that contained their personal weapons. They knew without exchanging words that there was no time to distribute the armory and use it in the battle that was raging. With an anxious glance at the clouds of gas that were starting to spread and clog up the air in the room, Doc knew that they had to get out. The filters in the air recycling system were taking out some of the toxins, but the majority was now beginning to blanket the room.

Doc's shout had been taken in by his companions, albeit on a subconscious level, and so they had tried, despite their exertions, to breathe shallowly as they fought. But even with this precaution, some of the choking gas was in their lungs and was absorbed through their skin, making their movements uncertain and erratic. To linger too long would risk the gren causing them as much damage as it was now inflicting on the remaining sec men, who had been breathing as normal, and the baron himself.

For Crabbe, by some supreme effort of will, perhaps at realizing that his dream was slipping away and determined to try to salvage something from it, had forced himself to struggle, still groggy, to his feet. He still grasped his blaster, waving it in a haphazard manner as though unable to control his muscles, which, if he had breathed in enough of the gas, was probably the case.

The door to the mat-trans unit was still open, and it was obvious what needed to be done. Doc and Jak half carried, half dragged the tarp with their weapons toward the mat-trans. The room was now a stinking mess of cordite smoke, nerve gas, and the stench of roasted flesh and bloodied wounds.

Ryan was grappling with McCready, the two men locked into a struggle where Ryan's injuries equalized his power against the smaller, stockier man. The one-eyed warrior was holding the arm that grasped the sec chief's SMG in a locked position, so that no matter how hard he might try, he couldn't level it at the man for whom his hate was almost palpable. As he breathed fumes of hatred and anger in Ryan's face, it was almost a physical presence.

"Fucker. Could have taken Crabbe. Could have been the baron. But you had to come along."

"I didn't want to be here. I don't want to be here now. Won't be." The one-eyed man was aware that Jak and Doc were readying to leave. The gas was growing, and he could feel it take hold of his body. There was little time. If he was going to end this, he had to end it now. For a moment he relaxed his tense muscles, allowing the sec chief to believe that he had the upper hand. McCready's grimace shaped to a grin and he pressed forward. It was what Ryan had wanted. The one-eyed man stepped back suddenly and pulled, toppling the sec chief off balance, bringing up his knee so that it caught the sec chief in the solar plexus as he fell forward. McCready grunted as the air was driven from his lungs. The SMG loosened in his grip and Ryan seized it, swiveling it and tapping a burst that took off the back of the sec man's head. Before he had even hit the floor, Ryan headed to the mat-trans, yelling to Mildred to join him.

But the physician had a task of her own to finish before she was ready to go. Unarmed in the midst of the chaos, she had taken cover, and had been able to observe what was going on in a way that none of the others could. J.B. and Krysty had wiped out most of the sec men, and were laying down a covering fire that was keeping the remainder outside the control room. Inside, there was no opposition left other than the baron, who was so dazed that even though he waved his blaster around, it was aimless and posed little danger. Ryan was about to join Jak and Doc in the mat-trans.

So she had to make sure that none of the remaining sec men, or the Baron, could follow. Once they were inside the unit, a random jump would occur. Her task was to make sure that this destination couldn't be followed. She dropped to her knees and crawled to where one of the fallen sec men had dropped his blaster. She took it and turned, tapping a volley that took out the computers in a shower of sparks. The baron was caught by some of them, turning and letting fly a shot that flew high and wide before he fell backward.

She didn't wait to see where he landed. Before Crabbe had even hit the floor, she was already in the mat-trans with Jak, Doc and Ryan.

"Come on, dammit," she yelled at Krysty and J.B., aware that the gas was starting to permeate every part of the control room.

The Armorer gestured to Krysty to fall back as he kept up the cover fire. The Titian-haired beauty dived into the mat-trans unit.

"Last destination," she gasped. "Safe—chilled them all."

There was no time to ask for further explanations. They knew they could trust that they would be going to an empty haven, no matter what desolation they may face.

J.B. backed into the mat-trans with a slowness that was almost infuriating, but the Armorer was thorough. That was how he had kept himself alive for so long. There was no way he would let any of the remaining sec men get into the control room and have the remotest chance of offing any of them with a stray shot.

"Let's go," he barked when he was in, only the barrel of the mini-Uzi protruding into the anteroom beyond. He whipped it back in, and Krysty slammed shut the door with a pained sigh of sheer relief.

As the mat-trans door closed, Ryan could see the baron. Crabbe was floundering around the room, crazed with the loss of his dream.

Ryan closed his eye, but the image of the baron as a defeated man, flailing aimlessly in a broken world, was seared into his retina. He opened his eye again, and took in his own people as they slumped on the floor of the mat-trans unit, battered but unbroken.

Another fight for survival had been fought and won. Through grit and determination the companions had again missed the last train west. But when all was said and done, Ryan knew that death was merely a heartbeat away for all of them. Like it had been for Althea, Dean's woman.

Life was a fragile thing in the Deathlands, snuffed out in the blink of an eye by friend or foe. Now that the friends were free to move on, free to relax as much as they could in this blighted land, Ryan's thoughts would turn to his son, now a strapping young buck with a chip on his shoulder, and a deep anger focused unerringly at his father....

The mist began to rise around them as they left the world of Baron Crabbe and his dreams of empire behind them, moving on to who knew what, other than another chance to stay alive.

And free.

* * * * *